I WRITE

Short Stories by Kids, for Kids.

I Write Short Stories by Kids for Kids, Volume 7
Copyright © 2016 by LongTale Publishing© in association with iWRITE

ISBN 978-1-941515-79-2

Cover Design: Tamara Dever for TLC Graphics
www.TLCGraphics.com
Interior Design: Sharon Wilkerson
Front Cover Illustration: La'Jasha Champion
Back Cover Illustrations: Zoë Brown, Zoey Hess, Michal Ilouz,
Nicole Pasterczyk, Jacqueline Poisot, Joshua Sher

iWRITE
Leading Through Literacy

The iWRITE Non-Profit Literacy Organization was founded in 2009 by children's author and public speaker, Melissa M. Williams.

iWRITE inspires kids to write their own stories and provides publishing and leadership opportunities to our youth. Since reading and writing go hand in hand, iWRITE encourages readers to use their imagination and communicate through the written word. Both reading and writing builds a foundation for our youth to become leaders among their peers and to become strong communicators. The *I Write Short Stories by Kids for Kids* annual publishing contest awards kids for their academic and artistic achievements. Since 2009, we have published hundreds of kids across the nation in the 3rd-12th grade in our anthologies, thereby furthering our mission to encourage kids to read, write and create daily. The act of being a published, young author or illustrator increases positive self-esteem and encourages our youth to become role models to others.

For more information about iWRITE, sponsorship opportunities and ways that your school and community can be involved in our writing programs please visit our websites:

www.iWRITE.org

Table of Contents

SEVENTH - EIGHTH GRADE STORIES

NINTH - TWELFTH GRADE STORIES

POETRY

3RD - 4TH GRADE
SHORT STORIES

1

An Important Lesson

by Finnley Benson

Robert Jay Elementary was a peculiar school. The kids were mean, rude, and disobedient. Their unruliness included messing up chalk boards, scribbling on walls, shooting spitballs, and coloring over the teacher's writing using markers. The bad behavior had been a long tradition that unfortunately made the school famous in the district with a terrible reputation. And the worst thing of it all was that the teachers too never cared. But after school one day...*poof!* The chalk board, the pencils, and the marker came alive.

"I can't believe the teacher is careless when the students totally mistreat her," said Marker.

"Yeah, I can't believe it! She needs to teach them manners," said Leader Pencil.

"Hmm...maybe we can make a plan to touch up on their manners," said Chalkboard.

"Should we straighten things up by popping out and telling them the expectations?" inquired Kid Pencil.

"No, of course not! We need a plan that really sticks in their mind," said Leader Pencil.

"I think we should just suddenly come to life, and give the students a little fright. Then we can start talking about what the students have done, and tell them to fix their mistakes, and to restart things," said General Pencil.

"Well, I guess we are going to have to vote," said Chalkboard.

"Okay, deal. Now who votes for Kid Pencil's idea?" asked Leader Pencil.

Chalkboard, Marker, and Kid Pencil all voted for it.

"Okay, now who votes for my idea?" inquired General Pencil.

"No one voted for it sir," said Kid Pencil.

"What? Why did some items not vote?" asked General Pencil.

"Ahem, we actually want both ideas combined," said Leader Pencil.

"Okay, the votes are settled, we are moving on with both ideas," said General Pencil.

"Now everyone, get some rest because we will need to perform well tomorrow," said Marker.

"Okay, good night," said Chalkboard.

The next morning in class the teacher greeted the students. "Hello class. May I have your attention please? I am your sub for the week and I don't like this bad attitude."

"Well, we don't like school, so leave us alone," said Timmy.

"Oh, your teacher was right. I can't believe I have to substitute for her for an entire week," said the new teacher. The substitute walked to the door, shut it, and left.

"Ah! Just like old times," said Carlos. As the class went on to shoot spitballs at each other, suddenly they heard a *poof*. The pencils came to life again.

"Oh, what! They are alive," said Kate.

"Uh huh, you foolish kids, you need to learn good manners," said Leader Pencil.

"Yes, and you also need to step it up now," said Kid Pencil.

"This type of behavior has been wild for too long. You dear students need a change of heart. You need to become kinder," said General Pencil.

"Chalkboard will talk you through what you have done, and how to fix it," said Marker.

The students heard another *poof*. Then, Chalkboard came to life! "Okay kids, you have been rude, mean, and disobedient to your teachers for all these years. Now you must change. What you need to do is to start with an act of kindness, like giving a compliment to someone else," said Chalkboard.

The kids were frightened, and followed the instructions carefully.

"I like your shoes," said Carlos.

"Thanks," answered Kate.

"I like how you laugh," said Roy.

"Wow, I really am funny with my laugh, thanks," said Josh.

"Well, that's just the first part, but, good job everyone!

Now you must go to all the teachers you have hurt," continued Chalkboard.

"But that's not logical! We are in fifth grade, and we have several teachers. We have Ms. Joy, Mr. Koy, Ms. Kron, Mr. Jeff, Ms. Smart, and Ms. Clane. That will take forever," said Bob.

"Well, if you want to be forgiven and make a change, that is what you must do," said Chalkboard.

"Okay, fine! I will do it," said Bob. After that, the others agreed.

The kids started walking down the hallway, when suddenly they heard a boom. All their teachers were lined up frozen in place in front of them.

"Uh guys, I thought our school was messed up already, but this is just plain creepy," said Carlos.

"No, I don't think so. It is the only way to help us with forgiveness," said Kate.

"Okay, let's do it," said Roy.

"I will do it first," said Josh. "Ahem, hello teachers, we have an announcement to make. We are so sorry for um... being uh...bad people when we were in your class."

"Wow, it's really you, changing your hearts," said Ms. Clane.

"Uh..., yeah, you can put it that way," said Carlos.

"Well, now we would like to present you with a gift," said Kate.

"Wait, we didn't make any gifts," said Carlos.

"Yes, we did! We gave them the gift of our changing hearts," said Kate.

"You have learned a lot," said Ms. Clane with a smile.

"Well, we have someone to thank," said Kate. Josh, Roy, Carlos, Bob, and Kate walked back to their classroom. When they got there, they thanked the school supplies for their help.

Carlos said, "Your kind deeds will be remembered."

The school supplies answered with a nod and said, "we will remember what you've done too. Take note! Be always on the good side!"

The kids replied with a big *we will* and said their goodbyes. Consequently, their hearts were now full of kindness and they promised themselves they would help others change too. After other kids in the school heard of all the things that happened that day, Bob suggested a plan to spread kindness to the whole school. Kate and Carlos talked to the principal and got permission to make posters to advertise their random acts of kindness experiment.

Roy, Josh and Carlos passed out fliers that called the other kids at school to action. Their fliers read, *Pay it forward today, and be kind to others just because you can.* At first, the kids at school felt strange to follow their example, but in a few days after just a handful of kind acts the whole school was changed. The principal, the teachers, and the students were all happily participating. There was a new atmosphere at school that spread to the community. Shortly after that, parents were being extra kind to each other and the whole school district had caught on in the new kindness trend.

Roy was so happy and said out loud, "If only Chalkboard and the other school supplies could see how much change they encouraged."

"I am sure they can see it," said Carlos. "Kindness is hard to miss when it brings so much change, order and friendship."

Bob agreed with him and added, "Don't worry I am sure the school supplies are very proud of us all."

And with that, the changed friends walked side by side with confidence in their hearts searching for their next opportunity to spread kindness.

2

The Story of the Saved Land

by Randii Carrell

My last day here before we go to the U.S.A! thought Mei as she woke up. *I hope people there are nice!* Mei wanted her last day in Japan to be the best. She smelled Matcha Green Tea Cakes being made, so she ran into the kitchen.

"Konnichiwa, Paris," said Mei as she walked toward Paris.

'I'm glad to see you," Paris said.

"Well Paris, thanks for everything!"

"You're welcome, but you better get going," said Paris.

"OK, bye, I'll skype you!" Mei said good-bye and she and her mom headed to the airport. When they got there, they boarded their plane.

"Mom, I'm tired, I'm gonna' take a nap," Mei said.

"Honey, wake up, it's time to get off!" her mother said to her. She had slept the entire flight.

"Oh, really, already! Yay! Oh, the sweet, sweet land!"

"Ok, now we need to go to the new house," Mei's mother said.

When they arrived in their new neighborhood, Mei ran to what looked like the new house.

A girl about Mei's age walked up to her and said, "Konnichiwa!"

Mei looked surprised and answered, "Konnichiwa."

"Hey, what is your name?" the girl asked.

"Mei, M-E-I," replied Mei. They started to converse.

"Mei, help me unload!" shouted Mei's mom.

"Mom, Mom we need to go to get things to make our new Zen Garden!" shouted Mei to her mom.

Mei and her mom got into the car and went to a store. They got stones, rocks, sand, rakes, and Bonsai plants. When they got home, the girl next door offered to help with their Zen Garden. She had her own Zen Garden.

"Mei, the Zen Garden is getting better! Well, I must get to work now. See you later."

That night in the Zen Garden, a portal opened up in the Bonsai Tree forest. Mei saw a seal type thing come out of the portal.

"Hey, I need your help. I am Bubbles, and I live in The Land of Zen," said Bubbles the seal, in a whisper.

"Ok. I'll help you because...look!" said Mei, pointing towards the sand about 2 feet away. It was turning gray. Mei followed Bubbles through the portal.

"The Zen Gardens are losing color and the Cherry Blossoms are vanishing!" screamed Bubbles.

"We need to find out why the Cherry Blossoms are vanishing then," said Mei.

"Ok! Well I think that if we go talk to the Tiki God he could give us a source," said Bubbles.

"Where is this Tiki God?"

"On the Tiki Mountain up there." Bubbles pointed to a huge mountain that looked like a Hawaiian Luau party.

"How do we get up there?" questioned Mei, her eyes set on the mountain.

"We climb," said Bubbles.

"Ok...we better go!"

Bubbles and Mei were halfway up the mountain when they heard, *Bubbles, nice to see you again. It's been so long!* They looked up and saw the Tiki God leaning over the mountain.

"Hello Tiki God. We must ask you a question," said Bubbles. By this time Bubbles and Mei were up the mountain.

"Anything, anything, but I may not have the best answer," said the Tiki God.

"You did hear about the Cherry Blossoms vanishing, right?" asked Bubbles.

"Yes," said the Tiki God.

"Well, it is taking color out of Zen Gardens in the human world," said Mei.

"I know about this," said Tiki.

"Do you know why the cherry blossoms have gone missing?" asked Mei.

"No, I don't," said the Tiki God.

16

"Do you know anyone who could give us some information?" asked Bubbles.

"You can ask Mr. Fuzz the elephant on Savanah Rock! He knows everything," said Tiki God.

"Wow, why didn't I think of that?" asked Bubbles.

"Thanks," said Mei.

"Bye Tiki!" said Bubbles.

"Bye!" said Tiki God.

Bubbles and Mei started to walk toward Savanah Rock, but Bubbles got tired and said that Mei should return to the human world and come back after school. Bubbles made a portal and Mei returned home, wishing she didn't have to go. The following day, after school, Mei told her mom she was going over to a friend's house, when she actually went to The Land of Zen.

She met Bubbles at Savanah Rock, and they went to talk to Mr. Fuzz.

"Hi-loo little Bubbles! What brings you here?" asked Mr. Fuzz.

"Do you know why the Cherry Blossoms are disappearing?" asked Mei.

"Yes I heard of a source," said Mr. Fuzz.

"What, what?" asked Bubbles, raising his tone.

"The Blob Fish in Fish Valley says he needs to eat them in order to stay alive, because someone stole his stone that kept him alive and also kept the Zen Gardens in the human world colorful," said Mr. Fuzz.

"Great, thanks Mr. Fuzz," said Bubbles.

Mr. Fuzz and Bubbles hugged. Mei decided to head home for the day. She didn't sleep well that night. She tossed and turned, thinking about the Blob Fish in Fish Valley. The next day she asked her mom, "Mom, can I go to Mimi's?"

"Well certainly," replied her mom.

Mei went out to the Zen Garden to go to The Land of Zen.

"Bubbles, lead the way to Fish Valley!" yelled Mei, as they walked towards a pond.

When they arrived at Fish Valley, Blob Fish was munching down on Cherry Blossoms.

"Hello Blob Fish! I'm Bubbles, and we want to know what happened to your stone," said Bubbles.

"Well, I was swimming, and set my stone aside on a rock," answered Blob Fish. "When I got back, I noticed it was gone and saw a man running away with it. I tried to catch him, but he was too fast. My men found him, but he won't give up the stone."

"Where is this man and what is his name?" asked Bubbles.

"Jaques. He is strong and brave," said Blob Fish.

"May I speak with him?" asked Mei.

"Why...yes!" replied Blob Fish and pointed over to Jaques,who had been over to the side listening.

"I am Jaques, ruler of The Stone!" said Jaques.

"Where is the stone and what is it for?" asked Mei in a soothing voice.

"It is in the cave in Captain Shark's island. I need it because it helps me make more money to buy things for my girlfriend," said Jaques.

"I need you to give it back. Tell you girlfriend the truth. Girls like the truth. She will understand and know that you did the right thing by returning it," promised Mei.

Jaques took Mei to the cave, and told his girlfriend the truth. She understood and Mei was right. Jaques took the precious stone to Blob Fish, and he stopped eating all of the Cherry Blossoms.

Mei was sad to leave, but happy to know the Cherry Blossoms were coming back, and the human's Zen Gardens would be regaining color.

Mei didn't tell a soul about her adventure, but always knew it would be with her.

Mei went to bed and slept well that night, thinking about how she saved The Land of Zen, and all of the Zen Gardens!

3

A Fairy Different Person
in a Fairy Different World

by Bella Chramosta

This is the story of the ultimate fairy princess and her journey into a Fairy Different World.

One day Princess Angelina and Cassandra, her handmaiden (who happened to be her stepsister) were shopping for her coronation gown. They saw a closed store, the princess' favorite, *Glitter Chic*. The two fairies went inside when nobody was looking and they found the perfect dress for the coronation. It was a puffy and glittery dress. When the princess picked it up, she found on the bottom of the dress a fairy cockroach, so she threw the dress on the floor and jumped on the counter.

On the counter, Angelina, the Princess noticed a key and a map. She picked the map up. She looked at her sister and asked, "What is this thing?"

"It's a map, SILLY!" Cassandra said rudely. "We should follow it."

The princess, not being that bright said, "OK!"

They followed the map down to the **CREEPY CATACOMBS** under the castle and found nothing. They continued and passed by a colony of bats. Angelina held her nose to cover the bat odor. The princess' high heels were killing her, so she leaned on the rock wall, which was actually a door. She lost her balance and tumbled to the ground. On the other side of the rock door stood a goofy looking gnome. He had one eyeball with glasses that only had one lens.

The princess screamed, ***"GNOME!!!!"***

"No. No. Don't be scared. I just want to help you. I'm Conner," the gnome said.

As they were talking, Cassandra, who was also the former champion fairy wrestler, left and put a bolder in front of the opening. She locked the princess and the one eyed gnome in the dark and scary catacombs.

Conner got out his magical gnome satchel and pulled out his light bulb. It lit up the entire creepy catacombs. The princess saw that they were in the old underground castle. She noticed a lot of skeletons who had gotten trapped after the fairy earthquake that took the castle underground.

"Your dress looks very nice, *snort*, in this lighting, *snort*," Conner said as he blinked his one eye.

"Thank you. You're awful nice for a gnome," the Princess said.

"All gnomes are naturally nice, but we have to protect ourselves from fairies like Cassandra," he said.

"What do you mean?" asked the Princess.

"Cassandra's great grandmother killed my family members!!!" he screamed. Then he started to weep and snort.

"Don't cry. And really, don't snort. Cassandra's not the same as her grandmother. She's nice," the Princess said.

"So why did she lock you in here with me, *snort*?"

"I thought I told you to stop snorting," she said sweetly.

~

Meanwhile, Cassandra went back to Fairyville and told everyone that the Princess got captured. "I am now the new princess of Fairyville," Cassandra said evilly.

The townspeople said, "Technically you're not the princess if she's still alive."

"Did I tell you that she was captured by a giant, so she's probably in his stomach," she lied. "So she is D to the E to the A to the D. DEAD."

"Fine. Hail the new princess, Cassandra," they said sadly.

~

Deep in the catacombs, the princess and Connor, the one-eyed gnome, were still walking through the tunnels.

Connor said, "I need to show you something." He took her to a secret room. "This is our only way out. Ladies first."

The Princess walked into the room and saw a bunch of buttons on a control panel and started to press them not knowing it was a teleporter.

"What is this?" she said as she touched the teleporter. The teleporter pulled her in before Conner could say anything. Conner ran to the teleporter to check which buttons she pushed and realized she set it to PLANET EARTH!

~

INTO PLANET EARTH WE GO
Angelina landed right in front of Mythology School. When she saw the school, she went right in. As she was walking in she tripped and fell into the captain of the football team's arms.

"I'm Bret. I haven't seen you around here," Bret said and smiled. He set her back down on the ground. "Are you okay?"

"Yes just fine." *Angelina suddenly remembered her fairy wings and patted her shoulder when she realized her wings weren't there.*

"Are you really sure?"

"Yeah. Fine, just fine," she said trying not to act suspicious. Bret and his friends walked away.

As they walked away, his friends said, "Real smooth, real smooth NOT."

"I don't understand how you get so many girls to fall for you when you're so dumb," his best friend, William said.

"I take that as a compliment and offensive at the same time," Bret said.

Later, that afternoon when Bret went home and looked in the year book for the mysterious girl's phone number, but she was not there. He didn't even know her name. The princess was also wondering what his name was so she went back to the high school the next day hoping to see him. She was also wondering about the kingdom and how miserable it was knowing Cassandra would have taken over. Angelina knew Cassandra's coronation would have to wait one week, so she worried that she was running out of time.

~

BACK INTO FAIRYVILLE
Cassandra had taken over Fairyville and turned all the fairies into slaves. All of the gnomes were sent to the Gnome Catacomb Prison. The new princess and her mother, Medusa, ruled the land. Cassandra went down to the one eyed gnome to ask where her sister had gone.

Connor was messing with the teleporter, trying to figure out how he could get the *REAL* princess back.

Cassandra came up to Connor and pulled him by his eyelid. "What is this thing?" she asked.

"Not telling," Connor said and snorted.

"Are you sure? I can do something to you like my great grandmother did to your family."

"I can do something to you too." Connor then barfed on her designer shoes.

Cassandra pulled out another pair of shoes from her fairy purse and smacked him over the eyeball with the shoe. Connor didn't feel it because gnomes can't be hurt. She walked over to the teleporter and saw that it was set to PLANET EARTH!

"You're going to regret this," she said and put him in gnome handcuffs. She jumped into the teleporter, but is wasn't on. So basically, she hopped to the other side of the room. Six hours later, she figured out how to turn it on.

~

(NOW BACK TO THE LOVE BIRDS)

Bret and Angelina found out each other's names and went on their first date! On their date at *The Chinese Panda* they fell in love over a bowl of hot and sour soup.

Bret asked Angelina, "Where are you from?"

Angelina stuttered while looking at the menu and said, "Asia?"

"I didn't know we had any foreign exchange students from there," Bret said.

Angelina excused herself and went to the bathroom. Cassandra walked into *The Chinese Panda* while Angelina was away from the table. She sat down in front of Bret and asked, "Is this seat taken?"

"Kinda," he said.

"Whatever! Let me show you something," Cassandra said.

"No, I'm not interested if you're selling anything."

"I'm not a sales person. I need to show you something important." She pulled out a fairy phone and showed him a picture of Angelina with wings as her sister came out of the bathroom.

"Cool special effects, dude," Bret said.

Angelina came back and asked, "May I have a word with you?"

"Sure," Cassandra smirked.

"How could you?" Angelina asked. Just then, Connor walked through the door.

Connor didn't look the same. He had on a suit and a bow tie. Angelina thought he looked like a dashing prince. She didn't recognize him. She went right up to him and asked if they had met before, *because she read in a book when ever you meet a prince you should always ask that.*

"Yes, we actually have." Connor said. Then he SNORTED as loud as he could.

"Ewwww! Connor. You only had to make a tiny little snort. That was disgusting! Grrross!!!!"

Angelina put her hands on her hips as she said, "I hope you're here to take me home. I've been miserable here." She turned around and saw Bret and Cassandra kissing.

Connor took Angelina's hand and said, "We're going home now."

"How are we going to get back?"

"I made a mini-telaporter for us," Connor said and snorted.

"You're my HERO!" Angelina exclaimed.

The prince and the princess went back to the fairy world and were crowned king and queen of Fairyville.

4

The Seven Leaders

by Wm. Patrick Cook

In the Beginning

There was a big island that took up almost the whole earth, about 400 million years ago. Until one day, big asteroids had flown down and crashed into the planet separating the big island into seven parts. It was dark, no life until about 100 years later. Gradually, people and animals started populating these seven parts. Finally, these seven parts were now known as countries. There were seven leaders of these countries.

Battle Ball

BOOM!! BOOM!! The seven countries were battling. "You'll never get out alive!" yelled a random voice. "Fire everywhere!" The problem was there was not enough food and land for all of the countries. So only one could survive. Ever since the drought there was no water. With no water, there were no plants for them to grow and eat. They knew one country had to stand.

Leader Sokoviac, who was a strong man and leader of the Country of Peace yelled above all the rage, "Guys, we have been battling for months and look where we're at. Less soldiers, less ammo, less everything! Because we're too lazy to get off of our lazy butts and go find food and shelter and settle our differences. We're leaders not battle hungry monsters...well, Leader Dawson is. But still, fighting doesn't solve our problems, we can share."

"Where are we going to find all of this?" Leader Dawson interrupted. Leader Dawson was a big man and the leader of the Country of Hate. Ever since he was a baby he had a scar running down his face.

"We are running low on food and materials. There's not enough for more than one country," argued Leader Dawson.

"I know a place we can move, but it will take weeks to get there," said Sokoviac.

"Let's go then," said Leader Bauge of the Country of Intelligence. Leader Bauge was smart as a child. He went to middle school at the age of 6. He went to high school at the age of 12 and received a scholarship to Harvard at the age of 14. His brain was oddly larger than the average human brain.

The Heroes Journey

The seven leaders gathered their people and left on their journey. They were traveling for weeks with no food and no water. Until they ran across a beautiful valley that was flowing with life. Now they had found it! Or at least they thought they had found it.

"Is this the place?" asked Dawson.

"Yes" said Sokoviac. "Let's settle in."

They were there for several days. Suddenly, there was a blood chilling *ROAR*! A greenish, brown dragon appeared out of nowhere. He was returning from his hunt for prey.

"This is my territory, *GET OUT*," he yelled as he blew fire from his mouth and lit his eerie scaly skin up!

The seven countries had to leave. There was no way to defend themselves against the dragon. They quickly left the once beautiful valley now destroyed. Later after the fire died down, the dragon realized he had burned down his own home. Not the smartest move by the dragon.

In the End

Now several months after the incident, the countries were still trying to find a home to settle in. The seven leaders were badly injured. Leader Sokoviac's knee was bleeding. Because of all of the walking, his legs gave out and he fell down on his knees. Leader Dawson's scar was opened up because of the fire from the dragon. He was bleeding out. The red blood covered his face. Leader Bauge had broken his leg from running into a Komodo dragon. The Komodo dragon tried to eat his leg but only broke it. Leader Dregg, from the Country of Strength was born with incredible strength and power. He could lift very heavy objects. He lost his eye during the battle with the dragon. The fire made it impossible to see and he stumbled into the fire. The fire burned his eye off. Leader Gresham from the Country of Star had chapped lips and a dry tongue. Due to the lack of water and the drought on their journey. Whenever he tried to lick his lips it would not work because his tongue was dry. Leader Kimarra from the Country of Song, as a child was a very talented singer and dancer. She also was very pretty. During the journey, her voice became weak and she lost her ability to sing well. Leader Duan from the Country of Light had broken his fingers due to climbing walls. When he was just a young boy, his mother was paralyzed. When the asteroids came, she could not escape. He watched her die before his eyes.

They all looked like they were done for. It did not seem like they would make it.

Sike!

Ha! Ha! You thought they died didn't you? Nope, actually when all hope was lost, the old settlers' spirits had come to guide them to the place they had been searching for. One of the ancient leaders said to them, "Seven Leaders, we see you are troubled. We've come here for guidance. We hope now you have been taught by all of this that fighting doesn't solve all of your problems. You should also not be greedy and learn to share. You should work together more to solve your problems. We see you have learned your lesson. We will guide you to your destination."

"Thank you" said Leader Duan.

In a flash, all seven countries were in a perfect oasis. There was grass, water, coal mines, and lots of space to build their homes. Leader Sokoviac's knee was healing. Leader Dawson's burn was closing up. Leader Bauge's leg was all healed. Leader Dregg was given an eyepatch. Leader Gresham was satisfied that he got water to drink. This cured his dry lips and tongue. Leader Duan's fingers were put back together. And finally, the beautiful voice of Leader Kimarra, the only woman leader, was heard singing throughout the oasis.

They had finally found a place to settle in and call home.

5

The Value of Life

by Karen Corral

A wealthy man named Carlos once lived in a big city, prosperous. He was the owner of a very successful company. Since he was so rich he started to become slothful. He came late to work, forgot to pay his employees, forgot to pay bills, and he did not pay attention to his costumers. Soon his employees started to quit so he had to run his company all by himself. Since it was too much work for him he decided to quit. Since he did not have a job he started to lose all his money. In a matter of time he started to lose his fortune. First he lost his job, then he lost his car, and finally he lost his house. So he decided to take out some loans, but he was not able to because he did not have a job to pay the loans.

Not having anywhere to live he made the dumpster his new home. He would go days without food. He knew that if his friends saw him they were going to laugh at him. He would wonder around begging for money from people and soon enough his clothes became all shabby. His hair that once was nice, short, and clean had become long and dirty. He found out that a restaurant named Copper Kettle would always throw out the leftover food, but since there was a lot of homeless around the area he had to fight for the food. Days later Carlos found a box since he used to work building furniture he was easily able turn it into a bed.

The man started to feel lonely. For many days he would hear a noise but he did not know where it came from. He thought it was a rat but he found out it was actually a dog looking for food. The dog like the man was dirty and shabby. The dog was unlucky because that night the man had only a slice of pizza he wanted it all for himself. After looking at the dog's big begging eyes the man decided to share it with the dog. From that day on the dog would come back every day hoping to receive some leftovers.

As the days went on Carlos and the dog became best friends, and he decided to give him a name. He named the dog Hope, because the dog has taught him that in life it is important to always think positive. As time passed the dog started to stay by his side. The dog and Carlos would sleep together on the cardboard to keep each other warm and safe. Not only did he feed him, but he also began to teach him tricks every day. Hope was so smart he was a fast learner.

Carlos started to do more and more tricks with Hope. One day as they were training a group of people were watching them. The group of people were so impressed of how a homeless dog and man could do such an amazing job. So they put money on a hat that Carlos had left on the floor. They also told Carlos what great dog he had and that he was a great trainer.

Carlos thought of a great idea that making dog shows would make him money. He would use the money to help homeless people. So one day Carlos went to the park with Hope to perform their tricks. People started to gather around them to watch the show. As people started to walk off they dropped money in the hat that was close to them. With the first one hundred dollars he took Hope to the vet. He wanted to make sure that Hope was healthy. The first few days they started to make enough money to buy real food for both of them. As days went on he had enough money to rent a hotel.

On a random day at the park Carlos and Hope were performing when a guy interrupted to ask Carlos if he would do an interview for him. Carlos said he would think about it. He thought about it so long he could not decide whether to do it. At last he had made his decision and his answer was yes. What he didn't know was that the man worked for a t.v show that is presented worldwide.

After his interview Hope and Carlos did a special show that they had been working on. From there on he became very popular and requested. People would pay him to come and perform for them. So he started to save the money that he was making from his appearances. By this time, he already had found a house to live in with his dog, Hope. He became so popular that he took his shows on tour. He went to China,

France, England, Texas, and Canada.

He even had a company where people can adopt pets that were abandon or lost in the streets. He helped the pets find a home and someone to take care of them. He was so successful that he even had his own TV show. If no one would adopt the pets he would show them tricks and put the dogs to do the tricks on his TV show. People would see the pets perform and they would want to adopt them.

He showed the homeless how to work for their needs. He would also help them find a job where they could use their abilities. If the homeless did not know how to work, he would train them. If they were lonely he will let them adopt a pet. He would also need someone to take care of the pets so they would not feel lonely.

Carlos had to learn the hard way that not everything in life is easy to get. That one bad choice can change your life forever. Carlos went through many things to get to where he is now, but he is thankful that he came back up in life with the help of his best friend named Hope. After all he learned his lesson to be grateful and to work hard in life. So now Carlos dedicate his life to help others.

6

My Big Blue and Green Eyed Boy

by Juliette Hess

Ring! "Yes!" Fin and I yelled together.

It was the last day of school at Pines Middle School, and you could tell everyone in room 304 was looking forward to two nice months of summer! I grabbed Fin's football right out of his hands and raced him to the ice cream stand. I am *ALWAYS* faster than Fin, so I guess I shouldn't call it a race, considering he is a 200 pound football player.

Fin and I met 3 years ago, the winter after my Grandfather passed away. I was sitting down in the front of my front door crying with my best friend, Max, my golden lab puppy. All of a sudden, I saw a big bulky boy who I recognized from the school football team. He was not the most popular guy at school, but you could tell he was a sweet boy.

Before I knew it he came and asked, "What's wrong Alex?"

I told him about my Grandfather and how he left me with my puppy, Max. Ever since that day, Fin and I have been inseparable.

That same afternoon, we walked back with our ice cream to my house as we talked about our summer plans. We lived in Colorado, so there were tons of things we could do. Summer was our favorite time of year because there was always good weather. I told Fin I was going to Aspen for a week, but I was free for the rest of the summer.

Later that day, Fin was gone, and I was playing with Max. I always look forward to seeing Max every day because I know he will be happy to see me, too! During the summer, I always swim and he always joins me, since he is a lab.

The next morning...*crash*! I woke straight up and realized Max was not in the bed with me. I rushed downstairs and went to the window and saw that trees had fallen and water was over the curb.

"MAX!" I panicked, I could not find him.

My parents ran into the room and said, "We can't find Max, sweetie."

Max always had a fear of thunder, and he would run around the house going crazy. He must have gotten out of the house! That's when I noticed the back door was open. I ran out the back door into the garage, and the wind immediately knocked me down. My parents grabbed me and pulled me inside.

"I'm sorry honey, but we don't have time to look for Max right now. It is too dangerous outside, and we need to go stay on high ground," my Dad said.

We were in the spare closet for about two hours, and finally, the storm passed. Everything was silent and still. My parents lead me to the front door, and immediately I started thinking about Max. I told my parents we have to start looking. As I walked through the door, I realized my front steps were gone. I looked around and saw furniture on roofs, toys on the road, and clothes everywhere you looked. The neighbors across the street were in front of their destroyed house on the phone, crying hysterically.

I suddenly remembered Fin! Everyone was out on the street. His house was still standing, but you could not see him or his family in sight.

"Mom, Dad, what about Fin?" I asked.

"Let's go check on his family," Mom replied.

We walked over a bunch of dirty trash to get to Fin's house. Once we arrived, I could hear yelling and screaming. We had to push through furniture, so we could finally get to where we heard the yelling. Fin and his family were stuck in a closet. It took an hour for my dad to get everything out of the way to get to them. Once Fin and his family were safe and out of the closet, we all started looking for Max. This was all too much and too emotional, but we had to find my puppy.

The rest of the day, we searched for Max, but could not find him anywhere! As a month passed by, I was worried that Max had passed away or that he found a new family. Once our house was finally remodeled, my parents convinced me to go to the shelter, even though I could not stop thinking about Max.

We got to the shelter, and I smelled the smell of animals who need to be adopted. We went to the big dog section and passed by the females, but nothing caught my eye. I did see a black lab that looked a little like Max, but she just was not the same.

My family and I got to the male side and passed by 2 isles of dogs that did not catch my eye at all. Before I got to the last kennel and looked down at my feet thinking that I am never getting over Max,

I suddenly heard a loud thumping of a tail and whining and crying from the animal in the kennel. My eyes met with the eyes of a big brown blue eyed lab. Was this really possible? Could this be real? It was my best friend in the world, Max!

My Mom and Dad came up to the kennel and immediately recognized Max too. All of us were overjoyed! I stayed with Max as my Mom and Dad went to get an employee.

"Where have you been buddy?" I asked as tears came rolling down my face.

As we walked out with Max, we all knew the missing piece of our lives was put together again.

7

The Last Monster Hunters

by Ethan Oropeza

Once long ago there were eight countries that united to keep the underworld from awakening, but seven of them have been lost to time. Now the Master of Fire, Kai of the underworld is rising. Can the last monster hunters stop the threat?

The Fall

"Hey!" Luke yelled Mike.

"What?" Luke asked.

"Do you know where Lucy went?" asked Mike.

"No," replied Luke.

Mike started walking to Lucy's cabin when there was a sudden shake of the Earth.

"What was that?" asked Mike.

"I don't know but it doesn't feel good," replied Luke.

Just then Lucy came running outside. A hole opened up under Mike, Luke, and Lucy. They went crashing down into the hole. As they stood up and dusted themselves off they saw a hollow cavern city. The city was quiet and the citizens seemed nervous and scared. There was one, big, dark building in front of them. It had a sign in front with the words Training Facility written on it.

"Where are we?" asked Mike.

"I don't know," whispered Luke.

Lucy noticed a shadow walking towards them. "Help!" yelled Lucy.

The Welcome

"Welcome," a strange voice said. "You have been chosen for this place." The strange man glided out of the shadow. He was dressed in gold armor with a golden spear. "Welcome to the Underground Monster Hunting Training Facility. We call it UMHTF. My name is George and I will be your mentor."

The three new monster hunters were speechless. "At least he has cool gold armor," said Luke.

"But can we just go home now?"

"No," said George firmly. "Not until you have been trained. The world needs you. You have a calling, a duty. Then you may return to your homes. But we don't have much time. Let's get started."

A Hidden Enemy

George introduced them to his helper. His name was Paul. Paul shook the three monster hunter's hands and smiled. As the three monster hunters walked away to go train an evil smile slowly spread on Paul's face.

"These three kids think they can defeat my master, the evil Master Kai?" sneered Paul.

"Well they are wrong. Master Kai must attack tonight." George interrupted Paul's evil thoughts.

"Can you come to training tonight to help me?" George asked Paul.

"Of course," Paul said, but Paul had no plans of helping the three new monster hunters.

Lucy, Luke, and Mike had followed George to the training room. They practiced under George's supervision for hours and hours.

The Attack

Boom! "What was that?" asked Luke.

"They are attacking!" yelled George.

"What?" asked Mike. There was another great rumble. This time it sounded much closer. Everyone was running, evacuating, and screaming.

"Get to the top!" someone yelled over the rumbles.

"No, to the bottom!" another yelled.

"Luke, Mike, and Lucy follow me!" yelled George. "We have to get out of here."

They ran out of the building just in time to look back and see it explode into a fire and rubble.

"Did everyone get out?" asked Lucy.

"I sure hope so!" said Mike.

"What are we going to do now?" Luke asked.

"Quick! This way!" said George. George's cell phone rang. "Hello," said George. "Paul you did this! Why? I'll get you for this." George sadly hung up.

"Paul has been working for the evil Master Kai the whole time," he told the others. He led the three new monster hunters to a warehouse. "We need to come up with a new plan now."

"So now we are going to creepy warehouse unarmed?" asked Luke in a whisper.

"Luke, remember why we are here," reassured Lucy. At the entrance Lucy yelled, "Anyone home?" There was no sound besides her voice echoing through the abandoned machinery.

"No one appears to be here," said Mike.

Once in the warehouse, George and the three new monster hunters started to make a new plan. George explained to three new monster hunters, "Master Kai is the master of fire. He had been terrorizing his beloved underground city for years. They have tried everything they could think of to defeat him, but nothing has worked and now my own helper has betrayed me and fallen into the fire."

Lucy had a great idea.

Fire and Water

"How do you put out a fire? asked Lucy.

"With water!" they all said together.

"Where will we get enough water down here to defeat the Master of Fire, Kai?" asked Mike.

George said, We need to go see the Master of Water."

"He has been in hiding in the shadows for years. How will we find him?" asked Mike.

The three new monster hunters went back to the city. They search everywhere. High and low, but they could not find him. Just when they were about to give up they saw a little house on the last hill of the city where no one ever goes. It had beautiful trees and bushes and flowers and water fountains.

"That looks like a place where a Master of Water would live," said Luke.

The three new monster hunters went to the house and found the Master of Water. They convinced him to help them defeat the Master of Fire, Kai.

The Defeat

George, the three new monster hunters, and the Master of Water traveled to Kai's lair. It was a hidden castle on top of Mount Black. It was dark except for the fire, which made it very hot. Kai saw them from a mile away and sent his fire dragon down to meet them.

"You shall not pass," said the fire dragon. He began to breathe fire.

The brave Master of Water stepped in front of them knowing that fire could not hurt him. He summoned all the water in the land behind him and threw it at the dragon. The dragon was stunned and could not breathe fire.

"Hurry!" yelled George. "We only have seconds."

They ran passed the fire dragon as quickly as they could to the large front doors. They pushed them open to see Master Kai waiting for them. No one had ever made it past his fire dragon. He started summoning fire balls and fire spells and throwing them, but the Master of Water repeatedly retaliated. Eventually all Master Kai's stamina had drained. He could not make any more fire.

The three monster hunters put their training into action. Lucy, Mike and Luke captured Master Kai easily and transported him back to the underworld where he belonged.

Luke, Lucy, and Mike vowed to George that they would keep his city safe from Master Kai and they underworld as long as they lived. Today the descendants of these three brave monster hunters keep the city safe.

8

You Are Still a Winner

by Alani Simmons

It was the beginning of March and everyone around the school was talking about the Chinese speech contest. My friends Jordan and Vivian said they were going to do it so I thought, *why not*? I was a little scared because I had never been in a competition before. Not for anything.

There were a few topics to choose from; Hobbies, Family and Things We Love. I decided to talk about family. Writing the speech was a little hard because I didn't know how to say all of the words I wrote in English. This meant practicing really hard.

I wrote about my stepbrother, my dad, my mom and how much I loved the things that we do together. I also wrote about my very close friends who are like family to me.

I had to practice A LOT! I practiced during school, after school and on the weekends. I knew that I was going to need some help so I teamed up with our school Principal Mr. Chang on the weekends and practiced with my teacher Miss Huang during school. My after school tutor was even kind enough to help me after I finished up my homework. My mom unfortunately could not help me with the Chinese part but she did help me to keep my hands by my side and to focus straight ahead. I spent almost a month practicing for this special day.

Finally, the day came. The Chinese contest was held in a very nice building not too far from our house. It's called the Global Federation of Chinese Business Women in Southern USA. That is a mouth full. We just call it GFCBW. When I walked in I saw lots of kids. Some I knew but most I didn't know at all. There were several schools participating in the contest that day. I wasn't' nervous at all. We ate donuts and drank orange juice before the contest began. It took forever to start because people had to sign in. I was just glad to see my friends there. We played around and took pictures in the hall. We got our order numbers from a little lady at the front desk and we headed off to our classroom. I was number 15. That meant 14 people were ahead of me so I am a long wait. Parents weren't able to talk to us either. The room was small with a lot of chairs. There were 3 judges for the contest. They all seemed really nice.

When it was my turn to go in front of the judges I knew that I would do really good. We weren't allowed to read off the paper because if you did you would lose points. I sat my paper on the seat so I wasn't tempted to look at it. I was one minute into my speech and I FROZE! I just couldn't think of the next word. I was trying not to cry. I stood there for 30 seconds just staring at the judges and finally it hit me! I continued my speech but I knew I had gone over on time. We only had 2 minutes to say the entire speech we had written.

Once everyone was done, we went into a big gym like room with a few rows of seats. We waited for the finalists to be called. 3rd Place was my friend Maddie. 2nd Place was my bff Jordan and 1st was NOT ME. It was Christian who also attended my school. I was super sad. I ran to my mom and hugged her. I cried. My mom said I still did very well but I was still sad. My teacher and principal both walked up to me and told me that I shouldn't cry because I did very well. I did get a trophy just for coming. That made me smile. I didn't exactly handle losing the right way though. If I could do it over, here are the 5 steps I would take!

STEP 1: Congratulate the Winner. You can shake hands; you can high five and all that good stuff. My BFF, Jordan was in the speech contest and she won!!!!! I screamed when her name was called because I was so happy for her! But I should have said congrats to everyone instead of being mad about not making the finals.

STEP 2: Try try again. When I lost the speech I was crying and decided that I hated the speech contest! But then I heard that there was another speech contest next year so I was pumped up. You are probably wonder how I was crying then,

I am pumped up. It's because It gives me another chance to improve myself so, I am going to try, try again! Just because you lost doesn't mean you should give up!

STEP 3: Find out where you went wrong. My mom asked me if I knew why I didn't make it to the finals. I told her it was because I froze and went over time. I wish I did not stop in the middle of my speech. If I did not stop I will at least be able to compete in the finals but I did. I had to be honest with myself and the mistakes I had made.

STEP 4: Practice makes perfect! We know that nobody is perfect but practicing can surely make you better. Practicing helps you memorize and prepare for the big day. What I learned by being a part of the speech contest made all difference. I know now that I could have practiced a little more on my own.

STEP 5: Know that you are still a winner! When I lost the contest I thought I was a total fool but I remembered my friends and family telling me that when you try new things, you are still winner. It was still cool to participate and try something that I've never done before. Some people won't try it at all. I stood in front of 100 strangers and 3 judges memorizing a 2-minute speech all in another language. I should be proud of myself. Some grown ups can't even do that! Trying is half the battle.

Remember, even if you lose...YOU ARE STILL A WINNER!

9

Bitten

by Elsie Williams

"*5326,5326,5326,5326,*" I kept repeating to myself. Okay, here it is, my locker. It was the first day of school and I was walking down the hallway of Sunny Dell High School. My name is Lila Peterson and I am 15 years old. I'm a tenth grader at Sunny Dell High School in Chicago, Illinois.

"Wow!" I said to myself as I put in my locker number, "This is huge!" While looking down the hallway, I noticed the football team walking towards me.

"Oh my," I said sarcastically. I just didn't understand why the football players got all the attention.

Lila! Lila! I heard someone calling my name. Wait that's no someone...that's Faith! She was running down the hallway with her arms outstretched. We had been friends since we were both two years old.

"Faith!" I gave her a big hug.

"How was your summer?" she asked as she pulled away. I needed to think about that. I had spent the summer in Idaho with my grandparents and cousins. So much happened to me that I didn't know how to put it in one brief sentence.

"So?" Faith asked while looking at me with her ice blue eyes. I could feel her stare going straight into my brain.

"Well, I did..." *RINGGG!!!!!!*

Since the bell rang I wasn't able to finish my reply. Instead we ran into our history class and took our seats. I noticed my new teacher writing his name on the board. When he was finished the board said *Mr. Chiller.*

When Mr. Chiller turned to face us, I saw his eyes. His eyes were red and his teeth were sharp and yellow. It looked like he never brushed his teeth! He was a very weird looking teacher.

"Good morning class," he said calmly. I could see his red

eyes looking right at me, and for a second it felt like my heart had slowed down.

"Um...Mr. Chiller, why is your face so white?" I asked, looking curiously at his face. He smiled a crooked smile with his sharp yellow teeth showing.

"Well, you see..." He never finished because Ms. Raven, our Vice Principal, came in. She told Mr. Chiller that he was missing the meeting for...she trailed off as she looked at all of us. I guess she didn't want us to hear what she was going to say. She bent down to Mr. Chiller's ear and whispered something. I couldn't hear what she said but I could tell by her serious expression that it was important.

"Okay, I will be there in a second," said Mr. Chiller.

"Very well then, but hurry," Ms. Raven said as she quickly stepped out of the classroom and sped back down the hallway.

"Okay class, I have to go to a quick meeting about F...," He said, but stopped before finishing his sentence.

I could tell he didn't mean to say that.

"Goodbye," he said quickly. "Behave and just read your books and I will be back soon!" Then he walked out the door. All the kids in the class were looking at each other with wide eyes not knowing what to do. I looked at Faith.

"Hey Faith, do you want to come with me to get a drink of water?"

"Sure," she said with a warm smile.

"Okay, let's go," I said. We went out the door. The drinking fountain was in the basement. Faith and I walked down three flights of stairs to reach it. All I knew about the basement was that the drinking fountain was there.

"Hey, Faith do you even know why they put the only drinking fountain in the whole school down here?" I asked, looking at Faith.

"No clue." She just shrugged her shoulders. We kept walking and we didn't talk, not even once, until we reached the drinking fountain. We turned a corner and there it was. I was just about to bend down and get a drink of water when I suddenly saw something move in the corner of my eye. I looked over my shoulder and started to ask Faith if she saw something move, too but Faith wasn't there. Where on earth could she have gone?

"FAITH!" I yelled at the top of my lungs. I felt so scared, my eyes were filling with tears, and my face was turning red. I was shaking and whimpering as I ran up the three flights of stairs. I kept shouting, "Faith!" I threw open the door to my classroom. "M-M-M-Mr. Chiller," I said looking around worriedly, as if something would pop out of nowhere and try to hurt me.

"Yes?" he asked looking at me with curiosity.

"I can't find Faith," I groaned. A sly smile came over his face. When I saw his teeth, blood was dripping from them. I felt like I was going to throw up. I hadn't felt this bad since I was 6 when I had a terrible fever. No one else seemed to notice. When he saw me staring at his teeth, he instantly closed his mouth.

"Don't worry, she will be back soon," he muttered, whispering something to himself under his breath which I couldn't understand. It was probably in a different language. I looked away and stared at the door, praying that Faith would come in. Exactly 13 minutes before the bell, she stiffly walked into the room. I ran to Faith and threw my arms around her.

"Faith! Are you okay?" I asked. I noticed her neck was bleeding, but I couldn't see where the blood was coming from.

"I-I do not know what you are talking about," she replied. It was like she was a robot.

"Lila and Faith, will you please take your seats?" Mr. Chiller asked impatiently.

"Yes," I replied. Then I guided Faith to her seat because for some reason she would not move. When we got to our seats, I was still wondering why Mr. Chiller's teeth had blood on them. RINGGG! The bell broke my train of thought.

"That's the bell for the end of the day kids," said Mr. Chiller. His face had a crooked smile, his lip curled up revealing his sharp, yellow teeth.

"I guess that's how he smiles," I whispered. Before I realized it, everyone was out of the classroom except for me. Even Faith had left. I didn't even notice that she had left. I looked out the window and scanned the entire front of the school.

I finally found Faith and she was looking up at the window

that I was looking out of. She waved at me and smiled her same old smile. Great, I thought, she's back to her same old self. I turned around to find that Mr. Chiller was gone, but I found a note on the floor where he was standing just before I looked out the window.

Suddenly, the phone rang before I could read the note. I didn't know if I should answer it or not. After all, it was Mr. Chiller's phone. Before I knew what to do the phone stopped ringing. I listened to see if there would be a message. After a few seconds Ms. Raven's voice came over the line, *Please meet me in my office.* Then the message ended. I stuffed the note in my pocket and ran up two flights of stairs and down four hallways. Finally I came to Ms. Raven's office.

I opened the door slowly and saw that Ms. Raven wasn't there. I quickly closed the door and looked frantically for a place to hide. Just as Ms. Raven was opening the door, I spotted a little space under her desk and darted over to squeeze inside. Ms. Raven closed the door to her office when I heard another door open from the opposite side of the room. Who could that be?

"I caught one person today," said someone with a heavy accent. My hand flew over my mouth as I realized it was Mr. Chiller. I listened carefully to what they said.

"Who was it?" Ms. Raven asked.

"The girl's name is Faith. I was aiming for her friend but I guess she will work too."

I held my hand even tighter over my mouth to keep from screaming. How could this be happening!

"Tell me how much longer until we have enough?" Ms. Raven asked eagerly.

"I don't know," Mr. Chiller replied.

"Well, how did you get her?" Mrs. Raven asked.

"I stepped out for the meeting and the two girls stepped out for a drink. Faith fell down the chute while her friend was bending down." It seemed as if Ms. Raven knew exactly what he was talking about.

"Did she have the right type?" Ms. Raven asked.

"Yes, exactly the right type of chemicals and nutrients," he said. It sounded like he was a college professor of science.

"Well that is great!" Ms. Raven said excitedly.

"Is that all you needed to talk about?" Mr. Chiller asked.

"Yes, you can go now," she said quickly.

I heard the door slam shut as Mr. Chiller and Mrs. Raven left the room. I peeked around the corner to see if they were gone. Sure enough, there was no one in sight. I scrambled out of the bottom of the desk. I was shaking from head to toe and my feet felt numb. I ran to the door and threw it open. I started running down the hall. As I was running, I ran into a teacher! I was afraid to look up in case it was Mr. Chiller. I slowly looked up and noticed it was Mrs. Clementine, one of the nicest and prettiest teachers in this entire school! I was so relieved.

"Hello sweetie, how are you? Do you need anything?" She smiled sweetly down at me with a concerned look on her face

"Uh...yes, I was just wondering what the meeting was for earlier?" I asked.

"Meeting? What meeting? Oh dear, are you all right?" she asked while feeling my forehead.

"I'm fine, thank you," I said feeling very confused.

"Well, bye honey, are you sure you're feeling ok?"

"Yes," I said as I walked toward the front doors. When I got to the doors, I swung them open and gasped as I stared at Faith. She was standing there with her face tilted a little to the side; she had a misty look in her eyes as if she were dead. I stumbled backwards and thought there must be some way that I could heal Faith. As I was thinking I saw a dew drop on the tree next to me and was reminded how thirsty I was. My throat was parched. That's it! The drinking fountain! That was where Faith had disappeared! I quickly ran back inside the school and down the stairs to the water fountain.

The basement was dark and spooky. There was a small breeze and it sent chills down my back. I looked for a light then found a lamp chain and I gave it a little tug. The room was lit instantly with the dim light. The room was full of boxes and dusty books and shelves with barely anything on them. I quickly made my way to the drinking fountain. I felt around it to see if there was some sort of trigger that opened a trapdoor somewhere. I heard a loud click and I dropped.

I fell into a room with chemicals and microscopes. It looked something like my school's science lab. I stood up and instantly cried out in pain. My ankle had twisted in the fall. I limped across the room. As I struggled to cross the large space, I heard a crack come from my pocket and remembered the note! I unfolded it and began to read:

Dear Raven, if Faith is not healed in a week or so, there is a medicine that can heal her instantly on the third shelf to the left in my lab. It is called Bloodroot. Your friend, Chiller

I quickly ran to the shelves of the lab and went to the third shelf and looked to the left. There was the Bloodroot! I jerked my head as a door slowly creaked open. I grabbed the Bloodroot and ducked under a table in the corner that was covered in shadows.

Mr. Chiller walked to the edge of the room and grabbed a photograph and went out the door. I hadn't noticed it there before. I climbed out from under the table and put my hand over my heart to stop it from banging against my chest. I ran to the door before it closed and dashed up the stairs. When I made it to the door I swung it open and looked around. I was in the classroom! I had always thought this room was the janitor's closet. I stepped out and ran out of the classroom and nearly ran into Mr. Chiller!

Luckily, his back was facing me and he hadn't noticed me yet. I tiptoed back towards the front doors. When I opened the doors I saw Faith still standing in the same spot she had been when I was there last. I opened the Bloodroot and poured a couple drops down her throat.

She gagged and coughed and fell to the ground. She clawed at her throat and I dropped beside her.

"Faith! Can you hear me?" I screamed at her as she slowly closed her eyes. I was so worried I had done something wrong. Then I felt someone grab my shoulder.

I turned around to see Mrs. Clementine. She had a worried expression on her face as she stared down at Faith.

"What on earth happened, dear?" she exclaimed with tears brimming in her warm brown eyes.

I felt a wave of hot tears come to my own eyes at the hopelessness of the situation. I was going to lose my best friend and it was entirely my fault. I hadn't worked hard enough to make things right and now Faith was going to pay for it.

While I felt myself plunge into despair, I heard a soft moan and a light tap on my hand. I looked down to see Faith squinting back at me in the bright afternoon sun.

"Faith!" I squealed in pure joy as I threw myself at her. Mrs. Clementine's hand slid over my shoulder and gave me a squeeze of reassurance.

"Wh-what happened?" Faith asked groggily. She put her hand to her head and moaned again. "I have a terrible headache."

" Long story short, you got kidnapped and I saved you," I said with a smirk. She smiled smugly back at me.

"Oh really? My hero," Faith replied, with a glint of humor in her eyes. "Would you be so kind as to be my hero twice and help me up?" She reached her hands up toward me. I grasped her delicate, pale fingers and gently pulled her to her feet. Mrs. Clementine did not hesitate to pull Faith into a long, warm hug. Then she helped Faith slowly make her way to the bus stop where the yellow vehicle was waiting.

As soon as Faith was securely on her way home, and Mrs. Clementine was on her way back to her classroom, I ran back inside to get Mr. Chiller and his special friend Ms. Raven fired. There was only one way I could do that.

There, I thought. I signed the second note with a flourish like Ms. Raven always did. Then I picked up the two notes that would set my whole plan into action. My plan was a smart and sneaky one. I would give one note to both Mr. Chiller and Ms. Raven, saying they wanted to discuss the situation of Faith. Then, when they met up, I would record the whole conversation and show it to the principal. I slipped out of Mr. Chiller's classroom and slowly made my way down to the library where Ms. Raven was. I walked toward her and slipped the note into her binder that was lying on the table, making sure she would be able to see it. I read through it one more time.

Raven; meet me in my classroom at 3:45. We have matters of Faith to discuss. Much appreciated, Chiller

Perfect. Everything was in order. I slipped out of the library unnoticed and went to find Mr. Chiller. Nearly ten minutes later, I found Mr. Chiller in the cafeteria. His tray was on the table while he went to get a cup of coffee. I stood the note up on his sandwich and slowly backed out of the room. Now all I had to do was sit and wait, so I crept up to the classroom and got comfortable for the show. I looked at my watch and it read 3:40. Time to get my camera out, I thought. I took it out and suddenly Mr. Chiller burst into the room, with Ms. Raven following close behind. I turned my recorder on.

"Why on earth are we having this meeting during my break?" Ms. Raven asked angrily.

"I didn't start this. I thought you wanted to meet up," Mr. Chiller said in a defensive tone.

"Oh, whatever. Let's just discuss Faith so I can get back to my break." Ms. Raven crossed her arms and sat back on her heels.

"Very well. All that happened was I took her to my lab and sucked out her nutrients. I was turning ashy, you know. Then I sent her back up here. She obviously wasn't the strong type or she would have been able to survive on her own." Mr. Chiller looked suspiciously at Ms. Raven.

"What do you mean *on her own?*" Ms. Raven's tone was slowly getting louder and louder.

"Well, didn't you take the Bloodroot to set her back to normal, like I said in the note?" Mr. Chiller asked, also getting angrier by the second.

"I heard of no such thing and saw no note about Bloodroot. What is that anyway?" Ms. Raven asked.

"Oh no," Mr. Chiller said under his breath. "We've been..."

"Caught," I said proudly as I stood from my hiding place. "Glad you finally figured that out. I've got your whole conversation on my recorder plus a certain witness named Faith on my side." I held up my recorder.

Mr. Chiller snarled and stomped his feet like a two-year-old throwing a tantrum. Suddenly, he bolted after me. I screamed and ran out the classroom door. As soon as I turned the corner, I bumped into someone.

"Mrs. Honey!" I shouted with joy. There, the most wonderful person I had ever seen in my life stood before me. Mrs. Honey, the principal, stared back at me with a startled look on her face.

"What is going on?" she asked, looking between Mr. Chiller and me.

"I think I'll just have to show you," I said with a grin.

A week later, everything was back to normal. Faith was her normal, bubbly self, Ms. Raven and Mr. Chiller had been fired immediately after I showed the recording to Mrs. Honey, and I had a new history teacher named Ms. Joy. Her name completely described her personality. She was by far my favorite teacher.

Even though I knew Mr. Chiller was gone, every once in a while, I would look out the window and see a bat and a raven flying close together out on the horizon, then I would shiver and turn back to my work. It's just my imagination. Right?

5TH -6TH GRADE SHORT STORIES

10

Rest in Peace

by Anna Hockett

I died two months ago. Please, don't freak out! Yes, you heard that right. My name is Dandy (Dandelion). Yes, my parents named me after a very unusual flower. Also, I am a ghost.

It was a horrible day for many reasons that were somehow all connected. I was failing all my classes which led to having a big fight with my folks, one that would change my life. One thing led to another, and I took a ride on my bike to clear my mind.

It turns out I wasn't really paying attention to my surroundings and *BAM*, I was hit by a truck, leading to instant death. The surgeons at the hospital tried to save me, but there was nothing they could do.

So now, I am here, stuck between life and heaven. All I have to do is figure out how to rest in peace, which in my case, means I have to see my parents happy. There's just one problem, I don't know where my parents moved. They left after I died; my guess is that they felt guilty.

I have to find them in order to move on to heaven. For all I know, they could be in another state or another country for all I know. The only thing I know is that they would go to a small town where the news of my death hasn't spread yet. Another problem is that I don't have access to a map. However, I remember that before death, I had a map hung up on my wall. This leads me to wonder if they moved any of my belongings.

~

After searching every nook and cranny in the house, I came to the conclusion that there's nothing, not even the tiniest clue as to where my parents went. I guess that means I have to start from scratch. The only thing I have going for me is that I don't believe they would ever leave Kentucky. My parents both grew up in Kentucky and it is where their childhood homes are, which means that despite everything, Kentucky is precious to them.

~

We used to live in Kentucky, and I've already searched half the towns in this state. I just want to see my parents again. I wish I didn't have to do all this searching, but I in reality, what else do I have to do. Remember, I am stuck between life and heaven.

These are the thoughts going through my head as suddenly I watch my hand detach from my misty form. It jerks itself forward as if to gesture to follow. So I do what any ghost would do and follow it..

I've been following my detached hand for hours. We (well I) finally arrived at the destination it was leading me to. I'm at a strange place called Lucky Kentucky Diner. There's a counter in front of me and small tables to my left. There's also a soda machine to my right. Somehow I can tell my parents were here recently, which must be one of the perks of being a ghost. This new feeling must mean my parents might be living in a town nearby. My first guess is Louisville. It is small enough to where the news of my death has not spread but big enough to be a welcoming community.

As I get closer to Louisville, I can feel their presence get stronger. It's like they are in my reach but I can't quite grasp them. However, there are so many possibilities that something could go wrong. I could show up at the right house at the wrong time. No matter how hard it seems though, I'm determined to find my parents.

~

All I see is a house. It has checkered brown, red and maroon bricks and a beautiful entry way. There's vines carved into the stained, dark brown, wooden entry way, atop the door. The door is burgundy with surprisingly enough, dandelions carved into it. It looks like my dad's handiwork; but, I am not going to get my hopes up that this is the house. I look throughout the house in hopes that someone is inside there; they're just not close enough to the window for me to see them.

I finally see her, I see my mom. After all those months looking for her, I finally see her. All I can do is watch and listen but that's better than before. I look more closely at my mom. She looks distraught as if she's mad at herself. She must think it was her fault that I died. I wish I could just run up and hug her. Soon enough, I see my dad come up behind her and whisper something in her ear. It looks like he is trying to comfort her.

I can hear her talking to an adoption agency. They're going to adopt someone. I just know that they are going to be happy. Now that they have someone to talk, listen, and play with.

That's when I noticed that I'm starting to float up, as I grow wings. It's marvelous in heaven from what I can see. The clouds are fluffy as ever, and I see many other good Samaritans up here. I even see my grandma, who had died four years ago from cancer. It looks as if she has been waiting for me. I ask her how she knew I was dead.

"I have always been watching you and I have always been with you in spirit, but also in here," she said. She points to my heart. I run into her open arms. It feels so good that I realize how much I missed being able to hug her.

I have a feeling I'll be fine up here, I think as I listen carefully to Me-ma as she gives me a tour of this heavenly place. They have everything from never-ending-soothing-music to frozen yogurt machines. Man, they thought of everything.

That's the end of my story as Dandelion Grace Robison. At least, that's the end for a while.

Illustration by La'Jasha Champion - Front Cover Artist

11

Forever Pompeii

by Haleigh Lechner

The day Mount Vesuvius decided to finally wake up was the same morning I was heading back from the black market. My family always sends me there to get three loaves of bread and some goat cheese. None of us saw it coming. We should have taken those earthquakes seriously. We never could have been prepared for it, even if we knew it was coming. Then it came.

"Good morning Emery!" Mr. Jones said.

"Good morning," I replied brightly.

"Clouds look kinda dreary, huh?"

I looked up. I never noticed it, but he wasn't wrong. The clouds looked like the color of fire and ash.

"Yeah," I responded. "I guess so." I started back home again. Mr. Jones is one of the regulars at the black market. He's a lot better than some other people around. He deserves better than to come here. But one day, his life changed. Just like mine was about to.

"Mom, I'm home!"

"Oh, good," she said.

"Just in time for breakfast." Mama took off her apron and my sister, Harper, set the table.

"When is Papa coming back from his work trip?" she asked.

"In two days and one week's time."

That set everyone in a good mood. He was in our neighbor city of Herculaneum. I pulled out my chair to finally start eating my meal. At the heart of the town, everyone eats while walking. The smell of warm, buttery toast got me jealous every time. But now, it's my turn. I crunched into the warm eggs and fresh milk. I waited for the bread to come out of the fire stove. But it would never happen.

"So, mom," I asked. "Have you seen the clouds lately?"

She shakes her head for no. "They're really dark and shadowy. I'll show you if you come with me tonight to milk the cow. It will probably still be there."

"Sure Emery. But milking the cow is still your job," she said with a chuckle.

"I know, I know. The goat is still gonna be Harper's job, though."

"Don't remind me," she said under her breath. We all laughed at that.

After we finished breakfast, it was still fairly early in the morning. People thought we were crazy getting an early start on the day. Surprisingly, it's a lot better than sleeping in. Everybody else in Pompeii disagrees.

"What's your plan for today, Emery?" My mother looks at me with questioning eyes. I have to think about that for a while. I would probably wander around town and see if anyone needs help with farming or kitchen duties. My mother knows that's what I normally do over the weekend. And so, with one look, with eyes matching mine, she knew.

"And you, Harper?"

"I don't know," she grumbled, picking at her eggs.

"Well, I'm sure you can help with something," my mom said.

"If you girls will be back before lunch, the bread will be ready by then."

I hardly gave her a chance to finish her sentence, I had one foot out the door.

"Yeah, looking forward to it. Love you too, Mom!" I shouted.

Harper dragged behind me. It wouldn't be long before I saw her again. But next time, it would be for all the wrong reasons.

The first house I was planning to go to was Mrs. Edward. She had two boys. One my age, one two years older and one girl also my age. Years ago, my mom figured out I liked Matthew, Mrs. Edward's youngest son. She joked about it, but now I'm planning to marry Matthew in a few years.

Suddenly, all the town villagers seemed to scream one by one. I looked around at other people's houses. They were staring out their windows in horror.

"Something's outside!" I pulled Harper by the elbow towards the heart of the town. My chin dropped to the floor and my heart leapt out of my chest. Beside me, I felt Harper grab my arm, her small arms shaking. The clouds were even darker now. Deadly dark. Was it possible that clouds could be as black as fire? If so, that would be a perfect description of what it looks like. Finally, the whole town was flooded by deafening silence.

My heart was pulsing 600 beats per minute. The world seemed to spin around me, becoming a blur. I slowly dropped to my knees. Everything around me slowed. Mount Vesuvius started to erupt. I tried to move the most I could. My trembling lips muttered the faintest of words. "Run." My sister grabbed my arm and lifted me up. My wobbly legs quickly stood up. I stared into my sister's eyes. At that moment, I realized I needed to be strong for her. The fear and desperation in her eyes made me stand up a little bit taller. No matter what happened today, nothing was touching my sister.

Red hot lava came pouring out of Mount Vesuvius in long, flowing waves. I needed to get Harper to higher ground, and soon. My first thought came to me. Mrs. Edward. She would watch over Harper. She would protect my sister. She would keep Harper and her own children safe. I continued on the path to her house. She seemed to understand what I was thinking. "I'll protect her. I promise, she said.

"Thank you," I whispered, giving her a hug.

I turned to Harper and said, "I'm going to find Mommy." I felt a single tear fall on my shoulder. "It'll be okay." Then I left to go find our mother.

I passed by many houses on my journey. Some were trying to live. Others were hoping to die. The waves were getting higher now, hotter. I was nearing our house and saw my mother. She was helping others. I found her about a block down from our house. She was helping an elderly couple get out. They made it out. She fell. Their house was built close to a ditch. Luckily, she found a hole to put her hands in. But, the rich soil was wet. I saw sweat dripping down her forehead. Whether it was from the heat or the fact that her life was on the line, I don't know of. Her hands were gradually slipping. She started to lose the will to live.

"Mom?" I asked questioningly.

The lava below her was rising. Finally, her fingers slipped off the edge. I heard a single scream of pain. And then, there was nothing. Nothing. She was still alive, no doubt, but there was still silence. I knew I had to save her, I promised my sister we would all be okay. I slowly lowered myself down the side of the ditch. I found my mother, unconscious, but alive, at the bottom. I found a grip around her wrist and slowly lifted her up. I carefully set her on the ground. The lava continued to rise. It touched my feet. The pain was unbearable. But not enough to break the ties that bind. I lifted myself up by my mother. By the time I got up, my mother was fully awake and well. She and I both agreed to stay with Harper and be strong for her. No matter what.

We set off to find Harper. The clouds seemed to be raining now, in the form of ash and debris. I was starting to question the people who built Pompeii; at the foot of a volcano. Impressive. We finally found Harper and Mrs. Edward. Mom stayed with them while I went to make sure everyone was okay. Mr. Jones quickly ran towards me.

"Emery, your father's alive!"

I ran towards him and hugged him. I cried into his shoulders. Not tears of sadness or agony, but of joy. Joy. The state of being happy.

The city that my father was visiting sent a messenger on quick time's notice. He is supposed to be in emergency shelter, but knowing my dad, he'll probably be here by tomorrow. Mr. Jones managed to escape, too. His house was completely destroyed.

I went to tell mom and Harper the good news about my father. They cried, too. We all look down at the town that once was beautiful. Now, it was changed. It was still beautiful in its own kind of way. It's still home to our family. Our dad would be coming home fairly soon. Mr. Jones would be staying with us. And we would realize that no matter how hard you try, you can never break the ties that bind.

12

Going Down

by Isabela Parra

April 10, 1912

3:00 pm: "Hurry up Abigail! The ship is about to leave! That's my dad. I'm about to board the Titanic with my older brother Joe and my dad. Dad says that this will be a great way to get our minds off of Mom. Mom. Just saying her name makes me sad. She recently died from lung cancer. Joe and I were very depressed, and neither of us had said very much since that. My dad was pretty sad too, but he remained strong and did everything he could to make us happy. So when he received three free tickets for the Titanic from work, he thought it would be a good idea to go together as a family. So here we are. We're headed up to our room to settle in. I heard that it's going to be a really nice room. I started to relax. Maybe this could be a fun trip.

April 11, 1912

10:00 am: This morning was amazing! So yesterday we didn't do much because we were pretty exhausted from the long day. All we did was explore the ship and relax. But this morning we were ready to have fun! The plan was to have breakfast, visit the deck, tour the ship, and then meet some people. This morning we had the most delicious breakfast I've had in years. Plus, me and Joe aren't depressed anymore! Dad was right. This trip is actually fun! I'm so glad we went.

4:00 pm: "Whoo Hoo!!!" I don't think I've ever had such an amazing time! After breakfast, we headed to the deck to see the ocean, and boy was I blown away! It was the most beautiful thing I have ever seen! It was like looking into a vast blue expanse of nothingness. The feeling of the ocean water splashing on my face was my favorite part. But after awhile

Dad said it was time to go. I was pretty disappointed, but then Dad said we could come back after lunch. So we explored the ship a bit more, and boy is it beautiful! Yesterday we were kind of sleepy and it was pretty dark, so we didn't get the full experience, and boy did we miss out! It was the most beautiful and expensive looking ship I've ever seen! Only the richest people were on board. My dad was one of the main architects so he was given free tickets, but that's about the only reason we're here today.

7:00 pm: "Yawwwn!" Joe and I are pooped from a busy day. We sure did have fun, no doubt. But now we're both sleepy and just about ready to hit the hay. As soon as I touched the soft blankets on the bed I thought I was in heaven. I am so ready for this day to but at the same time I never want this day to end. I'm really proud of my Dad. I couldn't have designed this better myself.

April 12, 1912

9:30 am: I love breakfast! We had another amazing breakfast today. It was delicious eggs with the juiciest bacon and some of the tangiest orange juice I've ever tasted. If there was a competition for best breakfast it would be a tie between yesterday's and today's. Then later on Dad is going to take us back up to the deck. I'm looking forward to that!

1:00 pm: I love this ship! There is so much to see and so much to do! I love to hear the musicians play their music and the chefs here must have been beyond better than just being good at cooking. I'm so glad Dad made us come. We were just at the deck and it sure made my day. Right now we're about to have lunch. After that Dad took us back up to the deck to socialize with other people. But Joe and I got bored of that, so we started a game of tag.

Other second class kids saw us and joined in. Soon we had all the kids playing and making quite a bit of noise. One of the employee's heard the racket, so they came straight towards us and told us off for being loud. We stopped playing and went back to Dad to relax.

April 13, 1912

12:00 pm: Today we just plan to relax. We already had some glorious breakfast and now we plan to just chill in our room. I brought a board game so we are going to play a few rounds of that. Then I'm going to sketch a picture of our beautiful mother. Afterwards we plan to head up to the deck once more to just look out at the sea. I think we have a pretty full schedule today, but you always do on the Titanic.

April 14, 1912

12:30 pm: Yesterday we relaxed all day, but today we were ready for some action! This morning we were begging Dad to let us stay up late. He finally caved in after an hour of begging, but he said we could stay up no later than twelve-o-clock. I'm not complaining though! It's been awhile since any of us have stayed up late. So that's something to look forward to.

7:00 pm: Once again Joe and I are tired but we are both determined to stay up as late as possible. It's just that with all the stuff to do on the Titanic it is pretty hard to keep all your energy throughout the whole day. But Joe and I are both determined people, and we will stay up late.

11:40 pm: "Aaaaaahhhhhh!!" Something happened to the ship! I don't know what, but water's leaking into the rooms downstairs! I am so scared, nobody was expecting such a surprise. I don't know what to do right now!

April 15, 1912

12:10 am: I was listening to the musicians when it happened. People started screaming and the crew members started telling everyone to calm down I'm already pretty panicky, but now I'm freaking out because I can't find my family. I am so scared! I'm heading out to the deck to see if I just stay at the top and maybe not go down with the ship, if that is what is happening.

12:35 am: The ship is definitely going down. The water is rising and I still can't find my family. I really don't want to die! I can feel the place where I'm standing going up, which means that I'm going to start to slip.

1:05 am: I've been here forever, and I still can't find my family! What's worse, the place where I am is still going up! Down below the ship is sinking and the rooms are filling up fast with water. Am I really going to die now?

1:40 am: I have been holding on to the side of the ship as I rose upwards and upwards. Plus no sign of my family. Did they leave me? Have they already died? Do they even care about me?

2:15 am: I can't hold on forever. I can feel myself slipping and once I almost fell into the freezing water. I don't think I'm going to make out. I've been praying for about an hour now, but I don't think it's working.

2:20 am: I haven't seen my family, and I'm worried sick about them. I hope they survive. I really hope that they have found a way out. There is no chance of me surviving, so I hope they escape to live a full life. I hope they know I will always be with them.

2:30 am: I am going to die. I feel myself slipping, so I turn around to reposition myself, but it's too late. I go down, down, into the deep blue abyss of water. As soon as the water touches me I go numb. I go underwater, but as I come back up I feel my foot got caught in something! That means I'm stuck underwater without any air! I try to free myself but it is no use. I am going to die. Then I start to see colors, then a light. I go towards the light, but it disappears. Then I see Mom. She is telling me to join her. I don't know what to do. I can't leave Joe and Dad, but I have no choice. I go with Mom, and then there is a bright light. Then nothing. Just silence and darkness. My soul is now free to visit Mom once more. And that's all I really wanted.

13

Never Alone

by Victoria Pluviose

It was a cold December morning. My name is Samantha and I am 10 years old. I knew it was almost time for the holidays because I heard the faint sleigh bells behind the big steel doors. They brought back memories of when I was just 2 years old walking down the snowy street while holding my mother's warm, soothing hand. But she's gone now, I still had no proof she was dead but she wasn't with me, she left me and I had no one. Apparently my father left my mom and I a few months after I was born so I never even met him.

There I was, in the abandoned orphanage, all alone. I was curled up in the thinest blanket on the cold, hard floor. My toes were turning blue, from the bone chilling breeze entering from a tiny crack in the wall. I was so hungry. I haven't eaten in almost a week. I survived by eating moldy bread but it made my stomach ache for hours.

"Help!" I faintly yelled knowing no one would hear me or just not care. I felt a tear slowly roll down my cheek like a bulldozer tumbling down a mountain. So heavy, and so full of hope. I knew no one would come for me. I was useless. I didn't deserve to live. Who would want me? I couldn't breath very well as if there were something wrong with my lungs, and I had a giant open wound on my shoulder that I got from a nail sticking out of the wall. I was the broken toy on the shelf. My shoulder hurt, but I didn't care about that. Knowing that nobody loved me was enough to comprehend that I wasn't worth anything. I'm alone, and will always be alone.

As I laid there waiting for the pain to go away, the big steel doors in the front of the room budged open, until *BAM!* They opened! That hasn't happened in weeks! Standing there was a woman in a business suit holding a clipboard and an ordinary construction worker.

"Help!" I said again more confidently knowing finally someone would hear me.

"Oh my gosh!" the woman said. She stood there in shock, then dropped her clipboard and ran over to me. She looked at me and could tell I was hurt. "What's your name?" she asked concerned.

"Sam," I said my voice so dry and brittle.

"Well, don't worry we're going to take good care of you Sam. Bill!" she yelled. "Call an ambulance. NOW!"

One second I'm lying on the ground next to a woman yelling at some man with a hard yellow hat, and the next I'm being carried away in some sort of bed getting loaded into a yellow and white truck. I was so confused but it was so adventurous (for me anyways).

The truck drove for miles, I still had no idea where it was taking me. I laid there looking around at all the medical equipment and first aid kits. The woman with the clipboard was sitting in a small chair staring at me with tears forming in her eyes. But I could see something in her as if she cared about me, something I hadn't seen in a long time.

I arrived at a hospital. Doctors wheeled me into a small room with computers and a big window to see outside. The doctors poked me with needles everywhere. One of them gasped when they saw me. I was so pale, with ribs popping out of my chest, and my arms and legs looked more like sticks.

"Get her an IV," the doctor said calmly but in a hurry. They stuck another needle in my arm, hopefully the last, and put medicine and a patch on my bloody wound.

"Can you move your toes?" one of the nurses asked. I shook my head. They hurt to much to even think about. I heard some doctors having a conversation with the business woman.

"We might have to amputate her toes," the nurse said.

"Let them sit for a while and we'll decide whether or not to cut them off," one of the main doctors said.

I passed out, but quickly woke up screaming.

"What happened!" The nurse rushed over to me. I pointed to my toes cringing in pain, I didn't know how to explain what was going on.

"She has frostbite, her toes are defrosting," another doctor said.

"You're gonna be okay," the business woman said with her soothing voice. She took my hand and gave me one of those smiles that made you know everything was going be okay. She reminded me of my mother with her soothing voice. I smiled right back.

"Thank you for saving me," I said.

"You don't have to thank me I couldn't just let you lie there," She said. I smiled again.

I've been in the hospital for about a couple days and this was the best I've ever felt. My ribs sunk into my stomach, and I was happy. I was abandoned and now I'm free from that rusted old orphanage, around people who care about me, people who don't just leave me behind like Margret (the rude woman who owned the orphanage) who practically left me in the orphanage to die. But the kind business woman, who soon I found out was Katherine, came everyday to visit me and brought me balloons and teddy bears. But one day she came in with story books and asked me if I ever learned to read. I realized I never did but never thought it was important. First she read me a cute story about a princess named Snow White who lived with seven dwarfs. The story was odd but fun. After she brought out a book with thin pages, little words but lots of pictures. "Do you know the alphabet?" she asked.

I nodded. "A-B-C-D-E-F-G...now I know my ABC's next time won't you sing with me," I sang.

"Great job, now what sound does this letter make." She opened the book and pointed to a C.

"C-a," I said.

"Good, now A."

"A-a."

"Correct, and finally T."

"T-t."

"Excellent, now put that together," She said.

I tried it. "C-A-T, Cat the word is cat! I did it I read cat!" I was so proud of myself for reading such a simple word but it meant so much more.

All day Katherine taught me new words until I could read my own books. I loved reading chapter books. I loved to read

71

in my cozy hospital bed, until one morning Dr. Fern told me that I was healthy enough to leave the hospital. I started to worry. "Please, please don't take me back to that horrible orphanage I hate it there I'm all alone I have no one!" I said balling.

"You won't be alone, at least not anymore," Katherine said as she smiled holding up an adoption form.

I quickly wiped away my tears,"Really, you're adopting me!" I said overjoyed.

"Absolutely, no 10 year old should be alone especially not during the holidays," Katherine said.

I smiled the biggest grin I've ever done. I was more than happy. I was ecstatic. Katherine bought me some clothes and told me we were going to our new house. I couldn't stop smiling, everything happened so quickly.

Katherine was the only person who understood me. She cared for me. She showed me that life was worth living and many new experiences will come your way if you just believe. I would always said to myself that all my life I would be alone, but now I know that I'm never alone and that no one is. So if you're an orphan or feel unloved and feel how I felt, remember my story and just have hope.

14

Life Takes Its Turn

by Mia Reyes

Monday August 29, 2005, was the day my nightmares became a reality, losing an important part of my once whole heart. I was content with my life in New Orleans. My family and friends were only a few minutes away, my grades were super (straight A's) and my environment was delightful. My life was just perfect, really. Ten days into middle school and the teachers went on about how much they loved me.

After this day, everything would be thrown away, simply taken from me. Every single day was horrid, scary and just devastating. I owe my life to Papa; he saved me, but of course life took a rugged turn. I was completely devastated. Too many emotions were coming over me and I just could not keep myself under control. Too many thoughts cluttered my mind, and those thoughts buried me under a wave of depression I could not overcome.

During that day, I was at home with my Papa and I was in my room watching TV, like any other normal 6th grader would do on a stormy day. I was watching the *Simpsons*, when all of the sudden the TV made an awful beeping sound, they started to announce that a catastrophic hurricane was approaching the U.S. coast. That's when I switched to the news and heard the alarming yet warming voice of the meteorologist about the given location and projection of where the hurricane was going to hit. Hurricane warnings are very common during these months, there was nothing new about this season, but Katrina had different consequences than we were used to.

Papa ran into my room. He asked, "Are you ok?"

I said, "Yes. Papa what's wrong?""

His face looked like he'd seen a ghost. "I think I'm the one who should be asking you if you're okay." Papa finally managed to smile. He told me everything would be okay. I was very confused, I didn't understand why he was saying random things. "Ma is still at work," he said. "She will be okay. She is trying to come home."

Katrina like all the other hurricanes, was announced days before and was forecasted to be a potential disaster to Louisiana. Much like most of the residents of this beautiful state, most of us believed that its route would had be different one. So, we never made plans to leave our homes regardless of the continuous warnings given by local and nationwide news. I helped Papa get water ready and canned foods. The food we found in the kitchen did not looked edible, but if it was going to helped us live, then I guess it would have to be okay. I was in 6th grade at the time, therefore I was aware of everything that was going on around me. I wish I could had been a little innocent 4 year old girl again where I was oblivious in my surrounding and I could trust Papa about us being okay during this nightmare.

By the time we were done collecting our mostly expired food, the rain and the wind started to rock the house just at the slightest bit. It was the early morning and I was really sluggish. The wind and rain started to whip up a storm. Of course I didn't stay there so we went up to the attic. Slowly the water was reaching all kinds of places around the house. I could see all of our memories and prized possessions being eaten by all the water. Looking at our washed away memories my heart cried out loud for Ma. I wanted and needed to know my Ma was safe just like Papa assured me through the event. I was afraid of losing her the same way I was losing many years of memories right before my eyes.

The storm was getting mad. It was rapidly killing everything in its path. Everything being swallowed, the storm was hungry and it did not care what was served that day. I was afraid I was also on the plate. I was truly afraid. The water was catching up. Papa told me to watch out because my foot was about to get stuck in a hole.

The storm was too strong for anyone to come and rescue us. I had one objective in mind, to stay with Papa, water was rising like someone was filling an aquarium to the top. Therefore, there was no time for any stupidity. We had to find high shelter soon to avoid the water that was everywhere, so we made our way to the roof. It was pretty scary, I was afraid I was going to slip off and be lost in the massive black hole called Katrina.

Few days later

I was wide awake. Papa asked me to take a nap several times, but I couldn't. Everything was on my mind, the pouring rain, our lost home. The storm happened too fast. Papa told me to write *HELP US FAMILY SOS* with an almost empty spray paint can. I wondered if it felt like me at the moment, because I felt dry, lost, and my energy almost gone. We hoped that it was going to send the right signal to get the rescuers' attention. One, two, then three days passed by like a pebble slowly making its way to the bottom of the ocean, it was horrible; much like a scene from one of Tim Burton's worst movies. Our food supply, empty cans, and all imaginable debris were floating near us like they were witnessing our last days here on Earth.

This hurricane was memorable and it sure was ready to leave its mark on my beautiful state. I had seen lots of hurricanes happening on TV, but I had no idea it was going to be this bad. I was very worried for Ma. There were so many indications that she was probably gone. One night my heart felt so heavy that I knew she was gone.

Five dreadful days slowly passed by. So many things had happened. The air felt melancholic as if the hurricane swept human life off the planet. It felt like Papa and I were the only survivors in this area. It felt like a war zone. The days I spent on that roof were as horrible as a rotting pea in a trash bag. Papa and I were trying to make our food last and avoid an uncertain future. I wasn't sure if we were going to survive this war between Mother Nature and humans, but in this battle it was obvious who would be the winner. My biggest fear was to go sleep, what if I took a nap and slid off the roof to be eaten by the still furious water around us? I just never felt at ease.

Knowing that Ma was probably gone, I made myself fight even harder for our lives, we had to win this battle for her. I wanted Ma to be happy in a beautiful place, where she could relax and finally have peace. She would probably tell me to keep moving forward without looking back. I had to win.

The storm was getting lighter. The rain was clearing up. The heavy feeling was slowly decreasing. The depressed feeling still hung in the air but a little smile managed to stretch across my face. I was ready to get off of this dump! I was ready to sit next to a fire place with some hot chocolate.

After a day or so, I heard the most beautiful sound in the world. It was freedom, it was our rescuers. I heard the beats of helicopter wings cutting through the air. They were shiny and pretty, ready to free me from this horrible prison; white, red and black were the color of freedom. The helicopter had the Red American Cross logo. I knew I was being saved.

They gave us instructions on how to get inside the helicopter and I followed. I knew we were saved, saved from a living nightmare. I could imagine Papa and I in the pool, but this time Ma was not taking pictures by the side of the pool with her feet in the water. I wish it could be that way, but life had different plans for all of us.

11 years later

To this day I remember my Mama. I remember how she cared and loved me. I remember her beautiful face looking down at me waking me up in the mornings. Now, I'm 22 years old, I love my family and spending time with them is something I treasure with all my heart. My dad is and will forever be there for me, if hurricane Katrina did not stop him, no one will.

After our horrid experience on our roof, we spent weeks in a stadium, a different kind of hell. So many people with no space to sleep and not a safe place to deposit waste our body no longer needed. To many experiences I can't describe. After those horrible weeks, we decided to run away from the memories that haunted and reminded that my Ma was no longer with us. Like many survivors, Houston was the city that helped us create new memories. My mom was among 1,830 people that died and never got to say goodbye. I loved New Orleans, it will forever be in my heart, but I had to let go. "Only know you love her, when you let her go," those were the lyrics the song "Let her go" by the Passengers. If the song correctly describes love, then my love for my Ma and New Orleans has not changed.

15

Unforgotten

by Emily Santos

"Good morning, Charlotte," Mom said as she opened the door to my room. "We have a special present for you!"

Little did I know that these words would lead to the greatest gift of my life. I was turning four that morning, I could barely contain my excitement.

"Come Chari," Dad said.

I rushed out the door, not knowing where I was going.

"Look in the barn, sweet pea," Mom said. I quickly ran out the back door leading to the barn, and there it was. I thought I was dreaming. I couldn't believe my eyes.

"Happy birthday, Charlotte," Grandpa said. There was a horse standing right next to him. It was a black stallion. It was so beautiful. "This little horse is for you, it's all yours. What do you want to name it?"

A horse for me? As a pet? I stood there in shock. I never had an animal all to my own before. We did have chickens and cows and a few pigs on our farm, but they were never *mine*. I stood there thinking about the perfect name. Charlotte Jr.? No, that's weird. Stella? Maybe. Then it hit me. Audelia, Lia for short. It was perfect. "Audelia!" I shouted to Grandpa.

By then, Mom and Dad were standing behind me. "Audelia, what a beautiful name," Mom said.

"How'd you think of it?" Dad asked. I shrugged my shoulders. I honestly didn't know how it came to me, it just did, and all I knew was that it was the perfect name.

It was about a year later that I started taking horse riding lessons. I was five now. I begged Mom to sign me up the morning I got Audelia, but she told me I was too young. Even though I didn't know how to ride Audelia, I still had fun with her. Everyday when I got home from day care, I would rush to the barn to see her. I talked to her like she was a person.

Sometimes I would spend hours in the barn with her.

Mom signed me up for riding lessons the day I turned 5. My instructor, Mrs. Tower, told me I had a natural talent for riding horses. I guess I got it from my grandpa, after all he is an amazing rider.

After a year of lessons, Mrs. Tower told my I was ready to enter the local youth horse race competition. I was shocked, I knew I was good, but not that good. Most of the competitors are 9-12 year olds, who have been training for years. I would be the youngest in the competition. What would people think of me? I don't want to be the center of attention. If I won, I would be known locally. I live in a small town where news spreads quickly. I would be featured on the news and on the newspaper. I don't want people thinking I'm all that special.

It was the day of the 11th annual McAlister youth horse race. Mrs. Tower wasn't there, because she had to teach that day. She said she would've come if she could, which means a lot to me. I understand that she can't be there. I remember walking into the doors of the sign in center. There were so many kids and parents and horses. People talking, competitors getting ready, staff setting up, it was all so crazy. Mom signed me in, and we had 30 minutes to prepare Audelia and me for the race. As soon as we were done, we headed to a room where all the competitors meet up before the race. The whole room was filled with horses and kids, most of them were 8-11 years old. At first they stared, but not for too long, which made me feel a kinda glad inside. Maybe my thoughts of them were wrong after all. Parents weren't allowed, so Mom went to find a seat in the arena. Before she left though, she gave me a big hug and told me I would do amazing. When the staff member finished telling us the rules and directions, we all headed out to the field. All of us got lined up in our position. I was so nervous, I almost felt like backing out. It's good that I didn't though. The race was about to start, and the second the whistle blew, everyone was off. I jumped a little when I heard the loud whistle. I was trotted behind the person in first. It stayed that way most of the race. Sometimes, I would be in third, other times I would be in first. I was going so fast I felt like I was running on air. It was the last stretch and I was in the lead, the person behind me was at close second.

I thought for sure that I was about to win, but as soon as I turned the last comer, the person behind me pulled up to first. By then, there was nothing I could do to win. I crossed the finish line at second. Even though I suffered defeat, I was still proud of myself for getting second out of six people. After all, it was my first competition. Mom said I did great, and some of the competitors even congratulated me. The person that won the race was a 9 year old girl and had been riding since she was six. Her name was Rocky Shore.

As Mom and I were leaving, Rocky stopped us and told me I was doing great for my age and that I should keep riding for a long time. I responded by telling her that she was great too and that she truly deserved that first place trophy. She said thanks and bye as she headed out the door. She was a pretty cool girl, but I never saw her again.

I was featured on the local news. The next day in school, everyone was congratulating me for my achievement. Some people even gave me cards. The next day I went to lessons, Mrs. Tower gave me a very shiny and small horse pin to put on my riding uniform. Mom and Dad were even so proud of me that they bought me a TV for room. I couldn't believe that I got all these things just for getting second place.

Fast forward to 5 years later, this was the most devastating year of my life. I was at school checking out books from the library, when I got called to the office. I was scared, I didn't know what was going on. When I entered the office doors I saw my dad sitting in a chair with tears in his eyes.

"Hi, Chari," Dad said sadly. "I have some news for you."

When Dad said these words I tensed up, I didn't want to hear the news.

"Well-well your mom-mom died of a heart attack earlier this morning," he said.

I stood there not knowing what to say, what could I say? Tears started forming in my eyes. I felt like a part of me was gone. It was about three days later that we had Mom's funeral. So many sad and wet faces everywhere. Seeing those people made me cry even more. Before they closed the coffin, I stuck my horse pin in Mom's shirt. I always wanted Mom to know that I loved her and that I'm thankful for all she had done for me.

Ever since Mom passed away, I haven't been going to any horse lessons or competitions. Dad encouraged me to start again, but I couldn't even if I wanted to.

A few months after Mom's death, Audelia ran away. I came home from school that day and headed to the barn to see Lia. When I opened the doors to the barn, she wasn't there. I was worried. I ran around the whole farm to find her, but couldn't. First Mom, now Audelia? How could this be? I finally gave up looking, and ran back into the house to tell Dad.

"Did you check every where?" he asked me.

"I ran all around the farm but couldn't find her," I said.

"Let's go check again, I'm pretty sure she didn't go far."

We spent all night looking for her, but she was nowhere in sight. I was heartbroken, I thought my life was over. A few days after Audelia ran away, Dad told me that we had to move to New York for his new job. I started to cry out of frustration.

"We're leaving the barn? We lived here since I was born. Leaving the barn is like leaving all the memories behind," I said still crying.

"I know, but I have to earn money somehow," Dad said.

I understood why we had to move, but leaving is beyond what anything I could imagine.

My dad and I finished packing up all our belongings and loaded the truck. I sat in silence the whole ride to New York. I thought about where Audelia could be. None of the gates were open, I don't get how she could of escaped. How?

Well, I'm 14 now and I've made many new friends at my new school in New York. We never found Audelia, sadly, and I haven't gotten a new horse since. I did find a new friend who also rides horses. Her name is Rochelle. She started lessons a few months ago. I go over to her house a lot to see her horses. She has three of them. They are so cute. I've gotten over moving, Mom's death and Audelia, but I still miss all of them very much. They are a part of me that will never go away.

Even though I'm probably never going to see Audelia or Mom again, I know that I played a special part in their lives.

16

Way Out West

by Genevieve Sheara

Like any other night, Kenny closed his eyes, planning to arise the next day and continue the pattern. Little did he know that when he awoke there would be not a single coffee machine in sight for his pleasure. Everything he took for granted would be missing and only tumbleweeds would remain. *I must be dreaming*, he thought, as he tried to shake his head rid of this world. No longer did a puffy quilt cover him, but instead, dirt stuck to the creases of his body. Flying sand that settled on everything clouded his vision. He trudged through the tornado of cacti and grains of sand. His head pounded, soon giving way to the booming laughs of those in the midst of this solitude. He tumbled through a large door, and the sandstorm disappeared. He could make out many people chuckling and playing small games of poker on raised tables, drinks in hand.

Immediately, silence struck the room as he was noticed, interrupting the noisy excitement with his presence. Kenny was never a friendly person and did not mix easily with others in general. Even though all the people were, when it came down to it, on their own, they were like single pages, but still bound together. A towering man confronted him, his shadow lurking over Kenny like a fierce lion about to pounce upon its prey. Though the savage weather had been contained outside, Kenny was struck with chills running up his spine. The man was nearly six feet tall, but Kenny's lowly stance made him seem two times as tall. The man grumbled something to himself under his breath, then reached down to Kenny with a bulky hand. Kenny went to grasp it, thinking that he may find one kind character in this mess, but the man had other ideas. He sneered as he lifted Kenny up by his collar and in a booming voice shouted something Kenny did not quite hear.

He just nodded his head, and to his relief, was let down to his feet. He shuddered and his knees clacked together as the man's gaze sharpened to meet Kenny's eyes. Kenny managed to ignore the constant stares in the room and brushed past several tables to a man he figured was the bartender. After the silence became too awkward for most people, they resumed their former activities, removing their attention from Kenny. The bartender stepped aside so Kenny could gaze at all the drinks, but instead Kenny just stood there shifting his weight from one leg to another.

"Coke?" he asked the bartender, who was polishing a glass.

"Never heard-a that one," he replied, still focusing on cleaning the smudged glass.

Kenny waited there for another few moments before realizing that he was trapped in the Wild West.

Another man, smaller than the first, approached the frozen Kenny. His hand was mutantly large with an undersized pointer finger that made his palm look like a balloon. It whipped Kenny around so that their eyes met. The man twirled his bushy mustache diabolically, glaring at Kenny with his deep, dark eyes. They were blazing with a fiery light, lit upon logs of rejection, flames made of a hidden fear. Kenny, although at first intimidated, felt a sudden sympathy though he did not know why. Inside the man was a light character, but it seemed as though he were toughened through the ignorance of others. The man grasped Kenny's right hand and firmly shook it.

"The name's Samuel," he shouted from under the few hairs of his mustache that fell into his muffled mouth.

"Kenny," he replied, twisting his hand in pain.

Samuel popped his knuckles, leading Kenny to a table. "You ain't really from around here, with those night clothes and all," Samuel said as he gestured to Kenny's pajamas.

"Umm, no," Kenny bashfully replied, awkwardly trying to cover his clothing with his slender arms. "I come from the future, actually, and these are called 'pajamas.' I woke up here and now need to go back to my home in the future and..."

"Zip it, midget!" Samuel cut him off before he could finish

explaining. "So what were you trailin' off about the future and all? Think you just had-a one too many drinks, son."

Kenny lowered his head in hopelessness and wondered if he would ever be able to leave this place.

"Nah, I'm just playin' with ya, kid. This thing is goin' on, happenin' 'round here. They go back in-a that desert and get to their home in a day or so."

Suddenly Kenny felt a surge of joy burst inside of him. *I could go home*, he thought as he straightened himself. He nodded and grinned in thanks to Samuel, stumbling in a hurry out of the door. As he did, though, a lass carrying a young child and holding hands with another, caught his sight. She had a smile on her face, though her clothes were old and torn. Kenny stood there gaping at the sight when he began to wonder, 'Why is that woman so happy?' She left the barroom and sat on the wooden porch of a rusting, crumbling shack, crooning to the child a melody he could not hear completely. It calmed him somewhere inside, sounding as serene as the morning dew settling on the fields at sunrise, as soothing as the pastoral rain dripping on a flourishing flower's petal.

As he stepped outside, the flying tornado of the desert became rain, fluttering on his window outside his bedroom. The image of the woman crept into his mind, gnawing at the strings of selfishness tying him together, day after day. He was stirred and could not escape the feelings he had by sleeping, nor eating, nor shopping, when it touched him. He took two packed wallets and emptied them at his local charity station. Finally, the nostalgic happiness he gained when seeing the woman returned, now he was becoming the man he was destined to be, the caretaker of the ones less fortunate than him.

Illustration by Zoey Hess - Back Cover Artist

17

Reality

by Jackson Swindle

Hey, my name is Cody. I wouldn't call myself normal. That would be an understatement. So, I guess I will start this (sort of) autobiography out with a fact. My dad is a government scientist. He can't tell ANYONE about what they work on there. If he did, he would have to kill whoever he told. Crazy, right? Well, so is the government.

It turns out the government has *Bring your Son to Work Day*. They must have not thought it through all the way because I was pretty bored. They pacified the little kids by giving them candy. The main age group the party was more aimed towards was 2-5, with its cheesy activities and a magician. I was the kid in the corner watching YouTube. I was about halfway through a really cool level on an iPhone game when my phone ran out of battery. I was so bored. I decided to walk around. I thought they wouldn't mind.

Dang, this place is big! I thought as I walked through the long bright hallway. I'm gonna need a map to get back! Some of the doors had tall rectangular windows on them so you could vaguely see inside the room. Nothing interesting, a couple of computers, filing cabinets, wait, hold on, what's this? I thought. It's some sort of metal circle, with a pool of purple fog inside of it. What is that? Is that a portal?

Wow. I thought. No wonder the government keeps everything a secret! Where does it even go? It must be pretty dangerous, I thought. Let's go into it! Testing lab 2, the door sign read. I cautiously turned the doorknob, hoping I wouldn't activate some sort of security system, and a cool blast of air hit me. Wow, I thought. This is a lot different from video games! I questioned myself on my thoughts of stepping inside. Then, I made a mistake that would change my life. I stepped in.

When I exited the portal, I eagerly awaited what I would

see, only to see the room I found the portal in. But, I thought, didn't I just come in here? I wasn't supposed to even be there, so I just walked back to the party room. I was hungry. I was craving my mom's chef cooking. When I entered the room, my mom burst out a set of double doors, wearing a white lab coat. "Cody!" She exclaimed, wrapping me in a bear hug. *What's mom doing here?* I wondered. And why is she wearing dad's lab coat?

"Hey mom! What are you doing here! Where's dad?"

"He had to work the late shift over at the restaurant."

Dad doesn't work at a restaurant! Did they switch jobs? That's impossible! I was pretty confused. But naturally as a teenager, I get confused a lot. So I just shut up I and got in the car. When I got home I opened the door to see my dad scrubbing dishes, whistling.

"Hey Cody, how's it going?" he asked, ruffling my hair.

"Good. Hey, can we go see that new movie tomorrow?"

"I have to work tomorrow Cody."

"But tomorrow's Saturday!" I exclaimed.

"Chefs have to work on Saturdays. I thought you knew that! Speaking of that, you want something to eat?

"No thanks. I'm not hungry." That was only half a lie. I ate some candy at the facility. I went to my room, to be greeted by my action figurine collection, TV and beanbag chair. I turned out the light and hopped into bed. I couldn't really sleep, I was overwhelmed with thought of the portal. Did it really not change anything, or did it change the definition of reality?

The whole weekend was pretty normal (despite my dad working on Saturday that was weird). But when I got to school, that was a whole other story. While I made my way to my locker my friend Bryce greeted me with a *hello*. He's my friend, and for the sake of politeness, I said *hi* back. Then this kid in my English class said *hi* to me. Then everyone in the 8th grade started greeting me like I had known them for centuries! What's going on, am I actually... popular? Well this is new. Despite the weird encounter that morning, I continued my day as if it hadn't happened.

After school when my mom was driving me home, she said, "Hey, Cody, could you grab your guitar from the trunk?"

"Hold on, what guitar?!" I asked.

"Your guitar Cody. You have lessons tonight. How could you forget?"

I don't play guitar! I thought. I didn't even know I owned one! Now this was confusing me like never before. Do all these strange occurrences have to do with the portal? I questioned. Did it bend the reality, or put me in a new one? We drove the rest of the way in silence. If i ask questions i might have to tell her about the portal, and that's not good.

When I arrived, I pulled the guitar out of the case and pretended to set it up. My teacher was a man with a tiny beard and long hair. He sported a blue hoodie and had a white fender telecaster. I got out my music. Enter Sandman. That was the name of the song. Nothing hard, a simple pattern on the 7th fret cage...wait hold on, how do i know this!? I didn't know how to play, yet it seems like my mind was born to read the music, and my fingers instantly knew where to travel. I somehow, no matter how confused I was about the portal, or anything else that was going on, enjoyed it. I managed to finish the lesson without cracking, and went home.

When I got home, I couldn't hold it in any longer. "Mom what is that portal over at the facility?"

She spit out her soda, and asked "How do you know about that! You didn't... go into it, did you?"

I slowly nodded my head. "We have to get you back through that portal," she said. "It was a experiment failed, that would send you through an alternate reality! No wonder you have been acting so strange!" I nearly fainted. Alternate reality!? "Get in the car Cody," she said sternly.

She drove me to the facility as quick as possible. "What is the other reality like?" she asked.

I opened my mouth to answer her when she screamed "Wait! Any information about the other realities could potentially create a ripple in the time space continuum!" So that's what's going on! I thought. They hadn't really switched jobs! And why I actually had friends! And why I could play guitar!

We arrived at the facility to be greeted by Mr. Doe. "Hi Clarissa!" He said in his gruff voice. "Why'd you bring your kid?" She whispered something in his ear and he said with urgency, "Get inside. Now."

I went in to be swarmed by doctors and scientists. Dr.

Mundy checked my pulse as Mr. Conager asked me questions.

"How old are you?"

"Twelve."

"Do you have any illness?"

"Umm...No?" It was all a giant blur of questions and scientists getting me to testing lab 2. When we arrived at the portal room, there was a woman in the room, Doctor Alphys, I later learned her name was.

"Mr. Doe! Guess what! I've finally fixed the portal for teleportation! Why is... Why is everyone looking at me like I'm crazy?"

Then, my mom asked Doctor Alphys a question. "Can you unfix it?"

Suddenly I changed my thoughts about Alphys not being crazy when she started ripping out wires and talking to herself. She was saying stuff like, "If we put this here, and add a capacitor here... Then it should..."

My mom must've sensed my discomfort, so she came over to talk to me.

"I know what you're thinking. She's not insane. She's a genius. This is how she works." Then she put my hands in hers, looked into my eyes, and said, "You may not be the Cody from this reality, but you're still my son. I love you Cody."

Then I heard Alphys confirm that it was done. I said goodbye and jumped through. When I came out I saw all the doctors, scientists, and my dad, wearing his white lab coat.

"Cody!" he yelled. "I'm so glad you're back! There was this other Cody that played guitar, and thought your mother was a government scientist!"

Then Alphys spoke. "No matter what happens, you don't tell anyone about this."

I gave her my word, and went home. And here I am, twenty years later, typing this out so people can learn about me and can see that no matter what, nothing is what it seems.

18

Little Star

by Bethany Tran

Adoption, to legally take another's child and bring it up as one's own. Legally, of or relating to the law. Lawyers, documents, papers, judges, why does it have to be so complicated? Jamie Jackson Coleman, male, age 11, African American, 55 inches tall, and 74 pounds. It didn't mention that I liked math, or that my favorite sport was baseball. It wasn't Jamie Coleman, a kid who wanted to go to college, become an astronomer one day, and have parents who loved him.

Have you ever heard of a stellar collision? It's when two star come together by the force of gravity and become one larger star. This only happens once every 10,000 years. I slept every night hoping that I would have a stellar collision of my own. I am the little star and somewhere in the universe mom and dad would be the big star. We would come together and become one larger star, a family. This only happens once every 10,000 years.

December 21, 1989 4:20 PM
"Four more days until Christmas y'all," the man on the radio said in a crackling voice.

As a new 8 year old I was super excited that not only today was my birthday, but Christmas was coming so soon! I had written Santa several letters about the new telescope I wanted, boy was I excited as a firecracker just waiting to explode!

Mama and I were walking around to find the best dessert there was in Manhattan. We stopped at Ferrara Bakery & Cafe to get one of their famous cannolis. It was a bit pricey, but Mama made an exception since it was my birthday. I don't know if it was my empty stomach or the cold air, but at that single moment it was one of the best things I had ever tasted!

"Papa wishes you a happy birthday from the heavens," Mama said. I shed a tear, not out of sadness, but of pure happiness.

December 21, 1989 5:15 PM

Mama and I are going home in a taxi as clusters of snow fall down faster than you could blink. We were playing red car blue car. I was red and Mama was blue. Every time we'd see red cars I'd get a point,and every time we'd see blue she'd get a point. We would share giggles every time I'd try to cheat. "Jamie, I...I heard a squeak and a crash and my whole life flashed before me, then I started to see a light, and it was silence.

December 21, 1989 6:00 PM

Hurry! Hurry! Yes...yes there is a boy and what seems to be his mother!...no I do not know them...uhhh the boy seems to be knocked out or dead!...the woman I'm not sure...okay PLEASE HURRY! That was all I had heard before I blacked out again.

December 22,1989 8:25 AM

Yes! Surprisingly the boy isn't harmed one bit! Such a big impact, you would think he would have at least broken something! "Excuse me ma'am," I say with my voice a little groggily.

The woman drops the phone and rushes to me quickly. "Are you okay, are you alright?" she asked.

I started to realized that I was in a hospital and suddenly my memory came back, "Mama, Mama, where's Mama?" I asked with worry in my voice. At that point I didn't care anymore. I didn't care about the cannolis. I didn't care about my birthday, I didn't care about that telescope I wanted. I didn't care about Christmas. I didn't care about anything except for Mama! She was the only thing I had left. Dad had died when I was younger, aunts and uncles, they didn't even know I existed. Grandma and Grandpa are gone. Everything gone, all my hopes, all my dreams, everything.

"Your...mother...is dead," the nurse said, sounding like she was about to cry. Just like that I had let go of the cliff and

I was falling down an abyss with no rope and no light. It was always mom and I versus the world, but now it's just me.

June 27, 1993

It has been almost four years since mama passed away. The hole in my heart has healed, but there's still a scar there to remind me. I had been in the care of 7 different foster homes. I had ran away from about 4 of them but the system always found a way to drag me back in. One time I was in a home with someone who did it just for the money. I never knew how selfish someone could be until I ended up there. What was that word I mentioned? Oh yes, adoption. It was just a word. It was something that was almost impossible. Nobody seemed to want a scrawny little 11 year old boy. They wanted the cute babies that would stick their bottom lip out when they got sad. I was still in the abyss there was no rope, no light, no where to cry, nowhere to hide, and no place to call home.

September 23,1993

Today was the day that changed my life completely, but i didn't know it yet.

"Jamie Coleman, we have someone we want you to meet," said one of the social workers in a pleasant voice.

I got up and followed her. "Jamie, this is Mr. and Mrs. Bassano," the social worker said.

Mrs. Bassano had fair skin and jet black hair. Mr. Bassano was so tall that I got a little bit overwhelmed. I tried to give a slight grin just to be polite.

"These are your new foster parents," the worker said. Mr. and Mrs. Bassano's smiles grew even larger as mine started to fade a bit.

Great, here we go again, I thought. Seven already and one more, I was already thinking about my escape plan.

"I promise you Jamie you'll love it here!" Mrs. Bassano said in a enthusiastic voice. I just slightly nod not wanting to be rude. As I entered the house, I was welcomed by 5 children and a sign that read *Welcome Jamie*. Lalani, a girl from the Phillipines who looked about my age. Ehud, a boy from Israel that looked almost 16. Ajaka and Adaka Twins about 6, a boy and a girl from Nigeria. Lastly Lilah, a little girl about 2 years old, that looked a lot like Mr. and Mrs. Bassano. Mrs. Bassano showed me around the house and showed me where I would sleep. The room I was staying in had paintings of stars on the walls. In the corner of the room by the window I saw it! The telescope I'd wanted ever since I was 8. I still didn't know if I could trust these people just yet, but whatever they were doing, it was working. I couldn't help but smile and gush *thank you* a million times. Mrs. Bassano just stood there and smiled.

That night, I had dinner with the Bassanos. Mr. Bassano had cooked a delicious meal for everyone. After the meal it was time for dessert. They had served cannolis for dessert. As I watched everyone eat the cannoli, I saw a sparkle in every one of their eyes, you could tell they were truly happy. They had the look I had back in the winter of 1989. The look of innocence and worry free days. The last time I ate with mama.

Lalani and Ehud politely sat and ate while exchanging smiles with me. Ajaka and Adaka made a mess with their food, getting it all over their faces, while Mrs. Bassano fed little Lilah spoon by spoon. Then there was me just sitting there, I hadn't even touched a bit of my food. I looked at them, then at my plate.

All the children were excused from the dinner table, and as I began to stand up Mrs. Bassano stopped me.

"Jamie, come here," she said, patting the cushion of the chair. "Why didn't you eat your cannoli."

I sat there for a few second thinking of what to say. "I'm not hungry," I lied.

Mrs. Bassano raised an eyebrow and I could tell she knew that what I was saying wasn't true. "It was the last thing I ate with her before...," I said struggling to get the words out.

"Jamie I've known you for a long time," Mrs. Bassano said.

I just stared at her with confused eyes. "About four years ago I was driving when I saw a white car smash into a taxi. I immediately pulled over and called 911 as quickly as possible. A mother and her son, completely knocked out. A few minutes later an ambulance had arrived. A few days after the crash they told me that the names of the victims were Lori and Jamie Coleman, and that was all I heard after that." Tears were streaming down my face, how did I not recognize her voice earlier! I bawled my eyes out. All of the bottled up emotion was let go at that moment. I could finally see the light and I was no longer in the abyss anymore. At that moment I realized that these people were different. I was going to be here for a while.

December 21, 2015

Adoption, to care and love a child as your own. Love, a special bond between family and friends. Death, regret, hatred, loneliness, and change, it all happened so quickly. Jamie Jackson Coleman Bassano, age 34, went to Harvard University, graduated with a PhD in Astronomy, had 5 children, and liked baseball. I had always dreamed of having a stellar collision of my own. I was the little star, and mom and dad were the big star. We collided to make one huge star, and there's still room to make an even bigger star.

There was one thing that Mama would always say to me every night. "Live your life worry less, strong, and brave. Cause you're not going to be my little star forever.

19

The Orb of Destiny

by Drew Turner

Virrilis awoke. His straw bed was uncomfortably comfy. As he sat up, he realized he was in the barn section of his hut. He couldn't remember the last night. All the memories were hazy and unclear. *Knock! Knock!* His friend Maximus, or Max, was knocking. Virrilis gradually opened the door. His eyes were heavy as the wooden door creaked open.

"Ello Virrilis," Max said, his voice cheerful as always. His voice was a little wavy however.

"What Max?" Virrilis gloomily asked, a dreary look on his face.

"Just saying hello... but now that you mention it, do you remember last night?" he asked.

"No."

"Exactly! I don't remember it at all. All I remember is something about an orb. But it's very hazy."

"Okay, by...," Virrilis replied as he started to close the door.

"Wait...I think we should look into this," Max interrupted.

"Fine," Virrilis said and rolled his eyes.

They set off trotting along the paved stone path, passing all the little peach (light brown) huts. They could faintly see the river Nox along the path. They passed the blacksmith's shop, where Jason, the blacksmith, waved at them. A small church glimmered in the sunlight as they strolled by. Finally they arrived at the library, which was a small, quaint little building with a tiny sign that said (obviously) *LIBRARY*.

As they entered the building, Virrilis had a weird feeling he was being watched. He was right. King Marth was watching them atop a hill, his black cape swishing in the wind.

The inside of the library was much bigger than it seemed. Velvet curtains hung from the clear windows. There were rows of wooden shelves, full of books. The books! Each one was different in its own way. Some were miniscule, while others were as big as a dog. Some had a shiny golden color, while other had a dark maroon shade. In fact, there were a multitude of colors and shapes.

Virrilis and Max headed into the nonfiction section. They skimmed all the books until they finally stopped at one. Its cover was mahogany red, and it felt like leather. On the cover was a monster-like face with one eye. The eye, however, looked strangely like an orb. It was a small pocket book.

They opened it and a horrid odor reeked from the yellow pages, which were, in fact, torn. It looked eerie. They flipped through the pages. The dusty pages were old. The pages were really thick and heavy.

They stopped on a page. "Here," Max exclaimed. The tattered page he had stopped on had a picture of a blue diamond orb that was sitting on a marble pillar. The page read *Beware the Orb of Destiny. If it ever gets off its pedestal, do*...the rest was ripped out.

"Do-what?" Virrilis questioned.

"Don't know," Max answered." But look, there's a map leading to the location of it!"

"I know what you're thinking." He rolled his eyes and continued, "and I'll go."

They quickly checked out the book and were on their way. They jogged along the stone path was a little bumpy. Mismatched tiles and broken ones made the road uneven and easy to trip. Max actually did every once and awhile. As they hurried along, they passed the blacksmith shop and stopped.

"Maybe Jason can help us," Virrilis said. "By making us some weapons."

They strolled into the shop. "Hello Virrilis," Jason said as they entered the dusty shop. "What can I do for you?"

"Weapons," Virrilis answered. It was one, simple word. It got Jason intrigued.

"What's the occasion?"

Virrilis raised a brow. "What do you have?"

"Emeralds,ruby,gold, diamond...," Jason replied

"I'll take a diamond...sword. Also a golden shield," Virrilis said.

"I'll have an emerald battle axe," Max asked.

"That was sudden," replied Jason.

"I've been wanting this for a while," Max said with a grin.

"Okay!" laughed Jason as he stuck out his hand. Virrilis gave him a sack of golden rupees. Jason quickly counted the currency, then got to work.

It was a long and boring wait. The clink of hammers could be heard from the distance. Sparks were flying like little snowflakes dancing through the air. Virrilis sat down on the waiting chair. He pulled out a Medieval Weekly magazine and read through it.

After what seemed like hours, Virrilis heard one last hammer blow before Jason came out, his hammer in his crossed hands and said, "Done."

Virrilis rushed in to see the sword, Max following behind him. There, on the metal table was a gleaming diamond sword. Virrilis touched the polished metal handle and grinned. Over the handle were leather straps. The reddish magenta-like diamond Jason used looked astonishing.

Max, like Virrilis with his sword, was staring in marvel at the emerald axe. The green texture glowed, almost like magic.

On Virrilis' sword, runes glowed. It was a peculiar glow.

"Had a Witch enchant them," Jason gestured at an old woman standing in a dark corner, a black robe covering her face. The symbols were lined up in a row.

"How do you activate them?" Max asked.

"Which weapon?" Jason asked.

"My hammer."

"Axe...Just concentrate on a ring."

Max concentrated, and sure enough, his axe was on his finger. It was a golden ring with a black axe embedding the top, with an emerald circling around it. Max touched it and it turned back.

"Cool," Max said. He flipped it back and waited.

"What about my sword and shield?" Virrilis asked.

"Your shield is impenetrable and can change into a necklace...so can your sword," Jason answered. "But your sword can light on fire by tapping the blue diamond on the bottom."

Virrilis touched the diamond on the bottom, and the sword completely changed. Meaning it changed from red to blue, and there was a red diamond on the bottom. Also, it was on fire. A blue flame was flickering from the iron hilt to the point of the blue blade. Virrilis changed it back and then to a necklace. "Also, take these...they might help too." Jason handed each of them leather boots.

"Thanks Jason!"

"Yeah, thanks!"

They started off on the soon to be perilous journey. They hustled into beautiful forest with lush green trees and a small creek where salmon swam along in their happy little world. As they left the forest, the ground suddenly shook violently. Cracks appeared on the surface of the ground. They widened until that entire forest with the dazzling plants and radiant trees fell. Where it once stood was a crater that led to a smoldering river of molten hot lava.

Not a good sign! Virrilis thought. They continued on.
They found a concrete path that led to a small village with an enormous tower on the edge. 'The Tower of Destiny, visiting hours: NEVER!' a small sign read as they passed by.

"Well...I know where we're going," Max said.

The tower was very tall with cobblestone walls. Moss was growing on almost every stone block. It had an old, dusty feel to it, kind of like they were standing on Stone Hedge.

A single guard stood by the entrance. In his hand was an electric spear. And no, I don't mean it was energetic. It was literally sparking jolts of electricity. To the side were some more guards, sleeping. We can take them, Virrilis thought, but I'd rather sneak by them. He motioned at Max to come on. Max thought he understood and willed his axe. Virrilis gave him a sour face, and Max frowned and willed it back. They snuck around to a narrow ledge leading to a conveniently open window and snuck inside.

The inside was bigger than the out! It was a creepily empty room. In the middle, a single pedestal made out of granite and marble stood. Max sprinted toward it in awe, Virrilis right behind.

"The pedestal that holds the Orb of Destiny!" Max exclaimed.

"But where's the Orb?" Virrilis questioned.

Before Max could guess its whereabouts, a guard screamed, "Stop right there!"

A bunch of armed guards circled them. Both Virrilis and Max willed their weapons. The guards charged. Maxed whacked them with his axe. The guards turned to dust. Virrilis lit his sword on fire and maliciously sliced, diced, and burned the guards. More and more guards came running in screaming, "You're not going to steal like Marth!" Virrilis deflected the electricity with his shield. His sword slashed and jabbed. Slash. Jab. Slash. Jab.

Virrilis finished off the rest of guards and sprinted towards the exit. As they were about to get out of the place, they were stopped by King Marth's minions. They were big and burly, and each carried a golden spear. They had one huge eye, right in the middle.

Virrilis dodged a jab by the minion. He quickly lunged and stabbed the minion in the eye. Meanwhile, Max took on the minion head-on. Literally! The minion jabbed at him, but he quickly jumped on the spear and took care of him. The minion turned into a miniature dust storm. Once it cleared, Max rushed over to help Virrilis. This minion was much quicker. With his eye out, he swung his spear randomly. He skinned Virrilis on the arm. Blood seeped from the spot. Virrilis fought through it and lunged at the Cyclopes. The sword burned through all of the skin fat before it stabbed his heart. The cyclops lumbered to the floor screaming in pain. He faded into dust.

Virrilis and Max left. "I only know one person with cyclops goons," Max told Virrilis.

"The Easter Bunny!?"

"The Easter...no! King Marthitious...or King Marth! Just follow me."

Virrilis and Max set off on their journey. They went over

the river Nox, its water glistening in the sunlight. Once they crossed it, Max led the duo through a small village called Sordune. As they left Sordune, Virrilis noticed a peculiar castle in the distance. He told Max who told him, "That where we are going."

As they approached the castle, they saw how heavily guarded it was. Minotaurs, cyclopses, and dragonets all covered every entrance. The only entrance that was unguarded was on the top floor.

"I wish we could fly," Virrilis said.

Suddenly, as if on cue, their leather boots grew wings.

"Jason," Max smirked.

Once they had practiced the art of flying, they soared up to the floor, where Marth was waiting.

"I've been expecting you." His voice sounded like a box of nails. He took out his double blade. "The world will be mine, thanks to the power of this..." He gestured toward the Orb of Destiny. "Do you want it? Just fight me. It's you and me," he told Virrilis.

"And me!" Max pointed out. Out of nowhere, Marth knocked him off the tower.

Out of pure anger, Virrilis wielded his sword and shield. He slashed at Marth, who quickly countered. He slashed at Virrilis, who almost dodged it. Marth had slashed him in the arm. He was bleeding badly. While Virrilis took a split second to examine his wound, Marth knocked him to the floor with the blunt end of his sword. As he went for the finishing blow, the ground rumbled. The ground split. A crack appeared under Marth. Virrilis managed a weak smile. He hoarsely said, "Bye, Bye." He waved at Marth.

Marth fell to the lava pit hundreds of feet below him. Virrilis was barely able to stand. Burn marks and cuts surrounded his face.

He limped over to the orb. "Fly," he said as he gripped the orb in his hand. His boots grew wings and fluttered. He jumped and started flying. As he left, the castle collapsed into itself. All that was left of the wreckage was a flowing river of boiling lava.

Virrilis flew past a huge chunk of land with forests, rivers, lakes, and plains on his way back. Virrilis maneuvered himself back to the tower. Virrilis saw only one face at the tower...Max! At first he was far away and blurry, but as Virrilis approached, Max smiled at him. His scarred face had blisters, cuts, and bruises.

They exchanged looks. No words were needed. Virrilis limped inside, his legs on fire from the pain. There it was, the marble pillar. Virrilis stretched out his hand. The pillar creaked. The shining orb flew out of Virrilis' palm.

"Done," Virrilis said softly.

They returned to their little village and couldn't believe their eyes. Their village was in smoldering ruin. Burnt marks ran through each house. Smoke was coming out of every shop.

"Marth knew we were here...so he destroyed it," Virrilis said softly.

They knew what had to be done. They started off to find a new village to settle in. Their long quest had finally ended. Time for a new beginning.

20

The Prismatic Prank

by William Wendling

There was once a school called *Butterscotch Academy*. It was a very normal school, one where the students had to wear a white shirt and black pants everyday to school. The school was on Ben Dover Lane and, they called it that because the strong winds always blew things out of your hands so you would have to bend over to pick them up. Or it was just named after someone named Ben Dover. One day something very strange happened at the school.

There was a kid that was always late to school and always wore multicolored clothes. He had to make his clothes start with the same sound like purple pants, teal top, brown beret, and lavender loafers. He would even wear his own colors to soccer games, parties and even to bed. His name was Alex Anderson but, everyone called him Alliterative Alex. The kids made fun of him a lot because he was different from them. Alex would always smile and hold his head high because he knew that being different meant people wouldn't always understand that what he was doing was harmless. He just wanted to bring color into everyone's life.

One sunny day, Alex showed up late to school as usual and the kids played a prank on him that changed how everyone thought of him. He walked into his first class, algebra, but everyone was staring at him that morning. All of a sudden, he felt something cold hit the top of his head and then run down his shoulders and finally he felt the wet coldness on his feet. He looked down at what used to be his colorful clothes and only saw black. The kids had set up a big bucket of black paint above the door so when Alex walked in, it dumped all over him making his colorful clothes all black instead. He was so embarrassed he ran out of the room, down Ben Dover Lane and back to his house.

He sat on his front porch, trying to gather his thoughts as to what just happened. He didn't know how to feel. He spent so much time getting his clothes right like scarlet slacks, chartreuse shirt, and fuchsia flip flops that he felt defeated in one prank. He was so sad he stayed home from school that day, thinking.

The next day Alex was not late to school. He showed up before anyone else. He sat at his desk waiting for everyone to come to school. As the kids filed into class they were surprised to see Alex sitting there at his desk wearing all black from head to toe. No one said anything to him. They knew they couldn't call him Alliterative Alex anymore. He did his work and kept to himself all day and everyone just watched him, waiting for him to be different once again.

As the days went by, Alex kept wearing black everyday and showing up on time with no exception. Days were boring and uneventful for Alex. The weather also seemed to be rainy and gloomy everyday. The sun wouldn't shine and the kids started to also get bored with school and started to miss the colors they used to see on Alex everyday. They started talking about how fun school used to be when they would be excited to see what Alex would wear everyday. They would always talk about the colors and how they were alliterations. They realized they actually learned a lot about colors they had no idea existed. The days at school started to blend all together and there was a feeling of gloom all around.

Finally one day a girl named Sally Smith asked Alex, "Why don't you wear your colorful clothes anymore Alex?"

Alex just said, "There's no point, Sally. I just want do my work and go home."

This made the kids sad. They started to realize that Alex had lost his spirit of being different and they knew it was their fault.

The following weekend, while some kids were sitting on their porch because their soccer game was rained out once again, they started talking. One of them asked, "Has anyone noticed how boring school has been lately?"

"I think everything got boring and gloomy after we played that prank on Alex," one boy said.

Everyone looked around at each other and started to nod.

"Well, what should we do about it?" asked Sally.

No one had any ideas.

She said, "I think I know what to do."

The next Monday, Alex showed up to school on time as usual, dressed in black. He was sitting at his desk in algebra class when the first bell rang. No one else was there. He thought "It's Monday, right? There's supposed to be school today. Where is everybody?"

He continued to sit there a few more minutes until he started to hear some commotion outside. It sounded like kids talking in a large crowd. He went to the window to see what was going on. What he saw was his whole grade outside dressed in every color imaginable. He saw red roller skates, blue bonnets, purple ponchos, white western wear, green gowns, jade jackets, denim dashikis, lemon leotards, beige belts, and so much more.

He was so surprised he didn't know what to think again. He turned and walked outside. When the kids finally saw him standing there in amazement, they cheered. As they cheered loudly, the sun started to peek out of the clouds. Sally walked up to him and handed him some colorful clothes.

She said, "We're sorry, we didn't realize how colorful you made our lives. We love wearing canary coats, cyan saris, viridian vests, jasmine jumpers, sage sundresses, turquoise togas, umber underpants and khaki kimonos."

Alex looked down at what Sally had handed him and smiled back up at her. He quickly turned to run back into the school so he could change. When he reemerged from the school, the kids stood quietly looking at him for a minute and then the cheers exploded again. He was wearing a rainbow colored shirt, rainbow colored pants, rainbow colored socks and a rainbow colored hat.

Sally said, "We wanted to make sure you were still different from everyone."

7TH - 8TH GRADE SHORT STORIES

21

Loss

by Nelson Aiken

The old, musty smell of rotting oak wood filled David's nose as he quietly crept along the wet grass, soaking his toes in the dew. A cool breeze swept right through him, making him shiver in his polka-dotted, thin pajamas. Only his right hand, which was gripping a big, heavy flashlight, wasn't cold. A big moon, almost full, shone above him, providing some natural light so that David could see where he was going, making sure that he didn't trip on the massive oak tree roots that surrounded his feet. David found that he was pulled to the trees, a pulling that he couldn't resist, nor did he try. He didn't want to. Ever since his dad died David found the trees gave him reassurance in life. A reassurance he couldn't find with his mother, especially since his father had passed away. Since then his mother had been dangerously near depression and he had never been close to her to begin with. But unlike her the trees emanated a feeling of power and strength. Since his dad died David couldn't cry. At first he merely sat in his room and stared out the window until he had the idea of sneaking out to the trees.

David loved sneaking out at night almost as much as he loved Hugo, his dog, who was walking beside him, giving him comfort. It was nights like these that he could lay back, stare up at the stars and imagine all the kinds of things that this forest had seen; maybe great battles or fires that had killed everything, and yet these trees still stood tall and proud because the bark of the oak trees can't be touched by flame for they are too thick.

David could go on and on about these tales that he had dreamed of before he crept back to his small and dusty house and climbed through the window of his bedroom, jumped into bed and fell asleep until the next morning when he would frantically pull on his clothes, gulp down some plain, tasteless cereal, grab his bag, jump out the door and begin his long walk to school.

During the day David would sketch trees of all shapes and sizes while Ms. Odouya, a gentle old woman whose husband had died in the Vietnam war, went on and on about grammar. Nobody knew why she hadn't retired yet but her age was catching up to her because David's class had to listen to her boring static voice throughout the week. David often thought of Ms. Odouya as a less lovable oak tree, old wrinkly and full of untold tales.

After school, almost asleep, David would half stumble, half walk back home to Hugo, his big friendly husky who would jump on him and almost knock him over, then lick his face, looking content.

David, feeling tired, would shuffle into their tiny living room where his mother would hand him a warm cup of cocoa. He would sip contentedly, staring out the window into the distance. This was a time where in his head he was in his own little world.

David would be snapped out of his dream by his mother asking how his day went. "Boring," he would reply, and then go back to his daydreams.

In the evening, he would go up to his room, open the door and plop down on his bed and start to write. He would write about adventures on small islands squirming with exotic animals and plants, lonely dogs or cats looking for a home or sometimes families getting reunited with their father. He would write until it was time to sneak out and return to his ancient trees again.

One day, not an important or particular day, David was led out of his daydreams and doodles in class by something Ms. Odouya said that had caught his attention. Something about the old oak trees. Something about the old oak trees being cut down. About his old oak trees being cut down.

It took a few seconds for David to take in this startling news. It couldn't be true, could it? The confused old lady didn't know half the things she said. But could it be true? Could it even be legal to cut down the trees?

David felt like crying just thinking about it. He had to

check, just to be sure. David stood up, a look of determination in his eyes, his chair fell behind him with a loud clatter.

The class was engulfed in a silence only to be broken by Ms. Odouyan asking if he was alright. He didn't respond, didn't even acknowledge her. He just took a few strides to the door, stepped outside and started to run. He passed a very surprised looking girl going to the water fountain but David didn't notice.

He burst through the doors of the school and kept running. Running and running through the park where the dogs started leaping beside him until their frantic owners started screaming their pets' various names. David never faltered, never tripped and as he neared the corner to his street where only his house stood, he sped up, the wind whipping at his face and gravel tearing at his old, weathered and beaten shoes. Sweat poured down him. He had never run that fast or hard in his life.

Finally he reached his house, and stumbled around to the back where he opened his gate and looked up and saw the stump.

In his shock, David did not take in sound, color or anything around him. He just stood staring at the huge, round stump. David collapsed onto it as though it were a hard bed, feeling its pain, anger and grief. It was as though he had lost his father all over again. Hugo came padding slowly up to him and licked his face as though to give his condolences, before climbing up to curl against him, his warm body pressed against his stomach.

And then David cried.

Illustration by Nicole Pasterczyk - Back Cover Artist

22

Shattered

by Sofia Bajwa

Poland 1939

It was a dark and desolate afternoon, raindrops slithered down the window as Dominique looked onto the cobblestone streets filled with murky puddles. There was nothing to do since the war had started. Everyone was forced to go into hiding but each day had been a bore, the same thing one day after another. Dominique missed the smell of the bakery outside and the soft blades of grass tickling her feet. It's funny how one man can change everything, your life and the world you knew. But the thing Dominique resented the most about him was that it had been over three weeks since she had seen her best friend, Lena. Their religion had never mattered until now. Lena was Jewish and Dominique was German. But, they had never been apart for longer than a week! They were inseparable when they were together. Lena was the complete opposite of Dominique. While she was shy, Dominique was outgoing. Lena had very long gorgeous dark brown hair that swayed perfectly in the wind, while Dominique's hair, usually very unkempt, was short and light. However, somehow they were perfect together. Usually they would've been outside splashing in puddles and dancing together in the rain, but all that had changed since the war had started. Everything was different now. Lightning illuminated Dominique's room, covering it in an incandescent purple. Abruptly she jumped up as an idea came to her mind. She wasn't going to let some tyrant stop her from seeing her best friend.

With a mischievous twinkle in her eye Dominique stealthily sneaked to her front door and discreetly opened it. Creak. Shoot, she cursed under her breath, but she hurried out of the house anyways hoping no one had heard. Fortunately, Lena was her neighbor. Dominique lightly knocked on the door, nervously, in fear that she would be heard and seen. Through the peephole Dominique could see one of Lena's huge mocha brown eyes through the translucent glass. Lena nervously let Dominique in. "Oh Lena, I've missed you so much," Dominique whispered as she clutched her tightly.

"Not as much as I've missed you," Lena joshed back, giggling. "Oh, I almost forgot, I have your birthday gift! Eek, I can't wait for you to see it, I spent so long making it and I just know it will be absolutely perfect," she squealed. With that, Lena excitedly took off with an ebullient smile. Just after she had left a heavy boot pounded the door. Dominique gulped, hoping that whatever was on the other side of the door wasn't what she thought it was. Two big burly men came barging into Lena's house. Dominique opened her mouth in horror, but she was so petrified that no sound came out. She cowered back in fear. The Nazis had come. They dwarfed Dominique in height and their roughness and merciless way made her cringe even more. Before she could even do anything they brusquely grabbed Dominique and harshly said, "Lena, you're coming with us."

Lena pulled out the present and dusted it off. It had been hidden under her bed for weeks since Dominique and her couldn't see each other for Dominique's birthday. Lena dashed back to Dominique bursting with joy. She couldn't wait to see the thrilled look on her face when she opened her gift. But as Lena turned the corner she dropped the present. Her face became pallid and Lena let out a soundless scream. Dominique was being dragged outside by the Nazis.

For the next five minutes Lena stood in the hall shaking, she was more than apoplectic, she was in rage. Why did they take her best friend? The war had taken away so many parts of Lena's life like her freedom, and her family. Her grandparents and uncle had both been taken to concentration camps. But Lena never imagined it would take her best friend away too. She was crushed, and felt like she had lost everything. Lena had no idea where the Nazis were taking Dominique and she had no idea what to do. For the first time in her life, she was completely alone and utterly helpless.

Dominique was shoved into a cart with at least 30 other Jewish people. The Nazis kicked and struck people with the butt of their riffles as they cried out in pain.

"Stay quiet you Jewish swine," a Nazi screamed in irritation. All around her was chaos. People were crying, kids were screaming, Nazis were shouting. Like jigsaw pieces in a puzzle Dominique pieced together what was going on. Lena was Jewish, but Dominique was German, but since she was at Lena's house and appeared to be the only one there the Nazis must've thought that Dominique was Lena and taken Dominique instead. Dominique felt like her heart was going to explode, it was thumping so hard. She was more than scared, she felt like she was going to faint. She was nauseous and her body shivered in fear. She had completely no idea as to what to do. None, zip, zilch, nada, nothing.

Throughout the train ride to the concentration camp Dominique's mind vividly flashed with memories of Lena and herself. Dominique remembered when they were in the school play together and it was opening night. As the lights dimmed Lena went out on stage. She began narrating the scene but under the blinding lights Dominique could suddenly see her statuesque figure frozen. Dominique could see the beads of sweat racing down Lena's forehead and the fear creeping into her eyes. Lena had always been shy but Dominique had never seen her this shy. Racing into action Dominique jumped onto the stage beside Lena and began acting out her lines for her, making it seem as though there was supposed to be two narrators. Out of the corner of Dominique's eye she saw her mouth the words thank you with a tiny smile. The fear slipped out of Lena's eyes and regaining confidence she finished her lines.

But it wasn't only the big moments that came to mind, Dominique also reminisced about the tiny moments of their friendship that she had treasured forever such as the time they had a sleepover and stayed up all night talking about things such as boys, boys, and well, more boys. Or even the times they went to the ice cream shop together jauntily singing and skipping only to get there and realize they had run out of our favorite flavor; chocolate.

Emotions clawed at Dominique tearing apart her mind and heart. How would Lena's family act if she turned in their own daughter? Lena was an only child and Dominique couldn't even bear to imagine how empty Lena's parent's lives would be. But Dominique also questioned what her own family must have been thinking now. Should she tell the Nazis she was German? But what about Lena? Would Dominique really sacrifice herself only to hurt her best friend? They had been through everything together, would she betray her now, only to show that while Lena meant the world to her for the past 10 years Dominique valued her life more? Either way one of them would have to get hurt, Dominique just didn't want to decide whom.

Lena paced back and forth in the hall. She knew that by sacrificing herself she may save Dominique but put herself in a grave. Guilt ripped and pierced at her conscious. Saving Dominique would be the right thing to do. Lena knew Dominique didn't deserve what she was going to face, but then again neither did she. Lena's head was whirling with emotions. she clutched it in agony. Fear, guilt, sadness, and anger mixed and muddled up inside her brain. Her whole life had been turned upside down. Lena wished that everything could be normal again and Dominique and herself could laugh and play like they used to.

She remembered the times when they used to dress up in the craziest costumes and pretend they were going to fancy galas. Lena remembered Dominique's hazel eyes and long brown hair tucked up in a fancy bun as they pretended to be royals. Lena couldn't think of a time when Dominique had not been there for her. Another memory came to her mind as a picture began to appear. They were teaching magic tricks to Dominique's little brother and... wait... what about Dominique's brother! He would be heartbroken if he learned about the whereabouts of Dominique. He had always looked up to her and was drawn to her by her irresistible charm and light heartedness. Guilt flooded Lena's conscious and she knew it would be wrong to not save Dominique but selfishness inundated Lena's brain, as she was afraid of what would happen to herself.

Every night the whole cabin was full of people crying, or soundless as most of the people were exhausted. Life at the camp was miserable for everybody. Their bodies would ache and their stomachs would remain mostly empty. They were ravenous. Dominique would constantly think of her family, especially her brother. She missed him so much, and her heart ached and longed to see him again. She missed his goofy little smile and the way he would laugh and play for hours. Despite all this, Dominique made the toughest decision of her life. She pretended to be Lena, and to be Jewish. Because Lena meant the world to Dominique, she was going to sacrifice herself. Being a friend meant putting yourself before others right? Every so often Dominique second guessed herself wondering if this was really the right thing to do, but she wasn't going to let her brain change her mind.

They had only been at the concentration camp for a few days but it felt like it had been a lifetime. As a result of the grueling labor everybody faced, most of the people were covered in mud, or their heads were taken over with lice creeping in their hair, and itching their scalp. Their fingernails were caked with dirt and bugs. One day however, it felt as though the Nazis were treating everyone with a little more respect, as they had offered to let the people shower! Maybe the war was taking a turn. Dominique was so happy that she would be clean again and she pushed her way to the shower room along with dozens of others. They were led into a large area with tattered, chipped walls. Above them hung a whole line of shower-heads hanging down from a metal pipe. They were told to undress and then wait for the water to turn on. Eager to feel cleansed, everyone crowded underneath, anticipating the cool water roll down their bodies. All of a sudden the shower-heads were activated but everyone was taken aback as gas came showering down upon them. All that Dominique could hear were screams as she dropped to the cold, hard cement floor, the world slowly fading and turning black.

Lena couldn't stop thinking about her own life. She didn't want to end up like her grandparents or uncle. She also didn't want to leave behind her parents. The truth was Lena was scared that she would be more alone than she already was. What if she couldn't save Dominique? What if she would just make everything worse? After long consideration, and the lingering guilt still in her mind, Lena knew in my heart that she would be doing the right thing. Dominique was one of the only people Lena had left, and she needed her. Lena began packing some necessities into a small backpack. She had never been in so much fear before. Anxiety crept into her body and rattled her brain. She had no idea what was going to happen to herself and she didn't exactly know how she was going to save Dominique either, but all Lena knew was that she was going to try. She had to try. As Lena slipped outside she embarked on the greatest and most perilous journey of her life, not sure of what was to come.

23

Regretful

by Tori Beuge

Maureen furiously rode her bike through the streets of her neighborhood, ignoring the water from the melted snow sloshing up and getting her feet wet.

Normally, Maureen would be rejoicing at the first signs of spring, her favorite season, but when her thoughts whirlpooled like this, staring at the same math problem on her homework wouldn't help her. So she got on her bike and told her mom that she would be returning books to the library. For once though, Maureen wasn't going to the library. Maureen's destination was up to her now rain-soaked feet.

She turned left at the large rock that she named Natasha when she was three and pedaled to the bike path next to it. Suddenly, she stopped. A large sack made of a rough-hewn material blocked her path. Maureen got off her bike and let it drop to the ground. Slowly, carefully, she walked over to the sack and gingerly prodded it with her index finger. She didn't know why she was being so cautious with this old rucksack, but something about it demanded respect like a religious tome.

After a few moments of inspection, Maureen pulled back a part of the sack and saw something odd. There was an old, blue, leather-bound book in it. Who would put an old book like this in the middle of a busy bike path, Maureen thought. Despite its look of fragility, the sack containing the book was somewhat haphazardly strewn across the bike path. Obviously, whoever left it there didn't want it, but Maureen was suspicious in nature, and understood that someone might be looking for it. It was best to just leave it on the path and let its owner come and get it. The one problem with this plan was that Maureen didn't want to leave it there. It was the wise thing to do, but Maureen was transfixed by it. Maureen was hypnotized. The book wants me to take it home. It was just a book though, it couldn't want anything. It didn't have the capacity to think, let alone have emotions. It couldn't talk to her, because it was a book.

Looking back on it, Maureen would say that it did kind of talk to her. It grabbed her attention, her actions, and wouldn't let go. She said it spoke to her in a kind of melodic, buzzing language that she could hear when she held it. It blurred out the rest of the sounds around her and sang to tell her what to do.

The book wants me to take it home. So she did.

Maureen took the sack with her book in it and sneaked it back to her house, avoiding her mom in the process, she walked into her room. Then she sat down with her book in her lap and waited. Her book seemed to have been waiting for this response. It began to sing. Maureen understood every single note of its melancholy tune. It told her what it could do, what it had seen, and what it wanted.

Apparently, this book was relatively new compared to what it looked like, it was twenty years old. Her book had traveled across the world changing hands all the time. Some of those hands were killed, others had mysteriously disappeared, but a few of them were breathing and could be located on a map. Her book said that its purpose was to show people what could have happened, and give them an entrance to it.

What that meant exactly, Maureen didn't know. She got the part about showing people what could have happened, that was like looking at the other path in a fork in the road. Giving them an entrance to what could have happened, that was another story. If the meaning was literal, that would mean that the book somehow transported a person to a different world where a different outcome had happened. At this point, the logical part of Maureen's brain would argue that this wasn't possible. Yes, there was a possibility that parallel universes existed, but a book transporting a person to one was improbable. Impossible. Could not happen.

Or could it? A book just happens to be talking to me right now. A *BOOK*. That's considered impossible by many people. Look at me now though! I'm talking to a book about life choices, and it's responding to me as if it was a person. Who am I to say something is impossible?

She studied her book more closely. It was a pretty midnight blue, with a fine, gold-leaf trim around the edges, the pages were blank, yellowed with age, and wavy. It did appear to be older than it said. If Maureen had to guess, she would say around half a century. Maybe sixty years, at the most. A book with the burden of looking at one's regrets would seem older than it was.

Then a question came to Maureen's mind, What does this book want with me? She whispered her thought to the book. Its reason wasn't a real surprise. The book wanted Maureen to see her regrets. This puzzled her though, because she couldn't think of any regrets she had. The book was indignant to Maureen's response, and said that everyone had regrets, even if one couldn't remember them. Of course, Maureen argued that if someone couldn't remember their regrets, it was kind of like they didn't regret them anymore.

The book said she was getting too philosophical.

"Future regrets are a different thing. Are you going to show me my future regrets?" she asked.

It didn't reply. The book was a temperamental thing, it didn't like being challenged. Maureen became alarmed by this. When inanimate objects get angry in books and movies, nothing good comes from it. She backed away, observing the book from a safe distance. The book finally answered with a feeble *sorry*, and a small explanation of what it wanted to show her. The translation didn't cover the full extent of what it said, but it basically told her that it wanted to show her a path to a world where what could have happened...happened. Maureen asked what did happen. In this world.

The book gave what could only be translated as an exasperated sigh, and told her she would have to see what was different herself. Then it proceeded to ask if she wanted to see her regrets or not.

Maureen hesitated before answering, "Yes."

The book shuddered before emitting a soft cry. Maureen widened her eyes, the air in the room felt thicker, and it seemed like there was no gravity. Something rushed through her, making her blood frigid, and her skin like a sheet of ice.

Fear grabbed hold of her heart, screaming at her to find a way out, any way out. Maureen could still move, but it felt like she was swimming in a lake. She spun around, looking at her room. Everything was fading away to a backdrop of blinding white light. The only thing that was visible now was the book. A million thoughts ran through her head while this happened. Where am I going? Why did I agree to this? How is this happening? How can I get out?

Finally, it stopped, leaving a ringing in her head and confusion in the forefront of her mind. Maureen was in an old, cabin-like room. It was a happy, airy, place, and it made her think of spring. The white light was still present, but it streamed through the glass windows like a warm ray of sunshine. In the middle of this room was a simple wooden table with the book laid open on it. Her book. The book that had brought her here.

Immediately, she shook off the comfortable charm of this place, and focused on her previous intent. How do I get out of here? Her attention was drawn to the book. She cautiously walked toward the book, taking every step into account. She stopped at a safe distance, then looked at its pages. A soft, spidery script in a satisfying mahogany ink peered back at her accusingly. It's your fault that you 're here, not mine, it seemed to say. Maureen crept closer, trying to get a better look at the writing. The first word she read was a bold signature. Her own name. Maureen. Elegant, intricate, meaningful, the handwriting stated; Maureen had never seen her name written like this. She wanted to read more.

So she did. Every gorgeously hand-drawn word. Every well-put sentence. Maureen's eyes glided through the page, right to the bottom. She then flipped the page over and read some more. When she reached the end of that page, she turned her head to the page on the opposite side of the crease, but the words were blurred; unreadable.

No. This one simple thought triggered a tidal wave of happenings. Maureen became aware again of her surroundings, she lifted her head from her book, confused, disoriented. She remembered how she got here and where she was. She looked back at the book, filled with awe and fear of how it controlled her. Then Maureen put the book down and sprinted to the other side of the small room. Now, instead of her favorite season, the room reminded her of a cage. Instead of coziness it felt confining.

For a long time it was just Maureen and the book in a staring match. Guess who was winning. The girl was only now aware of the room's foreboding; it leered and smirked at her, but in all reality was a normal room. It was her perspective that changed. The book who staked its claim on a girl riding a bike. The book singled out everyone though, it just seemed like a solitary deal.

In the end it was Maureen who lost. The voice distracted her. "Hello Maureen, it's nice to see you here," the voice simpered.

Maureen broke her gaze from the book and surveyed the room. No one. Except the book, but it couldn't be the book.

"No, I'm not the book. Smart girl, most don't get that right."

No reply. Silence was the way Maureen chose to answer the patronization.

A chuckle reverberated through the room. "If I were to formally introduce myself, I guess you could call me Fate. Destiny. Future, Past or Present would do too, whatever suits you."

Maureen shifted her stance to seem more confident. "What's with the book?"

"One could call it a record of sorts. The story of everything would be more accurate, a little preachy though." Maureen could hear it smiling. "And I decide everything that will happen to anyone, then I write it down in the book."

Maureen shivered.

"How are you?" The voice was trying to be polite. It didn't do polite very well.

"Fine."

"The clipped answer says otherwise. Truth can't be hidden from me, you do know that."

Maureen didn't know. To her, this omniscient presence was new. How could one know everything about everyone? No human would be able, that's for sure, and it scared her. What was this voice if not human? Destiny or any other names it went by didn't bode well with her.

How did it know her name? How did the book know her

life? That's what she read on the front and back of the page. She read her past, present, and future.

"Everyone is in there?"

"Everything is in there. Stars have pasts, presents, and futures, as well as a flower, or a dog."

Maureen made a quick and foolish decision. She calmly walked across the room to the book. "Can I read anyone else's lives?"

"No," the voice said suspiciously.

"Really?" Maureen asked, pretending to be surprised. "Why?"

"Someone reading another person's entire life could bring up certain ...complications. They could try to control someone else's life, to change it. People aren't meant to have that kind of power, and something of that nature would ruin both of their futures. The futures I so carefully wrote for them."

While Fate was on this tirade Maureen took the chance to casually open the book and gaze at her page. She firmly secured her hand to her page, then ripped it out. It was like she woke up from a restless dream. One minute she was standing in a strange room listening to Fate itself, the next she was sitting on her own bed in her own bedroom. Her room exactly the same as it was before she left, and Maureen melted into the normalcy of it all. The beautiful, safe, boring, sameness.

There was, however, one problem. Maureen held two separate pages in hand. One was full of familiar words. The other was blurry. Maureen wasn't alone anymore. Another person lay on the end of her bed. They seemed to be asleep. Maybe they were dreaming about their future, past, and present. Maureen wasn't sure, only you could be because it was you. It was you who lay at the end of Maureen's bed, eyes closed, a peaceful look on your face. It was you who might have possibly been dreaming.

Maureen did what any rational person would do, she checked your pulse to see if you were alive. You were. Then she put your page down next to you, and backed away to the farthest corner of her room, politely looking away from your sleeping form. Then you woke up.

24

Zinnia

by Bella Clark

They had named her Zinnia. She was true to her name, for she was the vibrant blossom in cool, forest damp, the shafts of light slicing shadows, and the lush grass against the dreary gray of the winter brush. A storm of anger or a flood of sadness was something very rare, for Zinnia would stand in a storm and smile at the rain, rejoicing in its blessing. She was undeniably gorgeous, and she was my sister, who had dreams of a bigger, better world. All my life, I watched her excitement grow, speaking of the different scenes and different people, and she made it seem that a life outside of our forest, with its variety and adventure, would be a better place for us. Though her name bespoke a shallow planted flower and mine, the river, in truth it was Zinnia who was the deep water. She tried to hide what was beneath. In contrast to her, I was always content with my simple life in the forest, and struggled to convince Zinnia of the danger of the villages, that her fantasies would leave her in the dark. But as she grew more envious of the villagers, who settled ever closer to the boundaries of our world, her eyes became bleak and cold. I watched helplessly as the blossom withered, the flame guttered into darkness, the lush grass blanched and faded to dreary gray. She had lost hope for her dream of living a different life. And like a winter storm, she only grew colder.

We had live amongst nature all our lives, and mine only a couple more than a baker's dozen. I did not know the things she did, or see the things she had seen. Zinnia was almost twenty years old, and on the day of her twentieth birthday, she did not stand in a storm. She created one.

I didn't think Zinnia had awoken and something about the morning seemed slightly off. For one, her normal, waking movements from across the tiny room were absent and though I was sure the sun had risen, its golden shafts didn't drape across the window and floor. The dawn was absent. The whole morning atmosphere was slightly depressing. I had gotten up slowly, stretching my limbs one by one and lowering my feet, my toes grazing the mossy carpet beneath me.

"Zinnia?" I yawned, lifting myself off the mattress and rocking sleepily. I assumed she'd be up at this time, before the sun had swept us from slumber, like my mother chasing away the errant leaves from the kitchen hearth. I ran my hand over her bedspread before lifting it, and there was yet another absence. Zinnia was gone. I knew this from the second I pulled her cover over, the moment I ran down the stairs calling her name, the moment frozen in sheer terror as I knew she wasn't coming back. Zinnia had left. I knew that she'd leave someday. And today was that day. My head pulsed until it ached, my legs started shaking and threatened to give way. My sister was gone.

Zinnia was like her namesake flower, and I, Mozella, was named for the river. Had I washed her away?

Another layer for warmth and I took off. I swept across the bank and just stared out at the river, not wanting to cross, not wanting to leave my home like Zinnia did. Sheer panic slowed me down, I halted, swallowed the threatening scream of terror and scanned the opposite shore. I squinted at the sun overhead, its warmth should be able to illuminate the shadows below, the path ahead, but the treetops were so dense. I had never left home. And neither had Zinnia. But she made her home within her head, equal parts fantasy and delusion. She did not know what dangers would face her when she left this forest. And I would not let her face those dangers alone.

I didn't need to guess where Zinnia would be, the siren call of the village was all she could hear. I wrapped my jacket closer to my chest, a breeze seeping beneath to chill my skin. I shivered. Naked sunlight was blinding as I drew closer to the village. Vivid greens grew vague and garish tones replaced the colors of earth. It was all so surreal, dream-like with a twist of fear and a twitch of a nightmare. Fear drove the pounding of my feet on the pavement. I was running for Zinnia. And her loss was all too real to be a dream.

The hive of busy streets bustled with life, I flitted to one corner only to swerve and approach another, searching in vain. I felt out of place, a smack of reality as I watched eyes flicker to the running girl. Me. The sting of their attention, their whispers and stares would have paralyzed me on any other day. I was too panicked to care. There were so many scenes blurred together, so many people, just like Zinnia said there would be. Briefly, I wondered if she enjoyed the spectacle around her, all the people in their element, the bold noise, mechanical movement, the cacophony of society. I wondered if she thought of me at all. They all dressed in bright colors and moved quickly, as if they had an important place to be, a place more important than this town. Their chaos made me long for the order of the forest.

I continued to run, my limbs aching. As I slowed down, the burning in my legs radiated to my head. I felt numb. And there was no one to look to, to stand up and ask where she was or where I was. I drew to a stop, panting. I collapsed on the grass alongside the road out of town. Breathing heavily, my eyes searched the sky.

Zinnia, can you hear me? Listen to me. Just listen. I felt like lying down, so I did. *There's danger here and I'm here for you. Running from the only place I want to be to find you.* I felt like crying, but I did not. Instead, I narrowed my eyes, sat up, and felt the sledgehammer of rage break through the panic. I didn't want to speak to Zinnia anymore. She wasn't listening. I crouched and sprang back to my feet. I needed to move. I was no longer running for Zinnia but running from her, away from myself. Because I knew myself. If I stayed myself, I'd sit on the curb and cry. So I'm not me. Even if I wanted to be. Zinnia had stolen a part of me, left me broken, and that wasn't who I was going to be.

I searched for an ending, a dead end, a place to accept losing Zinnia and a place to accept losing a part of me. But I never found it. And I began to wonder if it's really true, if I really did sweep my sister away from me, if it was the fault in me that fueled a fault in her. As I ran, I list all the things I could have done, all the things I could have said. But I drew a complete blank. My stomach started to feel sick with guilt.

All the people and their colors no longer exist, and all I see is blackness. And that's when I saw him. He's tall and slender, like I remembered him, but he doesn't look like he did in the woods. His clothes were nicer, and he strutted along with a smirk on his face. And that face triggered a memory.

"You should come out to the village square when you turn twenty next week. I could meet you there," he murmured, looking over Zinnia's shoulder at me, checking to see if I was aware of his plans, from where I stood in the kitchen. His axe was slung over his shoulder. Zinnia looked over at me, then murmured to him. She thought I couldn't hear her.

"I don't know..."

"Come on, you've never been outside this forest. There's a wide world out there. Time to join it." His smug voice boils my blood.

She nodded dumbly, leans forward and murmurs something I can't hear, and quietly shuts the door. My cue.

"You can't possibly believe him! He's a fool!" I yelled at her, and she rolled her eyes, still dazed by him. "He's a fine worker and he loves me, Mozella. He's going to marry me."

"He's a liar." I spit the words at the back of her head, clenching my fists. My own sister, leaving me for some half-stranger's promise.

In this flash, a split second, rage takes control. I storm over to him.

"Ash." His name hovers in the air. His smirk fades.

"Mozella...," he drawls, looking away.

"Where is my sister?" My voice was intense, and I narrowed my eyes to let him know how serious I was. And yet, he smirked to let me know how serious he wasn't. He looked menacing.

"The light was a little too bright for her here. Now run along, Mozella." Ash gestured me away, raising his eyebrows. I blinked back tears.

"She never should have trusted you," I murmured.

"It's not my fault she couldn't keep up," Ash replied. He didn't see the tears spilling from my eyes, because I shoved him away and started to run again. I ran from Ash, from the people and their bright colors, into the woods, across the river bank. I fell to the ground on the pathway of my home, letting tears spill freely onto the dirt. I wanted my sister home and whole and safe.

And as I lifted my head, there was Zinnia, lying on the earth.

"Zinnia?" I felt as if I'm calling her from a great distance. She whirled around and immediately my wish was granted. She hugged me, and didn't let go until she stared at me long and hard.

"Mozella, you were right about him."

Now the world was in color again, the light cast shadows in every corner. The woods were alive, and my search for Zinnia had shown me the world that I once was afraid to face. I no longer feared losing Zinnia, our world or my hope. My sister's smile grew bigger every single day, and her eyes no longer seemed cold and distant. Her warmth grew with each day, and even though when I awoke every morning I checked to make sure she hadn't run off or turned cold, I know that this world had something greater for Zinnia than Ash, than a colorless world or a tiny village. Zinnia was a flower, and I, Mozella, was the river. And together, we were the forest.

25

Inner Perfection

by Nia Gallagher

Out of all the thoughts that run through my head everyday, some are far more distinctive than others. Why am I unaccepted? What's so different about me? When will someone understand what I mean? Will I ever make friends? Why can't I be normal like everyone else? Some may say I have a gift, others don't even know my name. These people just know me as the *stupid girl, the weird girl, the autistic girl.* I hate that word.

Autistic. Autistic. Autistic. Autistic. Autistic. Autistic. Autistic. Autistic.

I hear it in school. In public. At doctors appointments. Everywhere. It follows me as often as my shadow. I wish I could snap my fingers...vanquishing it forever.

They call me stupid, but I'm not! Everyone underestimates me...even the teachers. Whatever happened to, *Don't judge a book by its cover*? I'm always surrounded by others with the same problems as me. Adults like it when kids like us are separated from the real world, but really it just makes it harder.

~

My hand slid across the tray attached to my electric wheelchair. I pushed the joystick on a built-in remote away from me, jolted forward and zipped down my driveway. Abruptly, I twisted it in a circle, spun around with great force.

Reversing onto the wheelchair lifter of my school bus is quite tricky. You have to have impeccable timing and speed, while also making sure you don't brake too early nor too late. With my delayed and spazzed movements, this is one of the most difficult parts of the day.

Once I hear the lift's low hum, I quickly waved to my mom as I slowly move upwards. I usually roll as far to the front of the bus as I can, allowing me to greet everyone in seats that I passed. My wheels satisfyingly clicked into the provided slots and locked into place. Now, I just have to prepare myself for the mundane journey ahead which takes me to the building of knowledge, with nothing more for me to learn.

Once we arrived, I reversed the lengthy process and eventually find myself zipping along the sidewalk. As I flew towards the glass double doors to enter the school, I watched my reflection grow rapidly. Once I finally came to a halt, the door quickly unlocked and I headed to my classroom. Adding to the troubles of this everyday process, I also tried to remain unseen by any other kids who may be walking the halls.

I saw a girl walking in my direction all alone. Her books seem to weigh an infinite number of pounds due to the struggle in her movements, along with her tiny size. I'm surprised the weight does not send her stumbling to the floor, papers flying everywhere like confetti.

She doesn't think I noticed her side glance at me. She doesn't know that I felt the one way tension too. I could nearly see her body stiffen. If I don't judge her, how come she still judges me?

Trailing the girl are two young boys. Here's the difference, they don't even try to hold back their stares. From a hundred paces away, I saw them looking me up and down, studying every abnormal feature of mine. Even worse, the second I heard their footsteps begin to fade behind me, a muffled burst of giggles exploded from their unfiltered mouths.

When I heard footsteps rounding the corner, the dread begins to build up inside of me, finally stuffing my throat with its anxiety. I can't help but wonder what this rude human being's reaction would be when they saw me racing down the hall. My heart beat in my chest faster than a hummingbird's wings. As the bodies cut around the corner, I saw the faces of two girl's appear and my body is washed with the sweet feeling of relief. I recognize these girls. How could I forget them? They are some of the few people that excitedly acknowledge me every morning in the hallway.

"Hey Ivy!" they chirp in unison.

Don't get me wrong, I loved the attention, but in the back of my head, I know they are only trying to be kind. In reality, they would never ask me to hang out, or invite me to their slumber party. I'm always going to be just Ivy.

I wanted someone that would think of me as more than just Ivy. I wanted to be a best friend. Someone who I could stand up for, and someone who would stand up for me. Someone I could paint my nails with and spend the night at their house. I wanted to have a true friendship. After I continued my ride down the hallway, I noticed Mr. Gilmore, our school guidance counselor, touring a new student around the halls.

"Hello Ivy, how are you today? This is our new student, Aaliyah. She will be in your grade," he exclaimed with an elated smile.

Why would it even matter if she's in my grade or not? Important people like you who run this school don't even allow me to be in the same classes as her. You don't seem to care about our education. She's probably just like the rest of the *normal* kids anyways. I pushed the negative thoughts out of my head, and forced my mouth to form a smile and moved my hand so I could wave. Suddenly, I was caught by surprise as unbelievable words can streaming out of Aaliyah's mouth.

"Hi Ivy! I'm Aaliyah...as you just learned. It's so nice to meet you. Hopefully we have some classes together because so far you're the only person I know. Maybe I can sit with you at lunch, if that's okay? You seem really nice and I'd like to get to know you."

Did she really just treat me like a real person? Am I finally not a total nobody? I've never had this feeling before, but I think it's the beginning of friendship.

As a smile broke out on my face, I nodded with delight and waved goodbye, zooming away with an energy I had never experienced before. I made the turn into my classroom, pulled up to my desk, and began a great day.

~

I can honestly say that I have never met anyone like Aaliyah before. She gave me a feeling of worthiness. It was almost as if without me, she wouldn't be able to have a fantastic first day of her new middle school.

I anticipated the bell after every class, and zoomed out into the hallway. I was looking out for Aaliyah. It took a while, but after fourth period, I saw her strolling down the hallway.

My heart sank as I saw several other girls surrounding her. Even worse, she seemed to love the attention, laughing so hard with the rest of the girls that the whole pack stopped to catch their breath.

I began to turn around and return to my classroom when I heard my name being called loud and clear.

"Ivy, wait! I haven't seen you at all today. What's up? I'm going to Math next, I hope it's not too difficult!" she yelled. All the other girls rolled their eyes and walked away, their faces filled with disgust.

"Hmm...I wonder what's up with them? I guess they don't want to be friends after all. I thought I did a pretty good job introducing myself. Well, I still have you," she stated with a grin, elbowing my arm.

My face lit up with excitement. She came back, stood up for me, and wanted to be my friend. Could this day get any better?

"Do you have a phone? I would really like your number so we could talk more often. It would help us get to know each other better too! I bet my mom wouldn't mind if you slept over some night...she absolutely loves meeting new people."

I ecstatically began screeching, "Yes! Yes! Yes!," and I threw my arms around her neck. I pulled out a pencil and paper, and began writing my home phone number as clearly as possible. It's as if she could read my mind...first being my friend, then sticking up for me, and now even suggesting we have a sleepover.

We both went our separate ways, and now I could not wait to get home. Even then, I knew that all night, I would plant myself in front of the phone, not letting my eyes off of it for a second.

~

The shrill of the phone echoed through the house for under a millisecond. The first ring didn't even end before my hand flew forward at lightning speed, grabbing the machine in one swift motion.

"Hello? Aaliyah? I've been waiting all night for this call. How are you?" I questioned, as I rolled out of the room into the office, closing the door behind me. For the next hour, I poured my heart out to Aaliyah. Our conversation escalated from my favorite color, to the most aggravating topic of my lack of opportunity.

Not many people know this, but my strongest subject is Math, and any other numerical situation. Whether it's solving an extremely hard equation like $6/2-\sqrt{3} = p(2+\sqrt{3})$, or knowing the exact number of Skittles a clumsy toddler spills the second they hit the ground, I have never been proven wrong. Perfection!

I told her that if I could participate in a math class like hers for one day, all my dreams would come true. I told her that I just wanted to show what I know and not only make life easier for myself, but for all my other *disabled* classmates. I told her that I wanted to show that even though I am different, I am still just as good as everyone else. I told her that I wanted to prove that I am capable of more than what everyone expects. I told her that I just wanted to feel normal.

Before I was even able to get another word out of my mouth, she paused and said, "Wish me luck! Bye!" and the line went dead.

~

As I replayed my long morning process, I wondered why Aaliyah was so quick to hang up on me last night. Maybe she realized how weird I really was. She probably thought that I made her look bad. She wouldn't want to be seen with me, and realized that she had made a big mistake. Everyone else gave up on my friendship, so why not her as well?

When I rolled into my classroom, all eyes immediately flashed in my direction. Never in my life had that happened to me before. As I scanned the room, I noticed Mrs. Ednels standing near my desk.

Mrs. Ednels is the math teacher for my grade. Her room is next door and I always found myself admiring the equations and other math related items all around her room.

"Ivy, due to your friend's actions, I would love for you to join our class during fifth period today. Now, just remember, you will not be permanently kept in this class. It is only a temporary opportunity."

Aaliyah. Oh how I love Aaliyah. How could I even think that she would no longer want to be my friend. I jumped to conclusions, and thought she was ending our friendship, but in reality, she was doing a good deed for me and all of my classmates, along with growing and strengthening our friendship.

I sat through period 1, period 2, period 3, period 4 and finally, I got to go to my first math class ever. I was thrilled. It' was amazing how much one person could change your life.

~

My hand shot up in the air. I answered. I'm correct. My hand shot up in the air. I answer. I'm correct. The process repeated itself several times. I haven't been incorrect once this class, and have answered exactly 23 questions so far. Perfection!

I watched as Mrs. Ednels uncapped her white board marker. She placed the tip on the board and began to write out an equation. I watched carefully as the red ink glided across the shiny white surface. Once the felt was removed from the board, I read the whole equation out and immediately knew the solution. Before I know it, I blurted out the answer.

"Uh...well...Wow! This is a first...that is correct," announced Mrs. Ednels. "That is the hardest problem I have ever given. It is actually a question you might find on the SATs someday. Good job, Ivy."

I looked over at Aaliyah and smiled, receiving a response of a wink. She reached into her backpack and pulled out a thin, red box, that seemed to have a rainbow cutting through the center, but I couldn't completely tell what it is.

It caught me off-guard when she randomly pushed her chair out from under the desk, and rose to face the entire class. Her hands were behind her back, hiding the box she had previously pulled out of her backpack.

Before anyone could stop her, she poured 56 skittles out of the box. Wait...56. *56!*

"56! 56! 56!" I yelled from my seat.

Everyone looked at me as if I had gone mad. They didn't understand, but Aaliyah knew.

"Alright class. Please settle down. Aaliyah, pick up those Skittles, and we will talk about this after class," Mrs. Ednels scolded, clearly frustrated with the current behavior in her classroom.

"But Mrs. Ednels, Ivy just counted the exact number

of Skittles that fell out of that container. I swear! See...
1..2..3..4..5..6..7..8.."

After what seemed like eternity, and fifty-six Skittles later, everyone was impressed with my abilities.

Without Aaliyah, I don't know what I would have done. Having someone love and respect me meant so much to me and I don't know what more I could have asked for. Now, we are best friends and go through thick and thin together. We even had the same schedule with all the same teachers and everything. The most important class is Algebra, fifth period. Don't judge a book by its cover, because even if the cover was ripped and crumpled, the inside could hold the best selling story. That's its inner perfection.

Illustration by Joshua Sher - Back Cover Artist

26

Run the Show

by Adith Gopal

Have you ever come up clutch in an important scenario? Have you ever choked in an important scenario? Have you ever been given another opportunity to come up clutch in that same scenario after choking? No matter what it is? Like a basketball game? For me, that was the case.

Basketball is a finesse sport. It requires the perfect angle of release, the perfect amount of power, the perfect backspin, and the perfect stroke. It is not easy.

Our team, the Dark Blue team, was playing an undefeated team; Pink team at the Governor Mifflin Gymnasium. Yes, Pink. They were 13-0, looking for 14 wins. We were looking for a playoff berth. Game time in 2 minutes. I did my normal routine, making a 3-pointer from all 5 places (top of key, 2 wings, 2 corners), watching the backspin of the orange rubber ball as it swishes cleanly in the long, white net.

The buzzer rings, signifying that pre-game has ended. Our coach, Coach Faccioli, made our starting lineups, which I was in. Coach had inspired us all year, but this was different. He advised, talking with his hands,"This may be the last game y'all ever play. Ever. Make it your best, and it may not be your last game of the year. Teamwork is key." We were ready, despite Pink's huge size advantage. Pink had 2 big, 6-foot guys. One was lanky, but the other just huge. Pink won the tip. Game time.

In the beginning of the first half, Pink had a lead 11-4 on us. I made a catch-and shoot 3-pointer early and a teammate made a free throw due to a hard foul. Their huge kid has all 11 points, on free throws and easy layups and didn't score from anywhere farther than 15 feet. Our bench was quiet, knowing that this was expected despite our confidence. Part of the crowd was ecstatic, while the other part had mouth's shut. They eagerly waited for our team to start a run.

There were 5 minutes left in the first half as our team got the ball. I got fouled driving to the basket for a floater. Swishing in the free throw made the score 11-5. On the other end, Pink's tall, lanky got blocked. Hard. It ricocheted off his face. 3 minutes left in the half. I grabbed the ball, sprinted down the court, stopped, and lofted a high 25-footer on the left wing. Taking my time, I swished it. 11-8. Could we continue the run? With 2 minutes left, could we end the half with a win and on a hot streak?

After back and forth possessions on both ends, results were fruitless. Still 11-8 with a minute left. We needed something to get back in this game.

I played the point guard for the minute left. A hand-stinging one-handed pass to a wide open teammate in the left corner tied the game at 11 with 49 seconds. The rest of the half resulted in failed efforts. At halftime the score is 11-11.

At the half, we decided to switch up our defensive strategy. They had no proficient shooters, so we decided to play a 2-3 zone defense. This intimidates their point guard as well as stuffing up gaps for the big guys driving to the paint.

This defense worked very well for a while. We went on a 10-2 run with five minutes left in the game. Now the score is 21-13. I brought the ball up after Pink scored their first two points of the half. The defense didn't expect me to shoot. They were playing laid-back defense. I shot a three. Three seconds later, the net gangling and ball coming out of the net, increasing the score 24-13, the Pink coach immediately called a timeout.

With 3:30 left in the game, Pink didn't seem to have an answer for me, my team, or the defense we were playing. I led my team in scoring with 10 points. We felt confident, thinking that their chances of coming back was fruitless. I was running the show.

Pink came back out of their huddle, desperately trying anything to get a 11-point comeback. They passed the ball in. Their huge guy got fouled. Before he angrily stepped on the free-throw line, the clock ran down. 3:24 left. The ball rolled in and out in both free throws. I got the rebound. 3:19 left on the clock.

After missing the free throws, the huge guy shouted something explicit. All of a sudden, it gets quiet. The bouncing ball stopped bouncing. The three refs called a timeout, and met up. All the parents, at this point, looked at him with steam smoking out of their ears like a factory.

After 5 minutes of serious discussing, the refs came out of their huddle like a challenged play. After that, they told the huge guy that this was his last warning. They asked him, "One more time, and you're done for the entire year! Understood?" Reluctantly, the huge guy kept his mouth shut, and the game continued.

At this point of the game, our strategy was simple. Nonchalantly climb up the court, don't lose the ball, and don't force any stupid, unnecessary shots. We only had to do that for 3 minutes before ruining Pink's perfect season and clinching a playoff berth.

On our first possession since the delay, we wasted nearly a minute just trying to miss shots, get the rebound, and keep the ball. Finally, that strategy died out, and the Pink team aggressively got the ball back. Only 2 minutes left.

Pink ran down the court. We knew they were thinking only about shooting 3-pointers. But they had nobody capable of doing so. After their futile efforts of wasting a minute trying to hack up 20 foot three-pointers, the score was still the same at 24-15.

With no shot clock, we just walked up the court with no effort, making sure we didn't lose the ball. We hustled around the three-point line and chucked shots off the glass to get the rebound and kept the clock moving. With only 30 seconds, there was no effort from either side. When each team gathered the ball after a rebound, walking up the court tended to be common. Pink had no sense of urgency. They had accepted defeat.

Although Pink was showing their sulky attitude hobbling up the court, they tried to jack up three-pointers as if they are Steph Curry! The nerve they had! My teammate even counted up how many misses they had. 0-20 in their last 20-three pointers! The score was still 24-15 with 20 seconds left, a low scoring game.

Only ten seconds until Pink's perfect season would go

down the drain and we clinched a playoff berth. Pink's point guard got the ball. Nine seconds left. The Governor Mifflin Gymnasium was silent, waiting to burst like a piñata at a party. The point guard slugged to half-court. Eight seconds left. He did a crossover move, trying to elude from my defense. Six seconds left. Spin move, crossover, double-hesitation. Two seconds. And he jumped like a rabbit, flicking his wrist and letting the ball go. A second later, a long, loud buzzer sounded like a bomb gradually sounded as the ball hit the steel rim and bounced off.

The final score ended at 24-15, and our team won. The crowd at the Governor Mifflin Gymnasium erupted like a volcano, with cheers and boos about the result of the game, and the attitude of both teams. We felt like we had won the championship, ending Pink's perfect season and us clinching a playoff berth. Many of Pink's players didn't shake our hands, so in return we gave them the salty sign behind them. All in all, it was a great day.

27

Butterflies in the Light, Beasts in the Night

by Divya K. Gupta

Lost Springs is a forgotten town with less than a hundred people. It was twenty miles from the nearest market or gas station. Inside one of the old farm houses lived a middle-aged man named Gordy Benedict. His life was full of gardening and fear. Gordy lived with his young puppy, Chipper. Chipper and Gordy were always together, doing everything. The cautious pair loved to climb trees, scuba dive, and row boats up fast rivers. Of course, all of these activities are done in the safety of their imaginations. One activity that would never occur in their house or minds, was laser tag. The dark room was an extreme hazard to Gordy. Ever since Jimmy Kine's tenth birthday party, Gordy hadn't gone outside after sundown. That night a group of seven boys told scary stories about aliens and monsters in the night coming to attack them. He imagined slimy creatures crawling up and down the pavement, waiting for the perfect time to attack. Gordy ran inside after the stories and locked himself in the well-lit bathroom for the rest of the night. Gordy eventually found a way to avoid the darkness as much as possible. Even now, if he walks outside at night, Gordy's mind transformed the trees, birds, and butterflies into horrible beasts. Every evening, Gordy came home from work at the library in a nearby town. He cleaned his house and tidied up his garden. He swept the dusty floors wearing his safety gloves and liked to mow the lawn with a gas mask on. Sometimes, Gordy dared to clean under the bed, but his fear of being sucked under it into the dark kept him from spending more than a minute on it.

Last Tuesday, Gordy came home to find his own personal garden filled with weeds. He grabbed his tools and pulled out the weeds one patch at a time with his trusty shovel. After a few hours, he noticed the sun starting to set. The sky was a canvas, filled with splashes of tangerine and scarlet, like a painting from Picasso. He whistled to Chipper and they both ran towards the door. Caught up in the excitement, Chipper accidentally crashed straight into Gordy's crimson tracksuit. Gordy's legs flew up from beneath him. His body hit the ground like a deflated basketball. The cold hard cement made Gordy's large, round aluminum glasses fall off. His deep brown eyes, filled with fright as he stared into the evening sky. The setting sun was a beautiful sight but not to Gordy. Life after the sun in his mind, was the most brutal and cunning world. Scaly creatures came out from the sea, spiny insects crawled out of holes, and large beasts jumped from the high branches of trees. Knowing that the sun was about to set, Gordy tried to revive himself. His eyes were hazy and he could vaguely see a large hairy animal racing around him. He watched the black dog run around him in circles. Around and around, he watched the animal like it was a spinning top. The fading grass, flowers, sky, and Chipper created a beautiful color wheel, but the radiant butterflies flew away as the darkness slowly approached. As his eyes faded, Gordy slowly tipped backwards onto the ground, falling into a deep sleep and Chipper ran off to explore the unknown darkness.

"Ahoooooo!" Chipper howled from the top of a tree. The loud noise woke up Gordy.

He sat up in the darkness. He looked around and noticed the speck of a glowing sphere in the dark magenta sky. He knew that soon the beautiful colors in the sky would become black and vile. His mind yearned for the house lights. The plastic, white light switch. Oh, the light switch! Gordy missed the feeling of it on his hands and the light it created.

"Ahoooooo!" Chipper howled for a second time. The one thing more important than light was still trapped in the dark. Gordy sat in between the house and Chipper. He could either help his friend or save himself. Soon, the trees would fade into the monsters that hid within them. Their arms of branches and hair of leaves would reveal the darkness taking over. The small tulips would soon become miniature creatures with large appetites.

"Ahooo! Ahooo! Ahooo!" Chipper desperately howled. Gordy didn't know what was within the trees. He didn't know the trouble he might face. As he thought about Chipper, he remembered his morning kisses and his cuddly hugs. He remembered how the sound of his bark gave him courage. Gordy decided that he would save Chipper, no matter the obstacles he had to face. To Gordy, the darkness was a way of revealing the troubles that the light hid, but he would fight through them and reach his best friend.

His head spun, looking first at the door, then at the dark garden. He realized that he could see much easier. He looked up to a small but bright speck. At first he believed that it was a rocketship aimed for his head, or a sky jellyfish, coming to sting his arms and legs. While trying to rationalize this unusual event, he heard another frightened yelp coming from the evergreen tree. "Chipper!" The poor puppy must be frightened! As Gordy looked back at the sky, he noticed the speck becoming a moon sized ball. The light sparked his hazel eyes. He was enlightened by this light. Although his brain told him to look away, his heart told him that the light was necessary. He was so in need of some form of light that he could not tear his eyes away from the mesmerizing spacecraft.

The beautiful light showed Gordy his garden's bright colors, as well as the trees. Although Gordy knew that the light was unnatural and mysterious, he could not resist its temptation. He had heard about UFO's from the television, but he had never thought that they were real, or this bright. His brain reached for an explanation, but found none. In the nearby tree, Chipper still sat whining and waiting for Gordy to save him. Gordy reluctantly pulled himself from the light and ran towards Chipper. He stopped and stared at his dog up in the tree. The fluorescent light from the UFO made his fur turn bright! Instead of being the black lab Gordy always knew, Chipper turned into a yellow lab! Gordy was struck by the beauty of Chipper, but he also loved Chipper's natural fur. His thoughts were interrupted by the loud rumble of the nearing spacecraft. The roar of the engine poured through his ears and made his heart sink. It slowly landed on the lawn and the wide door crept open. Gordy glanced to the top of the tree. Chipper barked. Gordy could see beyond the garden and into the pasture. The figures that were hidden by the dark there were not monsters, they were trees, and birds, and animals! Three large creatures stepped out of the UFO, covered in black robes. Underneath, Gordy could see a bright light, similar to the spacecraft. Cowardly, Gordy stepped away from the figures. The three moved in unison towards him. Gordy motioned to Chipper to be quiet, but the aliens caught Gordy's signs. They sent a light beam to pull Chipper down from the tree. Chipper and Gordy embraced and held onto each other as if they were on a scary rollercoaster. They looked back at the aliens.

The three figures growled together, "we...night...take...you...no...keep." Chipper whimpered and trembled behind Gordy. Gordy looked around at the bright garden. He could see every inch of it even though it was midnight. The thought of daytime, all the time, was a dream come true.

"Gosh, that sounds great! Take the night!" Gordy exclaimed. The peculiar aliens nodded as they ascended towards the starry sky in their spacecraft. As the loud rumble flew further away, the sky changed. Slowly, swirls of light blue and white completely masked the old indigo sky. The sun's shining rays pushed the moon aside and lit up the garden. Butterflies and birds revealed themselves from within the trees. The shining light from the unusually bright sun left Chipper's fur yellow. Chipper and Gordy stood in their lawn watching the UFO, until it was merely a shining spot amongst the shining sky. Gordy immediately jumped and ran around in his brightened garden. All of his fears were demolished. He could finally enjoy his garden without the strange aliens around. His mind thought of new ways to use the garden at night. He could build a pool in the ground or even get a trampoline. He was ecstatic! A world without darkness or night would give him the chance to work on his garden more often without being afraid.

Three days after the aliens vanished from the Earth, Gordy became a much more lively person. He took Chipper for walks at midnight, and barely ever slept. He expanded his garden, adding a stone walkway and fruit trees. The trees and flowers became emerald, filled with all of the sunshine they could store. Insects appeared from within the mud. Blue jays, cardinals, and hawks filled the sky. Gordy and Chipper were living a perfect life, they wished it could be that way forever.

"Golly Chipper, life is so perfect now. We have everything we could ever want or even need. The grass is greener, the birds are louder, and the sky is bluer," Gordy said. Chipper nodded his furry head.

"Woof, Woof" he barked agreeingly.

The sun's rays remained on the flora and fauna constantly, but after two weeks time, the beautiful and lush trees began to shrivel and the charming birds ended their songs. The once magnificent sun, was now the cause of a major drought. Without any precipitation or cool weather, the plants were dying and the butterflies were migrating away. Gordy realized the mistake he had made and fell on the yellow grass sobbing. He called out to the aliens, begging them to bring the darkness back. Then, the ground began to shake and the trees began to rumble. The sky became pitch black and cold. For the first time in his life, Gordy was not afraid of the dark. The UFO slowly descended onto the garden. Gordy immediately stood up and wiped his tears. He prayed that the aliens would give back the night. The three known aliens gracefully walked down the stairs of the UFO and stood in front of Gordy. He fell onto his knees and clasped his hands together.

"Please! I'm begging you to take this light back! Every living thing in my garden is desperate for the night, including me!" Gordy exclaimed.

"We...share...light...and...night," the three aliens stated. Gordy nodded his head, stepped forward bravely, and asked the aliens to leave all of the darkness with him. The three aliens declined this offer with no hesitation.

"We..take...one...hour...of...dark," they loudly spoke. Gordy was overjoyed. He had received most of the light he started with. As the aliens removed themselves from the earth once again, they left behind the dark they had brought with them. Chipper and Gordy danced around in their garden, in the pitch black. They slept in the grass and woke up to a shining sun and a peaceful garden. Gordy turned his head to smile at Chipper, when he noticed Chippers new fur color. The small portion of dark that the aliens took away was amazingly shown on Chippers fur. The yellow lab was now covered in black spots. The young puppy was no longer a black lab or a yellow lab, but a stunning dalmatian. Gordy could not have loved his new fur more. He remembered when he saved Chipper from the tree. He had faced his fear to save his friend. Now, the garden was more peaceful and with the darkness and light, it could thrive, and so could Gordy.

28

There's a Fly in My Stew!

by Kurt Kauffman

Why, hello there! Welcome to my award-winning restaurant, Ché Bayou, where I, Chef Pepé le Flyswatté, introduce humans like you with no taste to the amazing palette of the swamp! But, you know, I was not always so famous. Come, come! I shall seat you, and I will tell you of my magnifique story.

I came from a long line of acclaimed chefs, tracing back to my great-great-great grandfrog. While other little tadpoles were playing Frogger video games, I was being trained in the culinary arts! By 5th grade I could wield a spatula better than Toadgang Puck! I missed out on many childhood pleasures, but it paid off, as I jumped straight out of high school to take over my father's restaurant. Life was good, but something did not feel right. Only frogs and toads went to my restaurant. I wanted all creatures to partake of my dishes. So, I used the oldest marketing ploy ever created: coupons! At first I sent them out into the marshlands, to spread the word to the crawfish, turtles, and alligators of the swamps. Pretty soon, all kinds of animals were coming with "buy one swamp stew, get one free" coupons to try out this new amphibian restaurant. Business was soaring because everyone loved my food. Then, one day, I wondered if humans could get in on the action. So, I sent coupons out into the big cities. But apparently no humans were *ribbited* enough to want to try my food. Months went by with no humans coming anywhere near my restaurant. Until one day....

A highly distinguished looking lady waltzed in and took a seat. My best friend, Toadsby, waited on her himself. She ordered a piping hot bowl of my swamp stew, which I whipped up with all the gusto I could muster. I tossed in ingredient after ingredient: cattails, sautéed algae, and my not-so-secret finish, a smoked horse fly. Imagine my surprise when the lady shrieked at Toadsby, "AIEEEEE! THERE'S A FLY IN MY STEW! OH THE HUMANITY!" She flung her bowl into the kitchen, ran outside to her car, and drove off. I was crushed.

"Humans will never like my cooking!" I moaned and hopped home.

With my heart no longer in my cooking, ratings for the restaurant began to croak. My father could tell I was heartbroken and he consoled me. "Son, what is wrong?" he asked.

I sniffled, "I thought I was a wondrous cook, but if even one person doesn't like my cooking, then it is not perfect."

"Perhaps, but people have different tastes. That human did not know the fly was supposed to be in the stew, nor did she try the stew to see if it was good." I stopped and stared at him. I had never thought about it that way. He grinned and said, "Are you ready to reclaim your pride?"

"YES!" I shrieked. And I hopped back to Ché Bayou as fast as my frog legs could carry me.

I whipped together all the orders faster and tastier than ever, and Toadsby grinned at my renewed vigor. Weeks passed and ratings began to soar once more. Ché Bayou was back in business.

I was in the kitchen, when the usual chatter of the restaurant stopped. I came out of the kitchen to see a family of four humans, two parents and their children, come in and sit at a table. The tension was as thick as the bayou on a rainy day, because everyone else in the restaurant knew what happened the last time a human came inside. I received an order for four swamp stews, which I prepared. When all that was missing was a fly in each bowl, I hesitated. I considered leaving the flies off, but I changed my mind. I knew if humans couldn't take a little insect on their food, they didn't deserve my cooking! As Toadsby grabbed the platter, he looked at me nervously, but I nodded at him to continue. The food was placed before the family. The mother glanced at the stew and her eyes bulged out of her head. I winced at the outburst I assumed was about to come, but it never did. Instead, I heard, "Mommy, this is delicious!" Their little daughter was digging into the stew like a bulldozer into a dirt pile! The husband and the son had taken sips as well, but froze when they saw the little girl.

"You...You like it?" the mom whispered. The little girl nodded vigorously. The mom turned to me saying, "She won't eat anything at home. She won't even try mac and cheese! All she eats is crackers. But this..."

The girl set her spoon down and licked her lips. "Can I have another one?"

I smiled. "Sure. Tell you what, you can have as many bowls as you want today," I turned to her family, "As can the rest of you, should you so desire."

The mother cautiously picked up her spoon and tried a little taste. She immediately perked up. "This is delicious!"

She and the rest of the family tore into their stew with gusto. I was happy to give on-the-house refills, as well.

Within days, human critics were pouring in, wanting to examine this strange cuisine that had made the news. Everything was perfect, except for one detail. Almost every single dirty soup bowl that Toadsby washed had a fly in it. No one was eating the best part! This bugged me more than a case of the warts. So, in another clever marketing trick, I offered half-price bowls of stew if the guests ate the flies. Soon, the swamp stew was the most popular menu item, with cattail etouffee and mayfly pie in second and third. Many friends suggested I open other restaurant locations, but I decided I wanted Ché Bayou to stay in the bayou and be the only one of its kind.

So, now you know how my famous restaurant came to be. I'm sure all that storytelling made you hungry. I know I'm starving. So, what can I get for you today?

Illustration by Jacqueline Poisot - Back Cover Artist

29

The Winter Cabin

by Alexandra Killgore

It hit us like an icy volcano. The icy weather was merciless, and showed no fear in using its power against us. It was December, 2013. My father and I were headed up to the cabin for my birthday and time to bond before he left on his year-long journey to another state halfway across the country. I had my own protests about him leaving for the year, but they seemed to be as important as a dead flashlight. Ever since I found out he was leaving, I worried about my mother and what great amounts of stress it would put on her, but my opinion was overlooked, for it meant nothing to the people around me. However, through all the ignoring going on lately, I knew there would be many conflicts in his absence. We were driving up the steep road, pulling a small, two horse trailer behind us, and a 2 hour drive in front of us.

I was so excited for this weekend. We would get up early, go on trail rides, have warm campfires, and have nothing but time to spend with my dad and our two lovely Paint horses. Being in a big family, it is extremely rare to go away for a weekend without any of my sisters or brothers barging in on our limited time together. We stopped to get gas and let the horses out for some water halfway through the drive up to Lake Tahoe. When I got Tigger from the trailer he gazed outside the ice-crusted window. His breathe created a fog inside the trailer, and the reflection of the woods in his dark expressive eyes showed every single intricate detail of the scene. Hundreds of trees filled the forest, and the black ice between the gravel ground and the snowy, soft hills created a perfect shadow among the picture.

An owl sat on one of the branches near the top of the tall pine tree. He seemed so peaceful and protective, wise, and he whispered the secrets of the forest. As we climbed back in the truck, a light snow started falling from the dark clouds. With an hour more to go, I wondered if we would be safe to get to the cabin before the small flakes turned into mountains. I settled into the worn down seat and picked up an old book to distract myself from the dark feeling, but the picture of the owl through Tigger's dark chocolate eyes never left my mind.

After we arrived at our destination, I hopped out of the car. When I finished examining the weather conditions, I sighed in relief, for there were only a few inches of snow on the ground. We unloaded and settled in as fast as we could since night was approaching. My father and I brought the horses inside the small barn. After a thorough groom, I blanketed our tired horses, and my father cleaned the stalls, added fresh shavings, filled two buckets up with warm water, and put their hay on the ground. Just before we left, I turned on the heaters to keep our sweethearts safe from the shivers. My father and I hurried to the car as the air grew colder. When we got inside the nice, heated cabin, the pungent smell of dust and genuine memories came at me with a gust of wind. As we walked in the small house, the old cabin welcomed us as the old wooden floors creaked with happiness.

I took a minute to stare at everything I could lay my eyes on. The brick fireplace sat in the middle of the room, and nothing but old ashes lay inside it. A small couch and a chair faced the old humble fireplace, and a small stand was in between the two pieces of furniture. An old lamp, a family picture, and a hand radio sat on the top of the table. A bookshelf stood in the corner of the room, and inside it held our favorite horse movies, books, pictures, and games we have been collecting over the years. After analyzing the room, I went to my parents bedroom to prepare us for the night. I made the bed, plugged in the heaters, layered the mattress with tons of blankets, and then, I unpacked my small backpack. When I came out in my comfortable clothes, my father had dinner made and on the little table. We watched a movie that night and then went to bed, but not once did the snow stop falling from the sky. My alarm sounded, !jumped out of bed and woke my father up. We both got dressed, and it only took us 5 minutes until we were out the door heading to the barn. I rubbed my eyes.

The cool morning air hit me like a ton of bricks, and the snow had stopped, but the few inches of snow that were on the ground last night had tripled. When we got to the barn, I took our two paint horses out of their stalls, and gave them a nice brush while my father put their morning feed into their stalls and filled the buckets up with hot water. After he was done, the horses were eager to go and eat their delicious breakfast. I was too. My father and I closed the barn doors and went to go get breakfast at the dinner. My father and I went to the old waffle house that had been along the small town's main street for as long as I could remember. We talked all morning long about Tigger and Dusty, our horses, and what we had in stalk to do. When we got back, my father and I tacked our horses and went for a ride in the big indoor arena in the stable. The arena was huge, at least double the size as the biggest one at our house back home in Kentucky. That morning my dad coached me on my barrel racing. Since my father had won several national rodeo titles, it was safe to say he knew what he was doing. When two hours had passed, we decided it was a good time to end the lesson. Morning chores took up the rest of the morning. By the time we had finished everything on that long list of 'to-do's', it was noon.

It started to snow again by the time we had sat down for lunch by the fire. My father was listening to the news for weather reports while I made us tea, and sandwiches. We watched a movie and spent quality time together for a few hours as the snow picked up. Even with the freezing weather, nothing could get in the way of an amazing weekend with my father, and that was certain. We had put too much effort to let a little snow get in the way of it. After the hours passed, I cleaned the dishes as my father washed up. I overheard the sound coming from the other room, and what I heard is not what I wanted to hear.

A snowstorm was coming our way and a big one at that. In that very second, I knew that our fun, activity filled get away was going to face some struggle, but as my father always says, it isn't a great story unless there was a major conflict that came in its way. 12-15 inches were expected tonight and heading into next week. I looked outside the window. I worried for what was headed our way. When my dad came back, we discussed our choices. We could leave later today and risk running into the storm, which was a very dangerous thing to do with having two horses, or we could stay here until the storm passes, which would make our trip a little longer than expected. As the time passed, we realized anything was better than risking our horses lives and ours traveling through a storm like the one coming. It was decided, we would stay until the storm passed. I called my mother to inform her. We had quite a lot to do before the night arrived. My father headed to the store, and he came back with quite a lot. He got extra food, water, blankets, a radio, matches, batteries, cat littler (apparently, it makes walkways safe instead of slippery for going home and getting to the barn during and after the storm), and backup heating supplies.

While my father was at the store, I went to the barn. When I got there, I checked on feed and hay, cleaned and dried blankets in the dryer, to make them nice and warm for our boys, cleaned stalls, made a thick covering of shavings so we wouldn't have to worry about going out too far to get them, I filled 4 10-gallon buckets of hot water and split them between the two stalls, covered all openings to the outside with plastic (so the cold wouldn't get in or harm our horses), covered hay and feed in thermal blankets, and got the medical supplies down, in case of frost bite or hypothermia. I opened it up to make sure all supplies were there. I got out the stethoscope and thermometer, so I could check their rates to make sure they stayed steady during the storm. I recorded their rates in a notepad from the cabin, and I stuck it in the emergency kit. After I was finished, I gave my horse a kiss and a prayer to keep them safe, and I offered a carrot to my Tigger and said goodbye. I went back to the house. Before I walked inside, I shook all of the extra snow off of my giant jacket.

Inside, I felt the heat from the fire, and headed to the room to change into warm dry clothes. In there was my father setting up the heaters. A sound of heavy wind hit the house, and a loud creek sounded. I turned my head to look at the clock, then back at my father. It was 8:00. The snow seen from outside the window became heavier and larger in just seconds. It is coming, the storm is here. We went in by the fire. My father made me some soup. I turned on the radio.

That night, we didn't get much sleep. Every hour throughout the night, My father and I went to the barn to make sure our horses were okay. Every time we went outside, the snow came closer and closer to the porch. The porch outside of the cabin was 4 feet above the ground because of storms like this.

By 6:00 the next morning, there was two feet of snow on the ground, temperatures outside were very severe, being below zero, and the wind was blowing as fast as 35 miles per hour. Power died last night around 11:40, so neither my father nor I could contact anyone after our phones died, but at least we had the radio. The days blurred together in a very cold, dangerous, and nervous bunch. The expected amount of snowfall was 15 inches at most, but it was 37 inches by the time of Wednesday evening. The rooftops were covered live a cupcake with frosting, the trees shivered, roads, forests, big grassy hills, and mountains couldn't be told apart, and not another living soul could be found for miles. Though the snow storm was over, the struggle was not. Our food supply was running low, there was little to no more wood, our horses were achy and cold.

We could only survive like this for another day or so, but we had no where to go. Roads would be closed, heck our truck and trailer were probably frozen shut. Workers wouldn't plow the snow off the streets and the main highway until tomorrow. Although difficult, we would attempt to leave our cabin tomorrow evening. That night, my father and I packed up so we could leave bright and early tomorrow morning. Hopefully before another storm had a chance to become a conflict. I washed I the bed sheets, packed my backpack, and cleaned the cabin. Then, my father and I loaded tack, put fresh shavings into the trailer, a few flakes in each hay bag for our horses, and washed and dried the trailer blankets. By the time we were finished, it was dark out. When we got to the cabin, I tracked our trip out so we WOULD NOT run into any snow storm. I stopped to yawn and looked outside. It was pitch black, and when I turned to look at the clock, I was surprised when it read 1 :00.

I fell asleep that night on the couch snuggled up next to my father. That morning, I sauntered off the couch. The get away trip was over before it even started. At least the drive back home wasn't too long. My father and I ate breakfast then loaded our horses. As we left the white covered ranch, I said goodbye. The owl sat in one of the snow covered trees on an ice covered branch, As we drove off, the bird flew into the white woods. Though our trip didn't go as expected, I was happy I got to spend a weekend and four days with my father and our best friends.

Star
Author

30
The Art of Friendship

by Fiza Kuzhiyil

For the kids who choose to sit alone.

Dear Mrs. Rider,

Confidence has never come easy to me. As a military brat, I've moved more than I can count on one hand and every new school I go to, it seems as if I have less and less confidence. That's why on my first day at Hamilton High, I decided to have lunch with you. I had art class with you right before lunch, so it seemed less pathetic to have lunch with a teacher rather than alone in the cafeteria full of judgmental teens. I ate whatever my grandmother had packed for lunch for me that day, doodled in my sketchbook, and avoided eye contact with you.

It went on like that until the *WELCOME BACK TO SCHOOL* signs turned to *HAPPY HALLOWEEN* ones. On Halloween day, a girl with glossy black hair like yours but shorter walked into the room. At first glance, she looked like she'd just stepped out of a 90's movie. Her hair brushed her shoulders, like her oversized bell bottoms grazed the floor.

"I left my lunch at home," she said.

You didn't say a word, but instead handed her a floral patterned lunch bag.

"Thanks, Mom."

I wasn't surprised she was your daughter. She had the same high cheekbones and petite frame. She was so breathtakingly beautiful, I couldn't help but flip to a fresh page of my sketchbook and started drawing her bobbed hair.

"Are you drawing me?" a startling voice from behind me asked. Horror-struck, I instinctively closed my sketchbook.

"No-I-um," I stuttered with my nonexistent confidence. "Yes, b-but only because you're really pretty."

"Aw, thank you!" She extended her hand to me. "I'm Winona."

"Like Winona Ryder?" I asked taking her hand.

"Like Winona Rider with an i," she proclaimed like she was tired of explaining it. "Mom's into old movies. That's why I'm dressed like Uma Thurman."

Suddenly, the baggy white blouse and black bangs that hung over her eyebrows rung a bell in my head. It was the costume that Uma Thurman wore in the dance scene in my mom's favorite movie, Pulp Fiction.

"I'm Hollis," I introduced myself.

"I know. You're in my biology class."

I was too embarrassed to speak, so I let you chime in. "These are great," you said gawking at the pages of my inch thick moleskin sketchbook. I fought the impulse to snatch it out of your grasp and whispered an awkward thank you. You asked me about a few of my works and I gave you minimal information. You took the hint and left me alone. Winona didn't.

By the time the pumpkins went out of season and the winter coats came into style, Winona and I were thicker than thieves. Win and I would hang out at your house and you treated me like the second daughter you've always wanted.

But I still ate lunch in your classroom no matter how many times Win nagged me to go eat with her in the Cafeteria. I liked the silence you kept from day to day and never asked me anything. Once in a while, however, you would sneak a peek at my drawing and tell me that drawing the hair before the facial features helps sometimes or that the charcoal pencils are in the cupboard above the sink because that particular drawing would look better in charcoal. Your little tips added up to something more and by March you had helped me improve my work drastically.

March was the first time we had a real conversation. You sat next to me at my usual table in the art room, dropped a Shamrock Shake next to me, and took a sip from your own to-go cup. I muttered a thank you even though I don't like Shamrock Shakes because I wanted you to leave me alone. But you didn't. Instead, you started asked me about my drawings and if I had done any more of them lately.

"No," I lied.

"But you've been sketching away every day without even touching your lunch."

"My grandma doesn't exactly make the best lunches," I said trying to steer away from your interrogation.

You laughed and said, "I'm serious, Holly." I flinched. Only my mom called me that. "I think you could really do something with your drawings."

"What would I even do with the drawings?"

"Enter them in contests! I know a lot that you could participate in," you said enthusiastically.

"I don't know," I said tentatively.

"I'll give you time to think it over, but here's a list of contests I think will suit you," you said grabbing a stack of papers thicker than my sketchbook from your desktop. It was then that I realized that you had put more thought into my drawings than I had assumed. "I think this one in particular is perfect for you." You flipped to a page with a highlighted header, handed me the information of the contests, and quietly shuffled back to your desk to finish your lunch.

You asked the following days if I'd picked a contest, but I pretended like I didn't have time to. I didn't talk to you about the contests only because I wasn't going to enter one, but whenever you sat down with me and showed me how to fix the sloppy parts of the drawing, I felt guilty for not giving the contests any thought.

I didn't look through the contests that day or at all that month. By the time I had, the soles of my shoes were covered in cherry blossoms that the trees had shed and the sun shined through the open hallway windows illuminating the pollen in the air. Winona was helping me clean out my locker since there were only a few weeks of school left when she stumbled upon the contests. It took a lot of convincing from her, but I decided to enter the contest that you had highlighted.

For the first time all year, I started a conversation with you at lunch that day.

"Mrs. Rider," was all I had to say for your face to widen into a broad grin.

You helped me sketch a draft, make a final copy, decide I could do better, restart the piece, and make it the best that I possibly could all within the week that the contest ended. You helped me improve the art I made and who I am as a person. For that and your unconditional love I am forever thankful. I am thankful for you.

With love,
Hollis Boyer

Dear Winona,

When I met you I was friendless, lonely and tired. I was tired of being lonely and I was tired of making friends and then moving away from them. That's why, when I met you I was hiding in your mother's art classroom afraid of the world. My entire life my mom had moved our family from military base to military base and my dad had a very small role in raising my brother and me. So when my mom was stationed away for the army, my dad had no idea how to raise two kids by himself, so sent my brother and I to live with my grandmother in the town where my mom was born and raised.

I'm telling you all this because you never asked. You saw pictures of my mom in her uniform and her badges at my grandma's house when you came over, but you never asked about her. I would tell you funny stories that happened at the bases, but you never asked where my mom was. I told you about how my mom loved starting new at new towns every other year, but my dad hated it, but you never asked where my dad was. And that made all the difference.

You respected my privacy, but always knew when something was wrong. Once I missed Mom so much I wouldn't come out of the house. But instead of letting me sulk in my room, you brought Pulp Fiction, since it was my mom's favorite movie and made me hot chocolate like my mom used to make me. The best part of it all was that you didn't do any of this out of pity for the girl who missed her mother. You did it because you were- are- my best friend and you cared about me even though we'd only known one another for a few months.

You'd been in my biology class all year, but I'd only noticed you on Halloween when everyone, everyone but me, of course, was getting ready for the Halloween costume contest. You were a better Uma Thurman than Uma Thurman herself. We'd barely talked then, but the next day, you sat down next to me, snapped your gum, and asked me if I wanted to partner up with you for the lab. There our friendship began.

You supported me from then through the art contest in late May. You practically forced me to enter and then called me every night to see if I had gotten any word back from the contest officials. You even bought tickets in advance for the viewing where the top ten artists from the state presented their pieces and one winner was chosen.

"Scared?" you asked taking another sip of your drink. The viewing was in less than hour and you had made me hot chocolate to calm my nerves.

"Terrified," I replied.

It turned out that I was terrified for all the wrong reasons. Sitting on stage and listening to the guest speakers was easy and even presenting my piece was a breeze. When I sat back down after showing and explaining my piece, my nerves were still buzzing, but so was my phone. The last finalist was presenting, so I checked the caller' ID to see that it was my grandmother who was in the audience in front of me. I ignored the next call, but read the text she sent.

We have to go. It's an emergency.

I looked out to the audience and my grandmother was motioning towards the exit door.

Hollis Boyer! Came a voice over the speakers. I looked around me wondering why everyone was staring at me.

"Again, give it up for our winner, Hollis Boyer," the man at the podium said, waving a card air. I awkwardly strode to the podium gripping the frame my drawing was in so tight my knuckles turned white.

The winner was supposed to give a little acceptance speech, but my grandma's gesture to the exit, the audience clapping, and a man coming towards me with a check wider than I was tall disoriented me so much all I could do was mutter, "Thank you."

"You did it," you said coming towards me to hug me after I got off the stage.

"Yeah, I...I have to go," I said letting go of your embrace

though I didn't want to.

"Hon, I'm so proud of you," Mrs. Rider said to me. Her words filled me with pride, but I had no time to thank her before my grandmother pulled me away.

I'm writing this letter to apologize. To apologize for leaving the viewing without telling you why. I left because my dad called and he'd gotten word about my mom. I'm also writing this letter to thank you for all the friendship and love you have granted me. I'm writing this letter because I didn't say goodbye.

Your Best Friend,
Hollis

Dear Mom,

I miss you. I miss the hot chocolate you made me in the middle of the night when I couldn't sleep. I miss the way you called me Holly when you were proud of me. I miss the way you said my full name when you were mad at me; the syllables ending abruptly. Why did everything have to end so abruptly?

It's only been a week since the incident, that I am writing this. Dad wanted to the get service out of the way as soon as possible, and I don't blame him. With every passing day, the bags under his eyes grow bigger, the sadness in his smile stronger, and the twinkle in his eyes weaker. He wanted me to write a eulogy for you and that's why I picked up this pen, but I don't think I can. Instead, I'm going to put this letter in your casket where you should be. They said there were no remains to scavenge from, so we'd have to fill the casket with things you loved when you were still with us. But I don't want to bury your extensive stamp collection. I don't want to bury the old records Dad bought you for your anniversary or your first every military uniform. I don't want to bury the memory of you.

I will miss you forever and my heart may never stop throbbing, but I am holding on. Dad, however, holds in his feelings and smiles in front of Max and me, but one night I heard his sobbing through the walls and though I wish I had, I wasn't brave enough to go to his room to comfort him. It's the same with Max. He's 10 and old enough to know what's going on, but he pretends he doesn't. It breaks my heart to see them this way, but I know that there is nothing I can do but fill the hole you left with as much love as I can muster.

In other news, I won an art contest. All I got was a plaque and some money, but it meant a lot more to me than that. It was a drawing of you in your military uniform with a flag draped over your shoulder like a cape billowing in the wind. It was intended as your homecoming present, but I'll enclose it with this letter.

Mrs. Rider, my art teacher and her daughter were a huge help in the making of it, so I'm not going to take all of the credit for it. They've been very helpful and loving to me in the past year. I've already written a farewell letter to them, as Dad wanted Max and me to move back in with him. Grandma is holding on well, but Dad wanted to give her some space. While I'm sad that we are moving away from the friends I've made here, I don't think that I can live here knowing that you grew up here and you'll never be able to come back.

I've cried out all my tears, so I'm now left with nothing but my thoughts. I'm proud of where I am today and thankful for those who helped me get here. When I came to this town, I was a military brat that was too scared to eat in the cafeteria with the other students. Now I know that friends will hold you up until you build your own backbone. They will love you until you learn to love yourself.

Love,
Holly

31

Meltdown

by Arianna Papadakis

I stepped into the orphanage bedroom, breathing in the humid California air that seeps through the broken windows. The old wooden floorboards squeaked beneath my feet as I slowly walked over to my assigned bed, noticing how quiet the room was without squealing little girls fighting over who got to play with the Barbie that wasn't missing a limb.

Reaching under my bed, I pulled out the old keepsake box that I kept stored underneath. The box was falling apart and buried beneath dust that had collected over the years.

Setting myself up on the floor next to my bed, I tried to blow the dust away but instead it puffed up and lingered in the air next to me. I pulled the half torn lid off of the box and peeked inside.

Memories swirled inside my brain as I sifted through the old artwork, trinkets and photographs that lay at the surface. I ended up finding other things like my old teddy bear, a drawing of Camri running that I never finished, a poem about butterflies that I wrote in first grade and a small little photo in a gold colored frame.

I wiped the photo clean with the sleeve of my sweater, I stared at the picture of my mother holding my twin sister Camri and I at the Golden Gate Bridge. My mom's face had been crossed out with a black marker. A wave of guilt washes over me as I remember how ten year old me felt so powerful drawing that X across her face.

Setting the photo down next to me, I continued to search the box, still unsure of what to keep and what to throw out.

"Hey Beez," I heard a soft voice say. I looked up and noticed Ruby standing in the doorway. Ruby was like a third sister to Camri and me. She was our best friend.

"Hi, Ruby, what's up?" I asked as she walked into the

community bedroom.

"Ms. Margaret said that dinner's almost ready and that you should come down, unless you're busy."

"Nah, I'm just looking at some of my old junk and deciding what to pack for college," I replied as I continued rummaging through my stuff.

"Whatcha got?" Ruby asked me as she sat down next to me.

"Nothing much," I said. "You can look if you want."

Ruby peeked inside and began to dig through the box. It didn't take her long to find something. She handed me a small, half torn photo and asked "Who is this?"

My eyes started to water as I look at the photo.
"That's...he's," I stuttered. After taking a long, shaky breath, I continued, "It's my father." I finally managed to choke it out. Tears rolled down my cheeks as Ruby wrapped her arm around my shoulder. "At least you knew your father," she said. "What was he like?"

"I don't exactly know or remember what my father was like, because he died when I was really young. My only memories of him come from pictures or videos. He died in a car accident." I start to cry. "When he didn't come home from work later that night, my mom told my sister and me that he would be going on a long business trip, and that he would come back eventually."

"Oh Beez, I'm so sorry."

"The saddest thing of all is that I believed it. I believed he was still alive, that he would come back and we would be a normal family again. I waited by the window every day hoping that his little black car would pull up into our driveway, he would come through the front door, and my sister and I would jump into his arms just like when we were small. But that day never came."

My tears soaked Ruby's sweatshirt sleeves as I leaned my head on her shoulder. I didn't stop crying until I heard the footsteps of the little orphanage children marching up the stairs. Ruby and I quietly stood up and before I could climb into my bed she pulled me into a long hug. She leaned in and whispered in my ear, "Beez, I'll always be here for you. You know that, right?"

I pulled away and smiled at her, "I do. Thanks Ruby."

I turned my head and looked at Camri who stood in the doorway. She looked tired from her school track meet, but with her positive attitude, you would never guess how beat she really was. I was about to ask her if her team won, but before I could one of the children skipped over to her and asked, "Camri, can you tell us a story?"

Laughing, Camri walked over to her bed with the little children trailing behind her. One by one, she lifted the children onto her bed, and finally settled herself next to them.

I listened to Camri's woven, magical tale until she said the words, "And they lived happily ever after, The End."

And those were the last words I ever heard her say.

~

I woke up in an unfamiliar bed, in an unfamiliar room. The bed was comfy and had obviously been cleaned recently. The soft sheets smelled of lavender. Sunlight leaked into the room from a large window. Something tightens around my arm.

Looking up I saw a tall woman standing next to me, she was watching a shorter woman take my blood pressure. The cuff squeezed my arm tighter and tighter. The pain became stronger and I cringed. *Why are my arms so sore?* I asked myself.

The tall woman looks down at me and said, "Oh, good morning Breagle, how are you today?" She flashed me a million dollar smile of white, straight teeth.

"Um, I'm ok," I said. "But where am I? And why am I here? Who are you people?"

The tall woman chuckled, making me uncomfortable. "You're in the hospital, and you're here because you injured your arms."

I stared at her in disbelief.

"I'm Dr. Barbara and that's Nurse Lydia," she said and gestured to the shorter woman.

"100 over 62," Lydia said as she loosened the cuff from my arm. Dr. Barbara quickly jotted something down on a clipboard and turned back toward me.

"Do you have any questions?" Dr. Barbara asked me politely.

"What happened to me? How did I injure my arms?"

Both doctors don't answer me, it looked as if they didn't want to. I noticed that Nurse Lydia kept glancing at a newspaper lying on a bedside table.

"Give it to me," I said, pointing to the paper.

"I don't think you should–"

"Give it to me!" I yelled, cutting off Lydia mid-sentence.

She held out the paper and I snatched it away from her. *Why are they acting so weird?* I thought to myself as I read the headline. It said, *Local Orphanage Fire Devastates Many.* Confused and concerned, I kept reading. *Two nights ago, a fire was reported at a local orphanage in San Francisco. Fire fighters managed to put out the fire, but the building was left in ruins. "I honestly don't know how it happened," Ms. Margaret Smith, head of the orphanage said. "I was always so careful when it came to keeping these children safe." Camri Brown, was reported dead at the scene and many others were reported injured. Many of the injured children have been hospitalized and taken into intensive care.*

Tears blurred up my vision as I reread the paragraph. Blinking the tears away, I let them roll down my cheeks. I crumpled up the paper and threw it across the room, my arm was aching with every movement.

"Breagle, please calm down, it's very important not to make sudden movements if you want your arms to heal properly," Nurse Lydia said as she grabbed my arm and lowered it slowly.

"Camri's not dead," I said, and started to laugh. "She can't be dead! I know she's not! Why would the newspaper lie like that?"

"Breagle, sweetie, please relax, take some deep breaths," Dr. Barbara suggested calmly.

"I'm relaxed!" I screamed. Both of them took a step back, startled looks were plastered on their once friendly faces.

"Should I get a sedative?" Nurse Lydia asked.

"Yes, and hurry," Dr. Barbara replied. Nurse Lydia quickly jogged out of the room, and left Dr. Barbara and me alone.

"Breagle, I know this is hard for you, and I'm really sorry about your sister, but..."

"Why are you sorry?" I asked, my laughs turned into sobs. "She's not even dead!" I started to hyperventilate and tingling sensations moved up and down my body. I craned my neck and looked over at the heart monitor and noticed my heart was beating faster. Dr. Barbara came over and fumbled with the wires and gadgets stuck to my chest.

Camri isn't dead! Don't believe anything they tell you! She's alive! I repeat in my head, but somewhere, deep down, I knew I was just lying to myself. Hot tears streamed down and burned the sides of my face. Nurse Lydia rushed into the room holding a syringe full of clear liquid. Sweat trickled down the back of my neck when I saw the size of the needle.

"Ok, Breagle, I need you to relax. Don't worry, this will only pinch a little," Nurse Lydia said as she rubs something cold on my arm.

Nurse Lydia pushed the needle into my skin. Pain shot through my arm and electrocuted the rest of my body. My thoughts became fuzzy as the medication slowly took over me. The quality of my vision eroded away leaving me staring at colorful blobs that were once Dr. Barbara and Nurse Lydia. Their voices became so muffled I felt like I was being submerged underwater.

I then fell into a deep sleep.

~

The next few days in the hospital seemed to go by in a blur. Every hour a doctor or nurse came in and checked on me, and every time I forced the most genuine smile I could. I spent the rest of my days either sleeping or watching infomercials for some crummy product that no one would ever buy.

I pictured my life as a puzzle with missing pieces that were essential for the full affect. I figured my life would be like this forever.

But that was what I thought before today.

I was sitting on my bed, eating breakfast, when I heard a faint knock on the door.

"Come in," I said through a mouthful of jello, figuring it was just one of the doctors here to make sure everything was okay. The door squeaked as it opened and my mouth dropped when I saw who stood behind it. Ruby walked into the room holding a bouquet of flowers and a piece of paper.

"Oh my God, Beez, are you ok? When they were loading you into the ambulance, the doctor told me not to be surprised if you didn't come back, I thought I was going to lose you Beez, I really did," Ruby said.

"Ruby, calm down, I'm fine, I'm just a little sore," I replied.

"After you escaped the fire, you fainted and hit your head. The doctors said they didn't know when you would wake up. I was so scared that I couldn't sleep for days, and then I found out that Camri was dead and I just fell apart. I couldn't believe it, I refused to believe that she would never get to live her dream, she would never get to run in the Olympics, she would never run ever again," she said.

A tear trickled down the side of my face as I remembered how Camri's feet smoothly glided down the track. I remembered I read in her diary that she dreamed of running in the Olympics, she dreamed of crossing the finish line and having the crowd scream her name.

"That's why," Ruby continued with sudden excitement in her voice. "I wanted to show you this." She handed me a piece of paper covered with colorful drawings and sparkly letters. It read *The Camri Brown 5k on May 21st*. I looked up at Ruby and asked, "What is this?"

"I planned it. There will be games, food, raffles and everyone is going to run the 5k, all the money we raise goes toward building a new orphanage building and finding all the orphanage children good homes. All I need is your OK."

"How will we pay for this? It sounds very expensive."

"We have a whole bunch of people who volunteered to help. We are also having bake sales and car washes. Not to mention the countless donations we got."

I don't know how she managed to plan all this, but I didn't question it.

I looked at her and smiled. "Let's do it."

~

I tapped the microphone to test it, the boom sound echoed through the speakers.

"Hello," I said to the crowd of people, their eyes locked on me. "I am so touched that all of you wonderful people took time out of your busy schedules just to honor my sister. I know she is in Heaven, thanking all of you. She would have loved to be here."

My eyes started to water, so I wiped them with the tip

of my finger, then continued, "She loved to run, more than anything in the world. She had her future all set for her, she had a scholarship for college. After college she was going to train, until she was ready to run in the Olympics. But right before she was ready to leave, a tragic fire took her life away. I was a mess after she died, I couldn't sleep and eat, and I thought I would never be happy again. But with the help of my best friend Ruby, I have accepted Camri's death and I want to honor her. Camri, if you're listening, I just want to say I love you so much, and I miss you. I hope you are happy in Heaven, and I know you are running with the angels."

I paused for a moment and heard whimpers coming from the crowd. My heart retched when I see a woman sobbing in the front row. I took a few deep breaths, then continued my speech. "Now before we begin running, I want to thank my best friend Ruby Jonas for putting this together, I also want to thank all of you for coming and supporting the orphanage children and my sister. So now in memory of Camri, I think we should start." Now I'm sobbing, so I started to walk toward the end of the stage.

The crowd clapped as Ruby and I walked off the stage over to the starting line. I looked behind me one last time, all the smiling faces encouraging me to move forward. The pop gun sounded and I moved on, into the unknown.

32

Prove 'Em Wrong

by Nicole Pasterczyk

I stood on the court, taking a deep breath as I raised my arms, ready to block the ball. Through the squares of the net, I glared intimidatingly at my opponents.

You've got this, Maddie. I told myself, *don't give up.*

The volleyball flew over the net, and I felt it whiz by my head. I hear da bump echo behind me, the ball swirled toward the setter.

You can hit this, I repeated to myself again and again and again. With the lightest push, the setter set the ball above my head. A smile rose up my face.

I took a step and swooped down like a hawk, my hands back and my legs ready to boost off the ground like a rocket. I burst off my feet and smacked the ball to an empty corner, squeezing my eyes with hope as I landed back on the floor. After the squeaking of sneakers, I finally heard *thump.*

Fireworks exploded inside me as I ran to my purple and yellow team for a group hug.

"Nice hit, Maddie!" *and,* "You roasted them!" my teammates yelled, filling me to the rim with confidence.

I loved this game. This game was my life.

Finally, we put our game faces on and got low to the floor. I looked to my right, where I saw the scorekeepers scan the court. Our server, Sydney, was flipping the ball in her hands, getting ready to serve. The score was 24-20.

One more point.

Sydney smacked the ball over the net, and a girl on the other side struggled to pass the fast ball. Awkwardly, she shanked it over the net, where Carly, our libero, dove to pass it. As the ball came flying to the setter, I suddenly felt weak, like my arms were giving up on me. My vision started to blur, and all I saw were hazy shapes of players around me. *What was happening?* Suddenly, my throat closed up like a snake wrapped on my neck, and I fell to the dusty wooden court. I couldn't help but scream with my last breath. *God, please, help me.* I silently prayed to myself. Everything turned black.

~

"Maddie..."

I opened my eyes and looked around. I was laying in a hospital bed with an eerie blue light reflecting tubes up in my nose and body. I tried to push an annoying brown baby hair out of my eye, but as I lifted my arm, pain shot up it like lighting.

"Agh!" I screeched.

"Relax, Maddie."

I looked in front of me where I saw my mom, dad, little brother Tony, and a female doctor surrounding the hospital bed. Each of them had worried wrinkled faces.

"Mom, dad, what's happening? I'm supposed to be at the tournament. Why is everyone so worried...?" My rant came to a end as my mom cuffed her hand to my mouth.

"Honey," my dad said, scratching his stubbly beard. "You fell down at the tournament and fainted."

"I'm going to come back, right?" I asked.

"It's not that easy, Maddie," my mom said, trailing off as she held my hand.

"Let me explain," the young doctor said, pulling her hand out to shake mine. "I'm Dr. Ryan, and I'm here to help you fight your disease."

Disease? What disease is she talking about?

"I'm sorry to say this, Maddie, but after you fainted, we found that you had leukemia," the doctor said.

The word stabbed me in the heart. *Leukemia?* I've always been the strongest girl, able to lift more than anyone and very healthy.

"Th-that's impossible," I said, chuckling nervously.

"Sadly, it's true," Dr. Ryan said, scratching her blonde ponytail. "But we're going to cure you."

Relief crashed on me like a wave, and I took a deep breath and asked, "That means I get to play volleyball soon, right?"

Dr. Ryan bit her lip as she looked at my parents. Simultaneously, they give a hesitant nod.

"After a weakening disease like this, I don't think you will again."

My blood turned to ice. I waited for my family to say, *Surprise, we're kidding,* but that moment never came.

"This isn't happening, this isn't happening, this isn't happening." I said repeatedly, half chuckling, half crying.

"Calm down, Maddie," my dad whispered, softly laying his hand on my arm.

"I'M NOT GOING TO CALM DOWN!" I screeched.

I flailed my arms uncontrollably, my bones aching with each move. However, all of the mixed emotions of fear, denial, and anger numbed the pain. *Why me, God? What have I done wrong?* My family grabbed hold of me as Dr. Ryan clamped my mouth, but I'm untameable. I heard Tony whimpering in the back. Suddenly, my hand caught onto a plastic pipe and ripped it off, fluid sprayed all over the white bed sheets. Everything started to seem blurry and the cries of Tony started to sound muffled. I closed my eyes and lay unmoving. Before I saw darkness, the last words I heard were, *we're losing her.*

~

A few hours later, I woke up to the electronic beat of hospital machines. Turning my head, I saw that dad and Tony surrounded the bed, mom was rubbing my arm.

"Maddie, please, don't try to kill yourself again," she said, chuckling.

I managed to spit out a croaky laugh and said, "I'll try."

My dad sat back onto a creaky chair and asked, "So, are you okay that you can't play volleyball?"

I felt struck in the heart, but I calmed myself down so I didn't go insane. I had to face the fact that I would never get to play the sport again. I'll never get to hit that ball again. I'll never have the chance to play in front of millions of people in the Olympics. I had to tell the little girl inside me that it could never happen again. However, the little girl kept on saying *I can still accomplish my dreams,* and I couldn't help but grasp onto that hope.

"Can I still play in the hospital?" I whimpered, folding my fingers, almost begging.

"Of course you can, Maddie," my dad chuckled. "As long as you don't hurt yourself."

I nodded silently. I then saw a cross that hung over the St. Jude's hospital sign.

"Could you please hand me the cross?" I asked.

My mom picked up Tony and he picked it off the rusty nail. He skipped over to me and gave me the cross.

"Love ya, little bud." I said, ruffling his curly golden hair.

I held the wooden cross, feeling its smooth finish.

I prayed, *God, I don't know what you have planned for me, but I know it is for the best. Please fill me with the strength that you are doing this for the good, even if it seems to be a living nightmare. I will trust you.*

I handed the cross back to them, their looks were sympathetic as if they knew exactly what I was praying.

Knock. Knock. Dr. Ryan was standing at the door with a nervous look.

Patting the covers, my dad said, "We've got to run, Maddie. Keep strong honey, God knows what's best for you."

Each of them came to give a kiss on my cheek, dad giving his typical sloppy kiss, mom with her gentle touch, and Tony's typical choking hug. They left, Tony accidentally leaving the door ajar.

From the door's window, Dr. Ryan lifted her clipboard and said, "It's not looking too good. It turned out Maddie has *AML, or Acute Myelogenous Leukemia* where white blood cells grow rapidly. We must take more extensive measures. Honestly, I don't think she's doing too good, and if the worst comes, she could pass by March."

I felt shock jolt me and I gasped. I looked down at my arms, imagining leukemia infesting the bones that I once used to lift my team's trophies proudly. Am I just meant to wither away and leave my family to mourn? Holding my tears back in fear of death, I looked across the hospital room where I spotted a red, rubber ball laying on the bedside table, the St. Jude's logo stamped on. My arms were sore but not unmovable, I pushed the jungle of tubes aside and grab the ball.

I held the ball on my chest, rubbed my fingers across the familiar rubber surface. It felt safe to hold something that always has brought good memories.

I shot the ball out, setting it to myself with a gentle touch of my fingers. My hands gave a slight ache, but the medicine almost numbed it. Then, like the hitter I was, I threw the ball up and whacked it to the wall where it bounced back into my arms. Say all you want, Dr. Ryan. Faith in myself and God will win this battle, not leukemia.

~

I looked at the bedside table, the date was April 10th. I looked at my arms, spotted with bruises from the rubber ball I'd used from day to day. But my arms don't ache as much as they used to when I was first diagnosed. I thought back to the weeks of near death, like when leukemia almost destroyed me in March. All the tubes stuck inside of me, the pain begging me to let everything go and lose the battle. But I didn't.

I grasped onto the bed sheets, looking out of the window into the shining spring sun. Something told me that this would be the day that I could finally get out of this prison of fluids and medication. I couldn't help smiling at the thought of being able to laugh as hard as I wanted and dancing around without pain.

But death was always something I couldn't ignore. I heard the creak of the door, and I swiped my head to see my family and Dr. Ryan creeping into the room.

"Hi guys," I said, grasping onto the St. Jude's rubber ball on my lap, its logo crackled from all the days of playing around with it.

"Good morning my brave girl," my dad said, with my mom coming to me for a hug. They sat on the bed while Tony gives me a mischievous smile.

"What are you hiding from me you little rascal?" I asked him, chuckling.

Tony stayed silent.

"Well," Dr. Ryan said and came closer to my bed, smiling at her clipboard. "Your parents have something to tell you, and I'm pretty sure you'll want to hear this."

I glanced over to my mom, her rosy cheeks complementing her excited smile. "Well, Maddie, you've been in the hospital, and we know it's been rough," she said.

I sighed, remembering the aching pains I had to experience for days, the hurt gave me no mercy. The fear of having to go up to heaven without my family already there waiting. Losing my faith in myself and God.

"However," she started again, her hazel eyes giving me a warm look. "All of your teammates and friends from school have been raising money for you to fight through this battle. And through this, they raised $110,000 for you and others with leukemia."

Before I could say anything, I couldn't help but give the brightest smile I ever had. I imagined the hardships my volleyball team and classmates had to go through to make this possible. I imagined them having dances, food stands, spending so much of their time.

My dad started, "So with that money, we helped fix your leukemia until there wasn't even a speck of it living inside you. And we are so happy to say that we've won the battle."

I cupped my hands, letting the warm tears stream down my face. We did it. Arms wrapped around me, and I felt love from everyone. I even felt a pat on my back from Dr. Ryan.

"So," I said as they let go of me. "Does that mean that I can play volleyball again?"

Dr. Ryan gave me an approving nod and said, "It's a true miracle, but you've been cured almost completely."

I squealed. All of the memories of hitting, serving and biting medals would soon be back.

"Thank you," I said, wiping tears off my rubbery cheek. "Thank you."

~

Wham! The ball echoed up into the air, soaring to the back of the court like an eagle.

"I got it!" I heard a call from behind me, my hot pink dressed teammate passed the ball over to the setter.

I backed away quickly, feeling adrenaline pump through my legs. With the push of her rose-pink painted fingers, the setter, Amelia, set the ball.

I shot off my feet and jumped up, looking over the net to target an open spot.

C'mon Maddie, win this for the others. I told myself as I whipped my arm to the ball. I smacked it to the center of the court, my arm burning like fire as I landed back on the ground.

Boom. The game was over. I heard the rumbling of footsteps behind me, my teammates' excited faces as bright as their hot pink t-shirts. We then quickly shook hands with the other team. Together we ran to the referee, where we lined up to receive our medals.

"Sydney Smith," the old referee croaked, placing the shiny gold medal with pink ribbon details onto Sydney's neck. She gave a proud, cheeky smile and ran to the back of the line. One by one, each girl received their medal.

"Maddie Fortem."

I gulped and took a step toward the referee. I looked into his wise eyes as he placed the medal around my neck.

I felt the weight of the medal as I turned around to join my team, but the ref gently grabbed my arm and said, "Maddie, would you like to say a couple of words?"

I swiped my head back, the referee gave me a gentle grin. I replied to him, "Yes, please."

He handed me the microphone, smooth to the touch as a I turned to the pink-dressed crowd of people.

"If I have learned one thing from this, it is to believe in yourself. When my doctor said I couldn't play volleyball after I was diagnosed with leukemia, it felt like someone ripped my heart out. I eventually told my family that I was fine with not playing volleyball anymore, but inside I knew that I couldn't let myself down. With faith in God and myself, I believed that I could make it through this disease. I practiced with the ball in the hospital, passing, setting and hitting. Meanwhile, my fellow teammates and school friends were raising money for me and I was finally cured. Thank you all for the donations, and I hope you can give back to those who have been diagnosed with breast cancer so that they can have a chance at life again like me."

I handed the microphone back to the referee and smiled, knowing that I had let others know the importance of believing in yourself.

33

Neighbors

by Olivia Sacks

The gavel hit the wood plate and Mark won his case against Bill the flea.

"Of course I won," the cockroach remarked and opened his briefcase. He pulled out a big bottle of hand sanitizer to clean himself. Soon after Mark drove back, in his Beetle Bug car, to his law firm overlooking the Financial District.

He started his daily routine, which consisted of sanitation when he entered the lobby and another sanitation system in his office.

"Hi Mr. Germington, how did court go?" asked his secretary. He ignored her and kept walking. Mark entered his office and stared at his glorified 40 by 80 inch, framed professional picture of himself.

The cockroach's office consisted of a wall of awards from Harvard Law School. On the opposite end of his office stood a giant trophy case full of hand sanitizer, organized by expiration date. A week prior to expiration date Mark would throw out the *expired* bottle.

Later that afternoon Mark drove home, only to find an unsanitized pigeon in his backyard. Mark walked over to investigate with his sanitizing squirt gun.

"Hey neighbor!" the pigeon called down from his tree house.

Mark shot the infested bird with a shot of sanitizer.

"I've been hit!" exclaimed the pigeon as he fell out of the tree house.

While the pigeon played dead Mark pulled on rubber latex gloves and grabbed a stick. He poked the pigeon, but nothing happened. He poked again and the pigeon jumped up and screamed, "It's alive!"

Annoyed, Mark walked back inside showing no emotion

and slammed his glass door. The pigeon ran after Mark, hitting the door, and broke the glass. "Sorry about that, I'm Jeffery."

Mark grumbled, "You owe me $8,000 plus tax, for the door birdbrain." He walked back into his living room and made a fake phone call.

"Who are you calling?" Jeffery asked.

"I am calling the Rotisserie Company," Mark replied.

"Ooh, make it an order for two!" exclaimed Jeffery.

"Ok, well you pick it up at the corner of Time Square and 42nd Street," Mark demanded.

As Jeffery walked away, he happily said, "You got it neighbor!"

Once Jeffery left, Mark walked over to his hand sanitizing station. Then he walked over to his fridge and ate a single leaf, 100% organic sanitized, of Arugula lettuce for dinner. After he ate he went to bed.

The next morning Mark ate sanitized iceberg lettuce and was relived to find that Jeffery was not in his tree house. The cockroach put on his suit and tie and made his way to work. He worked on a new case and quickly closed it.

When he got home from work that evening he found his mansion a wreck. Everything was scattered around his home and another window was broken. He heard racket in the kitchen so he rushed over there. He found Jeffery hosting a cooking showing in his mess of a kitchen.

"What are you doing?" Mark asked.

He shushed Mark and said, "It's live!" Jeffery smiled and winked at the camera and said, " Sorry folks for that interruption."

Mark looked over and saw his video camera covered in cookie dough. He reluctantly touched the camera to turn it off.

"Why did you turn it off? My students needed to see the final result," whined Jeffery.

Mark grumbled, "What result? You only made a mess."

"What are you, the food police?" Jeffery questioned.

Mark replied, "No, but I am a personal injury attorney and I can sue you. So...get out!"

When Jeffery left, Mark hired a sanitation crew to clean

the kitchen, ate dinner and went to bed.

The next morning at work, Mark's secretary called his office to let him know that someone named Jeffery was there to see him.

Jeffery came crashing through the door before Mark put down the phone, knocking down his trophy case of hand sanitizer. Mark immediately smashed open his emergency hand sanitizer case and sprayed it at Jeffery. "How did you find me here?" questioned Mark.

Jeffery explained, "After my tree house burnt down, I went into your house to ask for legal advice, but you were not there. So I went through your mail to find you, and here we are now."

Mark said, "I can't help you. I have many reasons including that you don't have money."

"Well don't you do pro bono for broke neighbors like me?" Jeffery questioned.

Mark rolled his eyes and grumbled, "Fine, but I am not your neighbor."

Jeffery immediately jumped up and exclaimed, "Thanks! You are the best neighbor ever!" He then hugged Mark and said, "Ooh, maybe we can talk about this over brunch. I know a good brunch place."

Soon after Jeffery and Mark walked over to brunch. Jeffery took Mark through a hole in a wall to a trashcan and pulled up two cardboard boxes for them to sit on. "This is definitely not sanitized, we should get out," said Mark.

"Don't worry about it. It is just a hole in a wall," Jeffery said and then he poured some garbage on to two garbage lids and placed one in front of Mark.

Mark looked at his food disgusted and then asked, "Jeffery did you see who burnt your tree house down?"

"It was a small speck that talked, oh and it was kind of itchy. I think his name was Bill," answered Jeffery.

Mark quietly said, "Bill the flea? No it can't be, he is in jail, I won the case against him."

By the time Jeffery's attorney finished speaking, the bird had eaten both his and Mark's food. As soon as they both got up to leave something pushed them into a trashcan.

Mark heard cackling so he looked up, but he did not see

anything. And then he heard *Ha ha, I have both of you trapped, and now you can never get me!* He saw a jumping speck. It was Bill the flea.

Bill threw the lid up on top of the trashcan and hopped away laughing on how he was going to ruin Mark's law firm and career.

Mark and Jeffrey were both stuck in the trashcan and could not escape. Mark was disgusted and angry at Jeffrey. "This is all your fault!"

Angrily, Mark tried to climb out on his own, but he failed every time. The cockroach thought that he could get out on his own because he did everything on his own. He tried many more times, but never got out. He gave up and thought that he would be stuck in there forever.

"This isn't that bad, neighbor."

Two flies were buzzing above the trashcan. The flies knew a way for them to get out so they approached the two struggling creatures and said, "We know that you are stuck and we know how to get you out."

"How?" Mark yelled.

The flies told them that the only way to get out was teamwork and that two was better than one.

Defeated, Mark looked over at Jeffery and said, "I guess they are right."

The pigeon and cockroach figured out a way to escape. Jeffrey carried Mark on his back and then he pushed up the lid with an old pencil. The lid fell off and both got out of the trashcan. "That was a close one neighbor," said Jeffrey.

Mark immediately grabbed and opened his briefcase and took out his hand sanitizer. After he was done sanitizing himself, the tiny cockroach demanded, "We need to get back to the office now!"

At the office, after they were both sanitized, Mark rushed to his phone to call the police after Jeffrey informed him that he saw Bill walking into the Germington Law Firm.

The police arrived, arrested Bill and took him to court. Mark and Jeffrey had to appear as witnesses.

At court, Bill was convicted with property damage, terroristic threats and many other charges. He was therefore sentenced and put in a maximum-security prison.

Once the police took Bill away, both the pigeon and cockroach returned to Mark's mansion.

When they stepped outside, Jeffery saw that Mark had his tree house rebuilt. Jeffery jumped up with excitement and screamed, "Thank you neighbor! You are the best neighbor ever!"

"By the way, your rent is due, neighbor," replied the cockroach.

"Do you take checks?" questioned the broke pigeon, as he pulled out Mark's checkbook. "Oh, by the way, what's your name, neighbor?"

34

Child of Darkness

by Elian Milan Tee

I remembered the first day it happened. How could I forget the brief walk in the park that stole the one thing that made us feel human? It started off as an unnoticeable tingling. Then, came the similar sting of sun burn. This was followed by the unbearable, searing pain all over my skin. I remembered being rushed home screaming and kicking at the pain. I was placed into a tub of freezing water in an effort to relieve the pain. I was rushed to the emergency room, and stayed there for a week where they tested my skin and studied me. On the eighth day of being at the hospital, the doctors gave me a definite diagnosis. In other words, I received my life sentence. The doctors called it, *Erythropoietic Protoporphyria*. I called it, *EPP*. My life sentence, you may ask, is a life confined in darkness.

But that was 12 years ago. Since then, I had been forbidden to ever make contact with the sun. Hiding in the darkness for 12 years could really change a person. I'm 16 now. High school was all about fitting in with your peers. But it's kind of hard when you have to wear a sun hat, long sleeved shirts, dark glasses and gloves every day inside the the campus to avoid the sun. Being like everyone else was not just a priority to me, but a long lost dream.

I walked the hallways with many people huddled in their own separate groups of friends. I walked the hallway alone with my UV protective hat on my head. I heard occasional chuckling and snickering when I passed by, and although I'm used to it, I still feel rejected by society. Sometimes my mom would tell me that *I tended to avoid people more than I avoid sunlight.* And that's why she forced me out of homeschooling into this dump called high school. I walked the halls with my eyes averted to the floor to avoid any unwanted attention. I sometimes got a bump on the shoulder or a, *hey watch it!*

When I got to English, I headed straight to the back of the room. I watched as the empty seats in front of me began to be filled with other kids. Mr. Gonzalez came in the room with his red tie, ironed plaid shirt and neatly combed hair. English class dragged on by as I daydream about basking through a sunlit field. In the middle of daydream, I suddenly heard an echo that was calling my name. It was Mr. Gonzalez calling my name.

"Jonathan Staples!" he called with one eyebrow raised.

"Yes sir," I said, a bit dazed from daydreaming. The whole class is looking at me with smirks and concerned-pity looks.

"Well, I can see that you haven't been paying attention," he said with a clearly unimpressed face.

I gulped in fear. "I need to talk to you after class," he commanded. I groaned as Mr. Gonzalez returned to teaching his lesson. When the bell rang, I scrambled to grab my belongings and ran out of the classroom before Mr. Gonzalez could call my name again.

~

When I reached the cafeteria, I sat at the table furthest away from the large window. It's dark enough for me to take off my hat and gloves. I pulled out my sack lunch and munched on my chips miserably. Ever since I got my *life sentence*, my life was totally flipped around. No one in this dump understood how it felt like to never be able to go outside on sunny days. I heard staggered footsteps as I looked up from my lunch. A boy with messy black hair approached me. A wave of relief overwhelmed me as the only person that I've really known this past year arrived at my table and plopped down on a chair.

"Stephen, you know that they have combs for a reason," I joked around.

"The last time I checked, I don't fix my hair to impress you," he replied laughing. He grabbed my sack lunch and pulled out the sandwich and took a big bite out of it. Stephen is the only thing in this school that made it bearable. He didn't make fun of me or pity me like everyone else in this school. I don't pity him either. He struggled to walk because he used to have Polio, but I don't hang out with him because we both have or had something wrong with us. We were alike in almost every way. We enjoyed the same type of music, the same movies and we both wanted to be normal.

"Bro, I think Shelby might be into me," he said chowing down my sandwich. I snickered as I brushed my red blistered hands across my brown hair.

"In your dreams," I said, crumpling my potato chip bag. I heard a loud roar of laughter across the room as a football guy stood up from a chair and began to make his way towards our table. I gulped. "Your 6," I said. Stephen turned around to see who was coming. He jumped from his chair faster than any rabbit could and scrambled off faster than a roadrunner can run. I was left alone by my best friend. I saw the boy making his way towards me. He's muscular. He has blond hair, a letterman jacket and a smirk. I know him, everyone does. Football quarterback and Mr. Perfect. Chase Walker. I pretended to look cool as he took the chair right next to me.

"Hey buddy," he said, with a strong smell of cologne that made me gag. I could see his group of friends looking in my direction howling with laughter. I'm frozen with fear as he rubbed my shoulder. "You got a nice hat there," he said with sarcasm.

And like that, he walked off. No harm done, I thought. As the lunch bell rang, I placed my hat on my head. As I reached for my gloves, I realized that they aren't there. I panicked for a few seconds. I looked around. Then I see Chase and his group of friends playing catch with a pair of UV protective gloves, my gloves. I ran towards them with rage. They must've not seen me coming because I was only a foot away by the time they started running. They ran faster than me, of course. I didn't realize where they were running until I'm inches away from an allergic reaction. There was a block of sunshine from a window that they stood in like a force field.

"Give it back," I said choking back tears.

"Back up vampire, the sunlight is going to burn you," Case said sneering. I flinched at the word vampire. I shook in rage. I didn't remember stepping into the sunlight and getting grabbed by his group of friends. They wrapped their strong arms around my legs and stomach to hold me straight. Chase lifted me and forced my hands into the sunlight. The pain wasn't immediate, but I could definitely feel the tingling starting. I felt them drop me to the ground as they started running away.

"Scat, you bums." I heard the familiar voice of Mr. Gonzalez. He helped me up on my feet and put my gloves on my shaky hands.

"You okay Staples?" he asked.

I nodded. The pain on my hands screamed for relief.

"Here, let's go to my room," he said helping me up. My hands were shaking from the pain or the fear? I couldn't tell which.

When we get to his room, he pulled a chair out for me. "I wanted to talk to you after class, but you ran off," he stated.

"Well, I'm here now," I responded.

"I have an offer for you," he started. "I know about your condition quite well and I'd like to help you," he continued. He passed me a brochure. I read it. *Camp Shadow*, I read out loud. "Sounds cheesy," I snickered.

"It's a camp for kids like you who struggle with EPP," he explained.

"What do you know about EPP? You don't understand how it feels like to jump from shadow to shadow. You don't understand how it feels like to see all of your friends running in the sunlight while you have to stay inside and watch from the window," I stated emotionally. My mind is rushing because I don't know why I'm telling all of these things to Mr. Gonzalez.

"Well actually, I do. My daughter struggled with the same disease. She told me it felt like lava being poured on your skin. She was also confined in a life of darkness," he said with audible pain in his voice. "I wanted you to give this brochure to your mother and I'd like you to consider attending Camp Shadow," he ordered. I'm silent. "Now, you may go and take care of yourself buddy," he said with a smile.

When I got home, I handed my mother the colorful brochure. "This is a camp for kids like you," she uttered with great enthusiasm. I quietly listen and went straight to my room.

When June came rolling in, I felt like all the stress I had during the school year had finally been alleviated. I ran home with a blue umbrella over my head. I sprinted as fast as my legs could take me. When I got home I went to my room and saw a packed bag on my bed. Right on top of the bag was the Camp Shadow brochure. I'd forgotten about it. "Mom, what is this?" I asked.

Before I knew it, I was in a car heading to the camp. The sun was setting when I first reached the gates with the words *Camp Shadow* written on it. The first thing I noticed are the kids there. I couldn't believe that they also had EPP. They were casually playing a game of tag or soccer. *Could this be it?* I thought with hope blossoming in my chest. When my mother parked the car next to one of the cabins, I immediately took off my hat and my gloves and joined in a game of football. I felt something I hadn't felt for a long time. *Freedom. Belonging.* I talked to the kids around me. They had stories just like mine. They understood me. They also had a life confined in the darkness. They knew how it felt to be rejected by peers. They understood that feeling of great agony on their skin. We played outside until the sun began to rise. The sun forced us to enter our cabins. We sleep in the cabins and are required to keep up with a journal. While everyone else was asleep that first day, I pulled out a flashlight and a pen.

Many people take what they have for granted. Life allergic to the sun isn't that bad, honestly. Here at camp, we were just like everyone else. There were no people here to pity us, or to make fun of us. I know there are more of us out there so this was a calling for all of the children who were hiding in the shadows. Come on out. We have been in hiding for too long. We were all children of darkness here, but we are special.

Illustration by Alyssa Walker

35

Hearts and Stitches

by Alyssa Walker

"Amy, get up before your breakfast gets cold," my mom said.

I rolled out of bed and went to my stereo. As my finger slid onto the power button. In a flash the radio started to play gospel music. It filled my ears with delight which helped me to get my brain to wake up. As I did my daily routine, my mom called again.

"I just need to get my purple and green striped socks," I said. I rushed to get my socks on and raced down the stairs. My socks helped me glide around the kitchen with ease. I grabbed a small glass of orange juice. Ate my air cooled breakfast. Grabbed my books, binder, and sewing kit as I rushed out the door.

"Amy, you forgot your lunch," mom echoed through the house and tossed it to me.

"Bye mom." I walked with speed to make sure I got to the bus stop.

The air was foggy and thick, which seemed to be the usual Tuesday. The bus stop was like a slow clock during math class it took forever when you want to leave, but went fast when you're taking a test. Eventually the bus arrived and lurched to a stop. I climbed in and took a seat close to the front to avoid any mindless kids in the back. The ride was short, but long enough for me to do my math homework. Once at school, I avoided the morning rush by passing through homeroom to get to first period. I took my seat in the middle of the classroom. Math started on time. Mrs. May was always a nice teacher, but trust me, she gave a lot of homework. She went around and stamped our homework to grade. Then she went over it which was boring. She handed out new worksheets, and got started into the lesson. I started by listening to the problems and solving them. By about the sixth problem I started to daydream. Once I regained focus, I realized we are on problem ten and I tried to make it through the rest of first period.

The bell rang and I rushed to my locker to go to sewing. As I turned my combination with a quick flick of the wrist. I opened my locker and gently put it ajar. Pulled out my blue jacket. I swiftly tied it around my waist. Pulled out my heavy binder and snatched my sewing kit. Slammed my locker shut and went down the hall. Today we are working on upcycling old jackets.

"Hey hold on little squirt that's a nice jacket, can I see it?" a student named Alesha asked.

"No I need it for class."

"That's not good enough. You need to hand it over."

I gave Alesha my jacket. I didn't know what would happen if I didn't. She took off down the hall and into the bathroom. When she didn't walk out with it, I knew it was not dry any more. I still did not want to be late to class so I went in and pushed open the stall door. She had tried to flush my jacket down the toilet. Frustrated and sad, but trying to keep calm, I wiped down my jacket for class. The only good thing is I'm going to sewing. It`s my favorite class. We make scarfs, pants, skirts, and even upcycling which was my favorite. I slipped in the back and with a breath of relief realized that Mrs. Mattin hadn't started yet.

"Amy, you're not one to be late to sewing, you love this class," Sandy said.

"It's nothing, Sandy I just got caught up in the hall."

"What happened to your jacket? It's wet."

"Oh, well my water bottle spilled on it, and I tried to wipe it clean in the bathroom," I lied.

Mrs. Mattin was passing out papers. She never did that, The papers read, *I have a sore throat so you all will need to understand that I will help you but try to solve your own problems. That's all please go to work.* After reading the note, I went to the sewing machine closest to the design table so I won't have to go far to get buttons, patches of all designs, and sequins. First I sketched the embellishments I wanted to create. I thought of adding black buttons so they will pop.

With this info I went to the table behind me to search through the patches. It took awhile but I found a dark blue heart. I went over to my jacket it fit perfectly on the back in the center. I sketched it in for a perfect fit. With all of the class period spent, I moved on to study hall.

"Yo little girl, stop, I thought that was my jacket now." I heard a voice behind me say in an unpleasant tone. I turned around to see the same girls standing there.

"Leave me alone," I said in sort of a whisper.

"Oh girls, did you hear that she wants us to leave her alone?" The girl reached out and grabbed my jacket. Threw it in the trash, and took her friends milkshake and poured it on my beautiful blue jacket.

"Let's go, Lilith, our work here is done." With a turn and a flick of the hair, she went down the hall. Right after tha,t something strange happened. Her friend turned around to walk back to me, but Alesha took her arm and they went to class. I thought that's weird, why would she turn around?

In study hall, I asked the teacher to go to the library to look for a new book. My last book was Nerd Camp; it has an inspiring lesson in it. At least the hallway is safe now. This week of torment was the worst so far. Before I turned the corner, I heard an argument so I wait and listen to see if it's safe.

"Awful Airhead Alesha, why are you in my hallway?" asked a boy I don't know.

"I need a research book for a report. I'm going to the library."

"Well you still used my hall so you got to pay the toll, five dollars."

"I don't have that money," she said with a true hearted response.

I can't believe I'm thinking this, but should I help her? She's never done anything but be uncaring to me. What's that saying Mrs. Mattin always says. Oh, ya, *A kind heart to a problem makes an intelligent response.* So no matter what she's done, I still should help her. It's the right thing. Moving around the corner I reach inside my skirt pocket and pull out 10 dollars.

"Hear take this and leave her alone, you big bully," I said.

197

"I can handle this myself go away."

"Just run." We reached the library so that boy couldn't follow us. She followed me, but didn't seem to understand why I helped her.

I caught my breath, and asked, "Are you okay?"

"Why...would...you care?" she asked with a puzzled tone.

"Well as my teacher says, *A kind heart to a problem makes an intelligent response.*

"So that's why you helped me even though I've been offensive to you," she said with a smile.

"Right, kindness beats evil and people can change," I said with my arms out to hug her.

She reached out too and whispered in my ear, "I`m sorry." We picked up our books and went on with our school day. She really wasn't cruel, she just needed a friend. I`m glad I helped and maybe we can get closer. I might have an idea how.

So Thursday I put a box wrapped and bowed with cheer for Alesha at her locker. She walked up to it and opened it with care. Her face beamed with delight. The piece of clothes she pulled out of the box was a light blue jacket with a dark blue heart stitched on the back. She never hurt anyone again and always wore the jacket of hearts and stitches.

Illustration by Zoë Brown - Back Cover Artist

9TH - 12TH GRADE
SHORT STORIES

Star
Author

36

Rooftops

by Anna Boland

London, 1895. Generally, the only thing that can be heard on a cool London evening is the sound of police whistles and horse-drawn buggies creaking along the cobbled streets. It is a calming sound, really, once you get used to it. But occasionally, if the ear is strained, the faint sound of music can be heard up on the rooftops of the old homes that line the road like a row of perfect soldiers, with a sweet melody carried along the wind down to the busy passersby. I for one never paid any mind to the drifting harmonies, that is, until I met James Turner. It seems like long ago that I was walking home from my place of work when I heard a familiar tune from my childhood. I looked around for the source of the sound and my eyes moved up to the top of a townhouse. I caught sight of a young boy, no older than 14, moving along the rooftop in a merry jig and playing an old violin. I couldn't help the smile that crept upon my face as I watched the youth dance around.

"Hello up there!" I called.

The music and the boy stopped to look for who was calling him. "Who calls?"

"Down here! What wonderful music are you playing?"

I watched the boy hold the instrument to one side and the bow to the other, he moved closer to the edge of the house to project his voice better. "I'm just playing a lullaby from my childhood, sir."

"Ah, well it is a lovely tune. Might you come down so I can learn your name?"

For a moment the boy stood still, pondering his options, before moving back out of view to the edge of the alley in the back as he made his way down to me on the sidewalk. When he finally arrived I saw that he in fact was an adolescent, covered in soot from head to toe, his green eyes the only speck of real color on him while his bright smile contrasted the blackness that was smudged all over his face. I smiled in return and stuck my hand out for the boy to shake but he hesitated at the gesture.

"I'm dirty, sir. I don't want to get soot on your suit."

"Nonsense boy, go on. Take my hand." I insisted as I put my hand out again for him to take. The boy timidly grabbed my clean hand with his dirty one and gave it a quick shake before stuffing his hand into his pocket away from my sight.

"You'll have to work on that shake if you want to present yourself as a man," I remarked with a gentle smile as a shade of crimson came through the soot on his face. At that moment I didn't know it, but he would become the most important thing in my life, as I still had a long way to go before coming to that realization. "My name is Rupert Aldridge, I am a professor at the University of London. I teach literature there."

James Turner, was the only response I got from the lad.

I stared at him for a moment, recognizing the talent that coursed through his veins. I could only imagine what he could become if he worked at his talent. He could be a world famous violinist, actually; if only I help him get through.

"Have you ever considered playing that violin for people to enjoy?" I put the newspaper I was carrying under my arm and held my wrist in front of myself. James stood for a moment considering my question as if I had asked him a difficult math equation. His brows knotted together and he chewed his dirty bottom lip before looking back up at me with his bright green eyes.

"I have never, sir. I don't believe anyone would want to listen to a filthy chimney sweep play an old fiddle."

I frowned, "Oh really? I happen to believe the absolute opposite. In any case I want you to stop by the university and visit me after my lessons, Mr. Turner."

James looked at me, then nodded briefly before scurrying back to the townhouse that he was cleaning. I watched him until he rounded the corner and was out of my sight before continuing my walk to my house. It was a long time before James came to the university to see me. I guess there was a sense of avoidance in the talent that had been given to him and he didn't feel the need to build upon it to really enhance the gift. I had finished a lesson and was heading to my office when I was stopped by a colleague in the hall who told me that a young boy was requesting to see me. I immediately knew who it was and wasted no time shambling to my office before going to see James. As soon as I got to the front of the university, I saw James standing with his cap in hand. I hardly recognized the boy as he was bathed and groomed. Not a single speck of soot was to be found on him and his clothes appeared to be his Sunday best, albeit slightly worn.

I smiled at the sight, "Well, well, this is a wonderful surprise for a dreary Monday afternoon. I am glad to see you, Mr. Turner."

James stiffened at the address and began to wring his cap in his hands, "I came to talk to you about my violin."

I nodded and led him straight to my office. Once we were in, I closed the doors behind us. I went around to my desk and sat in my chair while James took one on the other side. He looked around at the multitudes of books scattered throughout the small room and curiously lifted the cover of a book next to him, I watched with my hand holding my chin as his brows came together as his interest melted into confusion.

"A good novel, *Wuthering Heights*. Have you ever read it?" I asked.

James abruptly pulled his hand away from the book and returned to wringing the life out of his cap, which was already covered in wrinkles. His eyes flashed to the window above my head and his cheeks turned a slight shade of crimson. I cocked my head.

"Are you alright, James?"

James stood up quickly, "I'm sorry Mr. Aldridge, but I'm afraid that this meeting was a mistake."

James moved to the door and was about to move through it before I could get up from behind my desk. It was understandable at the time to think his feelings out of place, of course, my ignorance was corrected shortly thereafter.

"Now wait a second, James. What is the meaning of this behavior?" I demanded, standing from behind my desk.

James stopped at the door and looked at me with a mix of

shame and anger, "I don't think it's your concern."

"I'll make it my concern if it causes you this much distress. Now tell me what has made you so upset."

James turned to face me and took a deep breath before answering me, "I can't read."

My mind drifted for a moment as I considered this. It had never occurred to me that the problem this boy was facing was one quite common to his type. Those that start work at such an early point in their lives often find there is no time for a thing like education. I immediately felt sheepish for my ignorance and asked James to come back to his seat. Thus began a long discussion that would make the bond between the boy and myself grow that much stronger. Soon, I set lessons up for James that were designed to teach him the basics of reading and we began the long task of perfecting his talent. Many weeks passed and he was improving with his reading but his music was not getting any better.

"Try again," I said gently.

James stood with his violin tucked under his chin and stared at the sheet music with hard eyes before starting again. The notes were short and unsure and the strings squeaked with every timid pull of the bow, the sound didn't coordinate with the music that was supposed to be produced. James stopped and slammed his bow against the stand and music with anger before sitting down in the chair next to him. I let out a sigh through my nose as I watched James chastise himself.

"Just start again," I said after a moment.

"It's no use Mr. Aldridge!" James cried out frustrated. "I'll never be able to read that blasted song."

I had never seen so much frustration in James, it had been a difficult couple of weeks for him; with work and lessons, all of it taking its toll on him. His frustration clearly radiated from him as he shook his head furiously. I placed a hand on his shoulder and gave it a heartening squeeze before putting the music stand back in its rightful position.

"Come on, James. We'll start from the beginning," I said calmly.

James looked up at me with a sad frown, "How can you have so much faith in me? I have failed you so many times and yet you continue to push me to go further."

"Because you have an incredible talent, Mr. Turner, and I know that you can achieve so much if you could only refine the gift that has been given to you."

James smiled ever so slightly before locating his bow upon the floor and dropped down quietly with his violin in hand, retrieving it quickly. He placed the rest under his chin and prepared to play by placing the bow on the string, allowing him to begin when ready. I counted him off and immediately following the fourth beat he began to play. His eyes followed the notes as he felt the music pulse through his body, moving to the rhythm and smiling at the flawless tone that came out of his instrument. I smiled widely and watched in rapt attention as James played the song with such emotion and musicality. Soon the song came to an end and James finished it with such phenomenal vibrato, it made the final note ring a little longer with sustained euphoria. When it had finally died, he looked at me with teary eyes and a triumphant smile and I couldn't help but return it.

"I did it, Mr. Aldridge, I actually did it!" James exclaimed.

"Yes, indeed you did," I replied. James looked at his violin with newfound awe and grinned at the sheet music with a respect that was long overdue. I gave him a strong pat on the back and moved the sheet music to my desk.

"Thank you Mr. Aldridge...for never giving up on me," James said happily.

"I never give up on those that have something valuable to give the world. Come on, let's go celebrate."

A couple of years have passed since that wonderful moment in my life and I am happy to say that James has moved on to display his talent for millions of people all across England and Ireland, even performing for Her Majesty Queen Victoria in the Adelphi theater. I confessed I have never been so proud of someone before, him having grown so much and I couldn't help but feel as if he were my own son. I knew that dormant talent rested within him and that he only needed to release it to become someone truly great.

~

I shuffled through papers in my office as I leaned back in my chair until I hear a knock on the door, acknowledging the caller but keeping my eyes on my work. The sound of shoes clacking on the floor approached my desk and stopped in front of me. I looked up and saw a pair of glittering green eyes staring back at me, crinkled by the smile on the face. I jumped up immediately and rushed around my desk to embrace the person.

"James, my boy! It's been years," I said as I squeezed the boy, rather the young man, before me.

James smiled and held me at arm's length, looking at my face and noticed the visible grays coming into my hair. "It has been a while, I will admit. I decided to visit my wonderful counselor and friend before I am to leave."

Little did I know this would be one of the few encounters I would have with the ex-chimney sweep after his success, I wouldn't get to see him as much as either of us would like but know that our communications would remain strong through letters and a new item called post cards. I would miss him dearly but I rested well knowing that the little boy I first met was now living a life others could only dream about and it gave me great comfort to know that I had given him a hand in his triumph. I will leave you with a tuppence worth of advice for free; no matter the challenge, no matter the feat, always push yourself to be better than you were before.

37

The Bookwyrm

by Claire Jones

"Need some help? You look stuck," said a quiet voice from behind Tara. She turned from the library bookshelf and found that the voice belonged to a tall woman with striking poison-green eyes and a name tag identifying her as Lisinda, Reference Librarian.

"Some help might be nice, actually. I'm trying to write a story, but I'm having writer's block and I came over here," Tara gestured at the nonfiction books surrounding her, "to maybe find some inspiration, and so far I'm not having any luck."

Lisinda smiled knowingly. "I have the perfect book for you. I'll be right back." She strode off through the shelves. Tara placed the few books she had been halfheartedly considering back on the shelves, which was technically not something she was supposed to do, but she knew the library very well and could re-shelf books easily. Despite her familiarity with the place, however, she didn't remember ever meeting Lisinda before, and in fact recalled the reference librarian being a short old man. *I suppose I can ask her about it when she gets back. Anyway, she's much more helpful than that man ever was,* she thought.

The reference librarian returned with a slim book and handed it to Tara. There was no title, author's name, or illustration on the pale gray cover, so she opened it to somewhere in the middle. It was full of writing prompts, characterization tips, and other useful information, everything a stuck writer could want. Thrilled, Tara grinned at Lisinda.

"Thank you! This is perfect."

"I knew it would be. It's not a real library book, just something us librarians like to lend to young writers in need." Lisinda stepped closer and lowered her voice. "And, as something extra, I slipped in some advice I myself have used. Don't share it with anyone else though, I wouldn't want my secrets getting around to too many people." She smiled.

"Of course, I can keep it to myself." Lisinda turned as if to leave, and Tara remembered her question.

"Wait, are you new here? I thought the reference librarian was some old man, Andrew or something."

Lisinda looked back, and her expression was almost angry as she replied in a cold voice, "Yes, I am new. Andrew left unexpectedly, so I took the position." The librarian walked away abruptly, and as she left, Tara noticed a tattoo of a snake winding up the back of the reference librarian's arm, its inked scales precisely the same color as Lisinda's eyes. Confused but grateful for the help, Tara gathered her things and headed home.

~

Three hours later, Tara sat on her bed, reading the book Lisinda had given her. She had tried to follow the advice in it, but that had still only resulted in several pages of discarded ideas and crossed out beginnings. She felt frustrated, her eyes almost leaking tears. She began skimming the rest of the book, looking for anything that stood out as useful. As she reached the end with no more progress, her frustration threatened to spill in salty waves from her eyes. But tucked in the back cover, only one corner sticking out, was a folded piece of notebook paper. Curiosity temporarily overcoming frustration, Tara tugged it free and unfolded it. Written across the top were the words, *Advice for a stuck writer*, and Tara realized this must be the extra advice Lisinda had warned her to keep quiet about.

But before she could read any further, the paper leaped out of her hands, completely ignoring both her grip on it and gravity, and drifted towards the ceiling. It ascended until it was about a foot from the ceiling, now definitely out of Tara's reach, even if she hadn't been too stunned to grab for it. Her last chance at writing advice began to curl around the edges, and Tara stared in disbelief as smoke and then flames consumed the floating sheet of paper, and its ashes slowly fell back onto her head, dusting her curly blond hair with gray.

"Sorry. It had to be done," said a deep voice. It seemed to

come from behind her.

Tara jumped off the bed, startled. She looked wildly around her bedroom, taking in the disorganized bookshelf, the rumpled bed with a few stuffed animals strewn across it, the window cracked open to let a breeze in, and her own reflection in a large mirror, staring back at her with gray-blue eyes, searching for the voice. Am I really so frustrated with writing that I'm hallucinating? What's wrong with me?

"Is there someone in here?" she asked the empty room, her voice coming out at half its normal volume, her fear expressed in its breathiness.

"Only the most powerful creature to ever walk the earth, here to save you. You're welcome." Above her bed, right where she had been sitting, a shimmer warped the air, and then a book the same size and shape as the gray one, only red, dropped out of nowhere.

"Open the book. I won't hurt you," the voice said. Tara cautiously stepped towards the bed and opened the book. It was blank except for a beautifully illustrated dragon with scarlet scales and silver spikes. At this point, Tara didn't even flinch when the dragon lashed its tail and spoke.

"Don't look so afraid, I'm really not going to hurt you. My name is The Bookwyrm. I'm a creature of pure creativity from an alternate version of your world. In that world, human souls contain creatures like me, which is where humans get their creativity. When a human dies, its soul is released and becomes free. I traveled to this world to find and capture an evil member of my society, whom I believe is going by the name of Lisinda." The dragon sounded slightly pompous, as if he thought very highly of himself and his cause.

"I met Lisinda. She helped me, and she would have helped me even more if you hadn't burned that paper!" Tara heard the pompousness in his voice, and any fear was gone. She hated people who were full of themselves, and even more so if they were going to call perfectly helpful people evil.

The Bookwyrm flapped his inked wings in annoyance, as though she was inconveniencing him by making him explain. "I burned that paper to save you. You have an unusually high amount of creativity for a human, so Lisinda was trying to steal it by hypnotizing you with a spell written on that paper.

She lost her creativity to one of the great enemies of our species, and she fled to this world so that she could steal it back without being caught. You would have been completely under her control if you had read anything else on that paper. Think about it. Didn't you notice something off about her, and doesn't it seem odd that you jumped to her defense so quickly? You barely know her."

Tara opened her mouth to fire off an angry response, but paused before the words could be spoken. She was acting oddly when I asked her about her job, and why would she tell me to keep her writing advice secret if she wanted to help stuck writers? She should have wanted me to share that and help others. And I've never been that quick to defend an acquaintance before, I usually try to not get involved in things. What did she do to me?

Her anger and defensiveness vanished, replaced by indignation and outrage at having nearly been taken advantage of. "So she was only trying to help me because she wanted to steal my creativity?"

"Yes." The Bookwyrm seemed relieved that Tara had realized the truth. "And now I need your help. I have to catch Lisinda before she can find anyone else to steal from. In her current state, she only has limited access to her abilities, which is why she could only trick you into giving up your creative power, rather than take it from you outright. But if she gets it from anyone else, she would be impossibly powerful, and once she takes one person's creativity, she will not be able to resist the power offered by taking more."

"That would be terrible." She imagined a world where people had no creativity, and her outrage grew as she realized she had almost been tricked into making that happen. "What do I need to do to help?"

The Bookwyrm stretched on his page and grinned, showing off long fangs in a dangerous, predatory smile. "I need you as bait. Take this book and the gray book to the library, and when Lisinda finds you, act like you still trust her and like her spell worked. Do whatever she asks you to until she tries to take your creativity. You'll know when that happens. At that point, take this book and open it in front of her, and I will manifest in my true form. You must keep me hidden until then, because if she even suspects that I am on this version of Earth, she will flee and I will lose my chance to catch her. Understand?"

"Yes." Tara knew she should be scared, or at least confused, by helping an alien race with incredible creative powers, but somehow she was just excited. If nothing else, this would definitely break her writer's block.

With both books tucked securely into her bag, Tara stepped through the library doors. She calmly walked through the rows of books and found herself in front of the reference librarian's desk, where Lisinda sat typing at her computer. The librarian looked up at Tara and smiled widely, but unlike her smiles during their last encounter, this one seemed triumphant and malicious. Tara suddenly felt much less calm and certain about her decision to help, cold tendrils of fear threatening to replace the outrage that had been fueling her. What if she failed and actually lost her creativity?

It was too late to back out, however. Lisinda stood up from the desk and looked over Tara, still smiling. "Follow me, Tara. I have something I need you to do," she said, and walked away towards the offices at the back of the library, not bothering to check and see if Tara really did follow. She seems completely confident in her spell, Tara thought. That's good for me.

So Tara ignored the fear, focused on her anger and indignation, and followed. Lisinda led her to a small, dusty room with only a table and two chairs. The librarian closed the door behind them and flipped on an old, flickering lightbulb. "Do you still have the book I gave you?"

Keeping her voice emotionless, as she guessed that it would be if she were actually under a spell, Tara replied, "Yes."

"Good little human! Your will was surprisingly easy to subvert, for someone with so much power." Lisinda laughed, a sound that came out more like a hiss. The snake tattoo on the librarian's arm slithered down, towards Lisinda's wrist, and then came off of her skin and formed into a real snake that lay limp on the table, its scales greener than any normal snake. Lisinda's body slumped, then disappeared into a swirling black cloud that drifted into the snake's slightly open mouth. The snake woke up, slithering across the table towards Tara, who sat frozen in fear, though she hoped Lisinda would think she was simply hypnotized.

"Set the book on the table," the snake hissed.

Tara removed the gray book from her bag and placed it on the table, where it too turned into swirling blackness. She went to close her bag so that the snake could not see the other book, but before she could, the snake darted forward and placed its fangs right above Tara's left wrist. Tara froze.

"What is that other book?" Lisinda hissed, lower and more menacing than ever before. Without waiting for a response, the blackness that had been the gray book reached for the red book, but Tara was faster. She snatched the red book and flipped it open in front of the snake, revealing the illustrated dragon. But The Bookwyrm no longer remained on the page. Out of the book rose the dragon, bigger than Tara, filling most of the space in the room. His scales gleamed, and for the first time, Tara saw things reflected in their surface, images of wild creatures both real and mythical, scenes from other worlds, and impossible things she couldn't even begin to describe or make sense of. The realms of human imagination showed themselves in this creature of creative power.

Lisinda tried to bite down on Tara's wrist, but looking at The Bookwyrm and the power written across his scales awakened something in her, and she imagined the snake being flung away from her, more powerfully than she had ever imagined anything before. Lisinda flew across the room and hit the opposite wall, and fell straight into The Bookwyrm's outstretched claws.

"Lisinda, you have broken the sacred laws of our people by fleeing to this world and attempting to steal its people's creativity. You will return with me and face our Elders, and be served a fitting punishment. Until you can be disciplined, you will be confined to the pages of this book," the dragon said, his voice carrying power in every syllable. He dropped the snake onto the red book, made a strange twisting motion with his claws, and Lisinda melted into the pages, becoming an illustration similar to The Bookwyrm's former self.

Tara sank back into one of the chairs, the fear she had

suppressed during the encounter washing over her, causing her to shiver. The magnificent dragon peered down at her.

"You seem to have some access to your creative abilities in a way I have seen from no other human, a way that can manifest outside writing and art. That is fascinating, although it may be due to your proximity to my power. Still, you are a very impressive human being, and you and your bravery likely saved your Earth's creativity. Well done, Tara."

She smiled. "Thank you. You have helped me too."

The Bookwyrm tilted his head in confusion. "How?"

"Now I have something to write about. My writer's block is completely gone. So I guess Lisinda giving me that book really did help me, in the end," Tara said.

"I suppose it did, young human." The dragon smiled as well, much more gently than before. "Make sure you continue to find the good things in bad situations. It is a trait that will serve you well. I must now leave and return to my people, but thank you for all your help, and good luck on your future creative endeavors." The Bookwyrm vanished into swirling blackness, as did the red book, and then disappeared entirely. Tara gathered her bag and headed home to write.

38

As the Earth Slept

by Alec Jordan

Ages ago, the world was still. It didn't turn or spin, it simply slept peacefully. The world was divided in half; on the right side there was a hot, sandy, stretch of land, and on the left there was a cool, dark, endless ocean. The sun was a burning ring of fire, turning everything in his reach into a dusty wasteland. The moon, a serene sphere of silver, holding a silent vigil over the waters she draped.

In the desert under the sun there was a small village consisting of two ramshackle huts, with one inhabitant in each. In between the huts was a covered well, where the villagers got water. Beneath the slits of the well covering grew the only wisps of wheat strong enough to survive the arid land with the well's moisture. The only villagers were two children, a boy and a girl. They dwelt in their huts without purpose, only coming out to drink from the well. For fear of the scorching sun, they never stayed outside, and only barely knew each other.

One day, the boy heard crying outside. He saw the girl kneeling by the well, weeping into her hands. He called to her, but she didn't hear him. The worried boy quickly ran and knelt alongside her. He gently touched her shoulder, and asked why she cried. Without raising her head, she pointed to the well. The boy peered into it, and saw nothing. He was suddenly struck by what the emptiness meant. There was nothing there. There had always been water in the well, but now it was as dry as the coarse sand which stuck to his clothes.

Shocked and scared, he stared up at the sun and called to it, begging it for water. The sun only laughed cruelly at his plight. He was suddenly overcome with an obsessive thought to find water. He helped the girl to her feet, and walked her back to her hut. He was afraid because he knew he would be on his own. He returned to his hut, took what cloth he had for a head cover to protect him from the beating sun, and fashioned a pole with a bucket attached to each end. He walked over to the girl's hut, and gently rapped on the brittle wooden door. It opened a crack, and he told her of his plan. She understood, and fetched a small cloth bag for him with precious bread inside. The boy thanked her, then he left the safety of the village for the merciless desert.

Within moments he realized that it was hotter than he imagined. He had never been under the gaze of the sun for long, and after just a few moments, he was drenched in sweat. He thought to himself, maybe the well filled up again by some magic like the wishes in his dreams? He knew this was nonsense, and so he kept walking, and walking, and obsessing over the thought of water. Finally, under the weight of the sun, he fell to his knees. Taking deep, hot breaths, he stood up and pushed onward.

The sun stared at him, as still as it had ever been, mocking him in the sky. The glowering sphere blistered his skin with heat, and it wickedly delighted in his struggle. As the sun fell away behind him, the heat became bearable. He ventured deeper into the sand, until he saw something in the distance. Squinting, the boy saw the end of the sun's reach ahead of him. He was filled with excitement, and reinvigorated, he jogged to the border of the light.

His heart leapt in his chest as he realized that before him stretched a dark mass of water. It seemed alive, churning with a natural rhythm. Running over to the shore, he dove his head into the water. He took in a mouthful, then noticed the briny taste the water left in his mouth. He couldn't gulp the water as he wanted to, his mouth was dry, more so than it had been in the desert. The well water hadn't carried this taste- something was very wrong. He spotted a small raft, barely big enough to carry him and his buckets. Recognizing it as a gift, he climbed into the small craft, and used his pole to propel him through the dark water.

He had entered a strange world filled with nothing but the cold, dark sky and the living water rolling underneath him. Still, the boy paddled on, determined to find good water.

So he paddled, until his arms gave out and he simply sat in his boat, adrift in the writhing sea. He closed his eyes, and dreamt of his home, of water, and the girl.

When he opened his eyes, he saw a silver-white sun above him. This sun wasn't the cruel, yellow tyrant that taunted him on his journey. As he inspected the cool, silver sun, he heard weeping. He was startled to realize that it was the gentle, silver sphere that wept. He stood up, and called to it. It opened its eyes, and looked back at him.

The boy asked, "What are you and why are you crying?" and the sphere responded, "I am Moon, and I cry because I am alone."

"You are not alone," the boy said. "I'm here."

A smile gleamed on Moon's face and he asked, "Why are you here? Surely not to visit me."

The boy's shoulders slumped, and he replied, "I came looking for water, but the water I found is harsh, like sand."

Moon closed her eyes knowingly as she said, "This is water of the ocean, not meant to be drank. However, I can bring you clean water."

Quickly clouds advanced on the small vessel, hovering directly above the boy. Then, something hit his face gently. It rolled down his cheek, to the corner of his lips, where he took it into his mouth. It tasted sweet, and killed the dryness in his mouth. The heavy clouds were dropping clean water! He grabbed the buckets and held them to the sky, then cried with laughter as they filled. When the buckets were full, he sat and the clouds receded.

"Thank you, thank you!" he offered Moon.

Moon only shook her head, "Those are only two buckets. How long will those last you until you return? Stay here, and you will never be thirsty again."

The boy shook his head, "There is another who needs the water, not just me. I have to go back and give it to her. I promise to return for more water, and to see you." Moon considered his words, and nodded. So she sent him back to the shore with a gust of wind, and the boy embarked on his journey home.

The sun seemed to have forgotten the boy, or didn't expect him to return, because walking back, he barely noticed the heat. He wound his way through the sands, his strides filled with confidence and purpose. The sun soon spotted the boy and turned up its heat in anger, but he pushed onward. Through the sand, through the smothering air he walked, until he could make out the shapes of the huts in the distance.

The village seemed lonelier than when he had left. Warily walking beside the girl's home, he could hear ragged and labored breathing coming from her house. He rushed to her front door, and flung it open. Inside, the girl was curled on the floor, small and motionless. He moved to her side, and propped her head on his lap. Carefully, he lifted a bucket of water to her lips, and slowly let water drip into her mouth. After a while, he stopped and waited with her, until her eyes fluttered open, and she tried to speak. He told her of his journey until she drifted back to sleep, and fatigue overtook him. When he awoke, he felt a deep anxiety in his heart. He felt responsible for the girl, and knew this companionship wouldn't last. He would have to traverse the wastes again and again, never having peace.

He prepared himself for when they were down to the final drop of water. He found comfort in the only home he knew, but he also longed for Moon's company, the cool breeze in his hair, and the nourishing water that fell from the sky. It was time to say goodbye to the girl, and trudge through the blinding desert, under siege from the malicious sun. He weathered the beatings of the sun, until his heart was lifted to see the dark shoreline ahead. The boat called for him, and he sailed again into the deep ocean. As he drifted, he thought of the gentle Moon, and the calm rocking of the vessel lulled him to sleep. In his dreams, a sweet moon song lit the pitch black night with peace and reassurance.

The boat lurched to a halt, and the sudden motion woke the boy. Rubbing his eyes, he looked up to see Moon smiling down on him. Without breaking the sacred silence, the clouds came, and filled the buckets with water, and Moon sent him back on his way. The boy hurried through the wastes, and faster than he had before, he made it to the village. Unlike the other times, he barely stopped after dropping off the water. He said goodbye to the girl, and then he was off again, into the sweltering heat.

This is how it went for some time, with the girl grateful and the boy pushing through the desert and floating on the sea. Each time was easier than the last, and the full buckets became lighter to carry. His steps became longer, his shoulders broader, and his arms stronger. After many trips the boy stopped to look down into the water, but he could not see the boy. In his place, there was the reflection of a man, weathered and weary, and he felt it, but pushed it away and sailed on.

Every time the man would make it to the shore, he would glance into the water, like a translucent mirror. Every time, his hair would be a little longer, his eyes more tired, and his mind more distant. The girl, however, remained unchanged. Youthful and energetic, she bounded around him on each return, oblivious to his changes.

The journey became heavier and slower with time. The buckets started to weigh down on his entire body. His reflection now showed the gray in his hair, and the fatigue on his face. This day he stumbled and fell to his knees. His lungs filled up with the choking desert air. He forced himself to his feet, and willed his failing body forward. He could see the shore ahead, and relief flooded his mind. He forced his aching muscles on, only to fall again. Not when I'm so close, he thought hopelessly.

The image of Moon began to fade in his mind, as he clawed and dragged himself to the shore. With one last effort, he heaved his body into the small boat. The weight of the man pushed onto the boat, and shoved it into the open water. The man fought against his exhaustion, knowing that if he closed his eyes, he wouldn't open them again to see Moon. He envisioned the well, the wheat, the huts, the girl, the sun, Moon, and then his eyes shut with neither the strength, nor the will to open them again. The vessel drifted among the waves, and Moon began to weep for him and his long struggle, until she received him knowing his sacrifice had now changed everything.

Days passed without the man returning to the village, and the girl worried. After waiting for what seemed like ages, she gave up hope. She was alone, and when her grieving tears hit the dusty floor of her hut, the ground rumbled. "What is wrong, little one?" a deep voice grumbled ominously.

The girl's eyes grew wide, and she looked around frantically for the speaker, when a gravelly chuckle arose from underneath her. "I am Earth. I am here under you, little one. I am the ground you walk and sleep on. I've been asleep for a long time."

The girl wiped her face with her hand, and asked "Why are you waking up now?"

"All had been still, then little feet turned me in my sleep as they trekked back and forth across my back."

The girl's eyes opened wide. "Have you seen him? The one who walks?"

Earth paused then replied, "He ended his journey a while ago, and now he's with Moon."

The girl's shoulders dropped in despair.

"Don't worry little one. Go to the well and bring me two blades of wheat and two small cups of water. Place them next to you when you sleep. All will be fine," assured Earth.

The girl did as Earth asked. A deep, despondent sleep overcame her, and she curled up on the ground. Many hours later a loud tremble, and the smell of moist air and earth aroused her from sleep.

Near her she found two tiny wrapped bundles cradled in an earthen nest where the wheat and water had been. She cautiously picked each one up, and unwrapped them. Two pairs of twinkling eyes stared up at her, taking in her face. Frightened, the girl nearly dropped them, but she composed herself, and held them tightly to her heart. It no longer ached with solitude, but filled with great purpose. She discovered a love she never knew, and these little ones grew strong with it. They grew wise alongside her.

The man looked down at the ocean below him. He felt young again, like the boy he had once been. He had found peace, but he knew that he could not, would not, return.

"What do you search for?" Moon asked.

"Nothing," said the man. Moon offered a gentle smile in response, pursing her lips knowingly. "You are worried about the girl, aren't you?"

"Yes, how can she get water if I'm not there?" he asked.

"Do not worry. I will provide," resounded a deep voice

below. The man looked down as the great Earth rumbled and turned in a slow, soothing motion. The oceans moved, the sands shifted, and dark veins of water began to cut through the bright, barren desert.

A rushing river ran right past the little hut, and the woman gave thanks to Earth. She pulled the two children close to her, and they watched as the water flowed past them. She had grown older caring for the children, but she had a happiness inside her, and a vision of the future for them. The children grew healthy, with the water bringing life to the land. The wastes filled with grass and trees, and the day cycled as Earth turned. Moon was never alone, and the sun could not abuse the ground with its incessant rays. Sun and Moon now knew their rhythm, and they pleased the Earth.

The woman grew old enough to know that time had stopped moving for her. She called the children to her, and kissed their foreheads. They feared the world without her, but they understood Earth's rhythm, and her hope for them. In a burst of Sun's rays and Moon's beams she was lifted beside the man in the sky, and they were reunited in a completed mission. Underneath they saw Earth awake and alive, turning through the ages at the joy of its Creator.

Illustration by Michal Ilouz - Back Cover Artist

39

Letting Go

by Sachi Khemka

Our lives are a sum of all of our decisions. The decisions we make today play a critical role in our future tomorrow. Therefore, we have to make choices that are wise and virtuous. So there I was, sitting on the cold, polished floor, staring at the rigid cage with no expression. My sorrow was bundling up inside me and pushing on the walls of my chests begging to be released. My heart was pounding as fast as a speedboat cruising across the rocky, tired ocean. The words, *we might have to give the birds away,* spiraled in my head inflaming it with confusion. The sound of my birds used to be so soothing, but now it was like needles at my skin. I burst into tears bewildered, heartbroken, and caught up in this spontaneous mess. Was it me to blame?

The melodious chirps of my two cockatiels wiped the bags from under my eyes as the aroma of fresh blueberry waffles drifted towards my room. "Honey!" my mom called. "We have a few errands to run. Get ready!"

I ran up to the silver cage, and watched as the yellow blob of feathers danced around, and a breathtaking grey cockatiel sat with its beak buried in its feathers. The relaxing sounds of the bells, and the subtle chirping of the birds were the complement of my day. My hand hovered over the door to the cage, and I felt the bird's feathers graze my finger. "I'll only be gone for an hour. You won't miss me that much," I whispered to them. I slowly got up and hesitantly lifted the cage and dragged it outside onto the concrete platform. I was convinced that the light, icy winds would give the birds some fresh air.

I arrived later to check on my birds after my hectic trip. I dashed out the door and was startled to find my yellow cockatiel, Fluffy, huddled against the corner of the cage with a slit in his right wing. Snuggles, the gray cockatiel, nudged Fluffy signaling him to get up and sadly chirped. Staring at the dreadful scene, I noticed familiar paw prints and displaced flowers and mulch which was only associated with one animal, a cat. I prevented the thought from seeping into my brain, but the closure of this situation was impossible without the thought. I imagined the cat with its hungry jaw dropped, and its saliva dripping out of the crevasses of its mouth. I could picture it inching towards the silver cage with its small and sly steps. A chill slithered down my spine and sweat trickled down my face; I gasped for air as reality hit me. I ran into my mom's room, my feet thumping against the wood floor as loud as the rumbling of thunder. "Mom...help. Injured," I wheezed.

My mom stared at me blankly, and I beckoned her to the cage. My mom's brown tangled hair almost traveled as fast as she did. My mom examined the condition of my birds closely and turned to me with a look of sorrow and helplessness and embraced me as we sat in a pool of my tears. Absolutely no discussion took place, no comments were exchanged, and there was no time for explanations. I felt like my youth had been drained and sucked out of me. I felt lost. I felt helpless. I briefly smiled at the clear picture of the day my birds arrived; it felt like decades ago. It was a scorching morning with the sun hovering over my head like an eagle looking for prey. I walked to this peculiar cage housing two strangers, and I could feel the cold breeze seeping through the cracks of the metal enclosure as my face got closer and closer to it. I unlocked the door of the cage, and watched the birds waddle up to the edge. I desperately wanted to relive that moment, where there were no worries and no thoughts or anticipation of misfortune. I curled up into a tight ball as my hot body heated the cold floor. I felt sensations of guilt and confusion overtake my sorrow. I could hear my mom's panicked voice as she talked to the vet over the phone. Even though I wanted to hear the conversation, my ears wouldn't let me. When the information from the vet was relayed to me, I was relieved but concerned. The vet had said it would be a fairly easy treatment and that time would ease the pain. I wasn't quite sure if he was talking about me or the birds.

Over the course of the next few weeks, I spent every waking moment watching and observing the birds. They chirped as if they were aching for relief and drank their water as if it was going to be taken away; their grace and ease diminished and I knew that my careless actions were the cause of this change. I truly hoped that with time their charm would reappear and they would dance and chirp like they used to before. By the end of the month, a remarkable improvement was seen. Fluffy and Snuggles playfully fought with each other, relished in their own music, and happily tweaked away. I had never seen them so carefree since the accident, and I wanted to ingrain this mental state into their bodies forever. The memories that I shared with them were so precious to me, and the bond and connection that had developed between my cockatiels and I could never have been stronger. By watching their unfading happiness and tranquility, I knew that I had to let them go.

Their happiness and their freedom was more important to me than the happiness I attained through my dependence and reliance on them. The bond that I shared with my birds could never be cut, and therefore I knew that by letting them go, I would be giving them a greater life while still keeping our connection strong. I looked into my birds eyes and saw my reflection witnessing the amount that I had grown and changed. I knew that what I was about to do would be painful but worthwhile. I opened the cage that I once considered peculiar and placed my quivering finger in front of their feet. Both birds, slowly perched themselves onto my finger as I carried them outside. I gently looked at them and thanked them for every moment that they experienced with me. I lifted my hand in the air and watched them take flight into the sky. The air lifted them higher into the sky, and I smiled as I witnessed this beautiful moment. The sight of their freedom, happiness, and safety liberated me from the strong attachment I had held on to. I knew I had made the right decision by letting go, but I also knew that the connection we shared will never be shaken.

40

The Smiths

by Harrison Kummer

Ash and smoke billowed from the chimney; this was a sign of war. The Smiths were a group of people that built outrageous inventions and alloys to assist them in protecting the world they loved. The Smiths were skilled with metallurgy and inventing and assembled maddening creations that could help anyone. Few people become a Smith.

A loud noise often clashed in the middle of the night, and I would rise to the metal on metal banging, before realizing it was my older brother Thomas hammering away on some odd invention. He would climb up the attic ladder apologizing for the noise and tell me to go back to sleep.

One night, Thomas shook me awake. "Nico, I got something to work," he said with a glint in his eyes.

We climbed to the crowded living room through the kitchen, and even though we shared the space between ourselves, most of the area had been invaded by Thomas' work. In the middle of the room was a miniature sized Gyroscopic ball. Thomas pressed the manky brass button.

A few seconds passed. "Nothing is happening," I yawned, but he just lifted a finger as if to tell me to be patient.

The steel ball began opening up, the gears and cogs ticking in perfect harmony to reveal a lens. Like a cat stalking its prey, I was drawn to a beam projecting itself from the invention. The light created an intricate design on the ceiling, but all of a sudden the ball closed up. Thomas groaned, but I simply said, "Maybe check the bottom screw by that one wonky gear." He gave a tired smile and put his hand on my shoulder.

"Thanks. Now go to sleep, we can talk in the morning," he said. I nodded my head and walked back to my room, excited for what the next day would bring.

The next morning, I walked into the kitchen and overheard my brother at the door speaking to a couple of men. They both stood like towers, but one had leaner muscles than the other.

My brother turned to acknowledge me. "You're up! Nico, these are my colleagues, Percival and Charles."

The man named Charles pulled out a manila envelope from his jacket. "Nice to meet you, Nico. If I were you, I'd start packing."

I looked at Thomas's haphazard bag already at the front door. My brother grinned at me.

"C'mon buddy. We're going to be Smiths!"

Bewildered, I raced up the ladder and stuffed clothes and tools in my personal worn leather suitcase before our ride showed up. *HONK HONK!* I ran outside in the nick of time.

"The train station please," Charles requested of the driver. I gazed outside the window of the car, nervously fiddling with the handle of my suitcase. The air was musty and smoky, and my nose felt like it was stuck in a wet chimney. Percival's face twisted after he breathed too deeply. I giggled to myself and began preparing myself to board the train. My brother was rambling to Percival about how excited he was and Charles had his nose deep in his journal.

We pulled up by the station and got outside of the car to retrieve our bags. Percival led us down the stairs into a broad opening. There were no doors or hallways, It was just a brick box.

"Why are we here?" I asked worriedly.

Percival smirked. "It's not open yet, young Smith." He walked over to the wall on the left of us and felt the bricks as if he was looking for something. His finger grazed over an old degraded cinderblock, and he looked at us proud of his success. Percival pressed his hand against the brick, triggering a chain reaction of stone movement. A large platform was revealed where the wall once was. Charles stepped on the platform as the rest of us followed. The floor began to lower. I heard the grinding of gears and belts. The brick wall began to disappear, unveiling a large open space.

"We're here," Percival said as we descended to the bottom of the room.

"What is here?" I asked.

Charles closed his book and looked at me, and said, "The Forge."

The Forge was the Smith's headquarters. No one outside of the Smiths knew where it was. Percival lead us to a front office and grabbed a small stack of forms for us to sign. After that, he lead us to our living quarters. "I can't wait to see what you two can contribute to the team." Then Percival and Charles left us for the night.

"Thomas, what did he mean by that?" I asked.

"Well, for us to be here, we both need to assist the team." said Thomas.

"Oh. I mean, I guess I can help you," I said.

Thomas smiled. "Don't worry bud. You've got a lot to help with, more than you give yourself credit for. I brought you in for a reason. This is a very special project. Now go to sleep, we can talk in the morning."

The next day, an alarm awoke the entire facility. Luckily I was used to Thomas waking me up early, so I wasn't too startled. "What's going on?" I asked Thomas.

"Facility wide alarm clock. It keeps going until everyone is present at breakfast."

In the middle of my plate of scrambled eggs, french toast, bacon, and hash browns, a stoutly man walked up to our team table.

"Hello Quincy," Percival greeted in the middle of his Eggs Florentine.

Quincy turned to me, and said, "Thomas has told me a lot about you. I was hoping I could have your input after breakfast Nico." I glanced at Thomas nervously, but he gave me an encouraging nod.

My hands were sweating as I walked into Quincy's office, and I severely regretted that extra pancake I stuffed into my stomach.

"Thomas really is more of the inventor." I tried to explain before I disappointed Quincy.

"I know," he laughed. "But I need someone who can manage a group, and see the things that our wonderful inventors miss. Thomas tells me you have that insight."

While I may have helped Thomas from time to time, I still

had doubts I could do what Quincy was asking. I mean it sounded like he wanted me to be a...

"Project manager. I want you to oversee the work of Team 54, Thomas' group."

"I can try," I said, as an attempt to sound confident. I wanted this opportunity. Quincy lifted a paper with some blueprints. It was a mixture of body suits and zeppelins.

"Our agents fall off zeppelins because they don't have proper footing or grip, we're stumped. Do you have any ideas?" Quincy asked.

I stood silent for a couple of seconds before blurting out, "Magnets." I explained, "If we had magnetic gloves or boots, that problem would be fixed because Zeppelins are dominantly made of magnetic metal." Quincy gave me a wide grin.

"That's the best answer any prospective project manager has ever given me, and the fastest. You've passed the test." Quincy had been testing me all along! The bigger surprise was that I passed.

I walked out to meet the team in the work room. Thomas, Percival, and Charles all looked at me expectantly. "Okay team," I grinned. "Let's get smithing."

41

The Fact of Life

by Amanda Paz

"Luna, pick up your back leg! Come back and do the combination again," Mrs. Sasha yelled as I finished up my last leap.

I ran as fast as I could to the back of a huge studio classroom to begin the combination again. After doing the combination at least three times, we sat on the floor panting and sweating our butts off.

"Good class, everyone your dismissed," Mrs. Sasha announced. The room roared to life as people cheered from being let out early. "Don't forget to stretch and practice your dance girls. The Winter show is coming up in about 2 months," Mrs. Sasha reminded us as she walked towards her office.

The girls and I all chatted as we went to the dressing rooms and began to chat as we got dressed and got ready for our next class. I began to get distracted in my thoughts as I walked out of the cubby.

"Hi everyone. I wanted to introduce myself. My name is Luna Hazel. I'm 17 years old and I'm a junior at Kerr High School. Just to let you guys know a few facts about me I'm a huge nerd that loves theater, dance and video games. Most of my time I spend dancing because of my district's dance program called Alief Jazz Ballet which is the class period I'm in right now."

"Yo Luna." I heard someone shout which brought me out of my thoughts. I turned around to see a girl that was medium height with dark red, dyed hair yell for me across the studio.

"What is it Daniella?" I asked knowing that she would hear me because of my loud voice.

"Bring me back white milk," she commanded. I just nodded my head as I followed my two other friends to the cafeteria.

"Hey Luna, how has your finger been doing? Has the swelling gone down?" my friend Leilani asked.

I held my right hand in my other hand and looked at my middle finger to see that it was still swollen. For the past few months or maybe even longer my middle finger on my right hand has been swollen and I have no clue why.

"Nothing's happening really. It's still swelled up but my mom and I are going to the doctor next week to figure out what's going on," I said to Leilani as I smiled and she smiled back at me. We quickly went to the cafeteria and came back to the studio room and I gave Daniella her milk. I sat down during the rest of the period talking to my friends and worrying about my finger in the back of my mind.

After a few days of nonstop dance rehearsals and theater performances it was finally time to go to see my doctor. Through the last few weeks for some reason my swollen finger started hurting. Some mornings I wake up and my finger would be stiff. To get some movement back I would have to stretch it out.

"How's your finger today Luna?" my mom asked as we turned into the parking lot of my pediatrician.

"Well, when I woke up today it wasn't stiff and it's not hurting so I think I'm fine today," I said as we headed into the office. I signed myself in and sat down next to my mom on my phone, reading my little heart out.

"Luna," my nurse said and smiled at me. My mom and I got up and followed her in and she did all of the routine stuff like checking my height, weight and asking health questions and then she left. A minute or two later my doctor came in and she looked over my finger and said that we should go the Texans Children's Hospital to get x-rays done. My mom and I quickly headed over there with the x-ray form and we got it done in a flash and left.

"Ok Luna, they said it will be a day or two until we get the results so just don't worry," my mom said as we began our journey back home.

Another few weeks have gone by, all of the major stuff like shows have happened and we were getting close to winter break. My finger has been hurting here and there but not that much. The results from the x-rays said that it was broken, so I went to a bone specialist, The specialists took his own x-rays and he had a different idea, and said that it wasn't broken so he made me wear a brace *just in case*, so I wasn't able to use my right hand for a while.

At the next appointment. I remembered sitting in a lobby of UT Physicians to meet with a hand specialist to figure out what was really going on with my finger. I could feel my worry and uneasiness grow as I sat there rubbing my casted and uncasted hands together. My mom took notice of this and put her hands on top of mine to calm me. I turned to her and she tried putting on a fake smile to comfort me but in her eyes I could see the worriedness come through. I smiled back at her just to give her some comfort even though on the inside I was screaming in fear. *Paz*, someone called out. I looked up to see a middle aged lady who smiled at me as my mom and I walked up to her. She led us to an ordinary doctor's room and I sat on the bench in front of the desk. When the doctor came in he felt my fingers and said that like everyone else he has no clue what's going on and just as precautions that I should go see a rheumatologist. He wrote me up a prescription for anti-inflammatory pain medicine.

Before we left the office my mom set up the appointment with the rheumatologist in the waiting room. When she finished we walked out to the car and when we got in my mom called my brother to tell him what was going on. She finished up talking to my brother. One question ran through my head. Why can't anyone figure out what's wrong with me? I felt my eyes began to water as fear overcame my mind and heart as I started to think of the worse possible things. My mom tried comforting me as she was driving telling me everything is going to be alright.

Another week passed before we finally got to see the rheumatologist and he quickly sent me to get my blood drawn and go through the RA test. Even more unbearable weeks had come by until one normal day during dinner it was just my dad and I. I served myself a small T-bone and some potatoes and went to go sit down at the table.

"Luna why didn't you make yourself a salad? You need to eat some spinach because your test said your iron is low," My dad said as he began putting dishes into the dish washer. It took me a minute to process what he said in my mind and I instantly perked up.

"My test? That means my results came in. What did they say?" I asked as I felt a surge of hope bounce through my heart.

My dad stopped putting up the dishes and turned to face me as he said the words I didn't want to hear. "You have RA," my dad said calmly as he went back to doing the dishes and I sat there in shock.

When those same three words repeated in my head the dam that held my tears back exploded as I felt my world began to crumble around me. All of the hope which had once filled my body, vanished in an instant, I thought of my now even more distant future.

"Hey it's alright, don't cry, everything will be alright," my dad said as he ran over and comforted me. No matter how many times my dad told me everything was going to be ok I didn't believe him because on the inside my once stable hardly cracked world fell apart.

That next day I went to school like any normal day but on the inside I was emotionally unstable. If one little thing messed up, then the whole day was a horrible day. I got excited when 3rd period rolled around I can feel excitement bubble in me as I walked into the large studio room and got dressed.

"Girls, today is ballet, so go get dressed," Mrs. Sasha said as I walked in. I walked over to cubby 6 and while changing I was chatting with the other girls. When everyone finished we pulled out the extra ballet bars and I stood next to one of them ready to hear the combination. Mrs. Sasha started the music and we began doing relives, but as I started going up on my toes I felt this unbearable pain coming from my big toe on my left foot. I ignored the discomfort and kept going up. After about the fifth relive the pain was too much to bare. I told Mrs. Sasha and she told me to sit out for the rest of the class. When I sat down in her office I pulled off my left ballet shoe to see my big toe was swollen, like a tomato and I could feel a few tears slide down my checks.

The next day I had an appointment with the Rheumatologist and he basically said I couldn't dance until the swelling went down in my toe. If that news wasn't bad enough I had to get a shot in my finger which was swollen too. This shot was the most painful thing I have ever experienced in my life. The painful shot left me crying afterwards, and more broken hearted than ever due to the fact a part of myself was being taken away from me. During that time, I thought everything was falling apart. I felt like my life was over, and I wouldn't have the future that I had been dreaming of since I was a little girl.

Three months later, my toe was still swollen a bit, but it didn't hurt when I got on relive any more. I'm able to start dancing again whenever I want to, but I cannot go overboard. I had to change my diet. I've cut out most of the gluten in my life since it causes my joints to swell up. I take pills and vitamins out the wazoo now, some in the morning and some in the afternoon. I still get pain in my joints due to the Rheumatoid Arthritis, but it doesn't happen often, which I'm very grateful for. I still live a normal teenage life. I go to school, I have my friends, and I procrastinate on my homework. For anyone that is going through a tough situation here is a quote for you which helped me out, *To win the game, just remain in the game.*

42

The Day My Life Changed

by Colin Pearce

It was Friday and I was sitting in the last class of the day watching the second hand, and waiting for the minute hand to hit the twelve. The teacher droned on until I heard the sound of freedom, the bell. I quickly packed up my things and sped walked out of the classroom and out of the school to my car in the parking lot. I took the ten minute drive home from my high school and walked in the front door of my small house in the suburbs. My mom won't get home for another hour, so I plopped myself on the couch and laid there thinking about my life. I thought about how I got two days of freedom and then five of the same thing every single day and this cycle will continue for another year and a half. People always say high school was the best years of a person's life, but the statement was false because high school was too uniform and boring for anyone to have fun. People always say we high schoolers were lazy and all we did was play video games and watch internet videos. This was true because high schoolers were so bored and stressed we needed a form of escapism.

As I was just about to fall asleep, I heard a tapping on the side of my house. I assumed it was just an annoying woodpecker and tried to fall asleep again. The tapping continued, but this time it was louder and sounded more urgent, as if someone was trying to get in my house but, it's just tapping, not pounding. The tapping began to turn into pounding. I jumped off the couch and grabbed a knife from the kitchen and headed out the back door. I sneaked to the corner of the house and jumped around expecting to see something there, but nothing was to be seen. Beginning to wonder if I am going crazy, I walked towards where the pounding was, and all that was there was a small hole in the side of my house where a woodpecker pecked a hole. I slowly and cautiously leaned in and peeked inside the hole. I saw something very strange; I was looking through a peep hole into a hotel hallway. I stepped back to take a gravity check and then I looked in again and saw the same thing. I reached to where a door knob would be and grab it. I turned the doorknob, pulled and stepped into the hotel hallway.

I looked to the left and to the right down the hallway, and it seemed to be just an endless corridor of doors. The hotel was very retro with a worn down green carpet, red paneled walls and off white doors. I heard a door open and slam shut to my left and turned that way. I saw a red headed girl running towards me. I asked as she ran by, "Do you know where I am?"

She turned her head and said, "Run! Follow me if you want to live!" I obeyed and ran after her.

She ran till the hallway unexpectedly dead ended. She looked frantically around and bust down the door to our left, grabbed my hand and pulled me in. After running through the door, we were in the middle of a dark oak forest. Confused, I asked, "What the...?"

She interrupted me and said, "No time for questions now, keep running!" She ran in one direction and I followed.

After running for about ten minutes, we came into a clearing and she stopped.

"Okay, I think we lost the chaser," she said, out of breath.

"Lost what?" I asked, even more out of breath.

She exhaled in annoyance and said, "That hallway we were in is a connection between multiple parts of the earth and even other planets; we humans are not supposed to be there so monsters called chasers hunt you down if you are found in the hallway."

"Okay," I said, very confused. "But how do you know all that?"

"I am not allowed to say, but you need to get back where you came from; it is too dangerous for you here."

"Why? You're here."

"Because I am trained to be here and to protect the world from chasers."

"But..." I am once again interrupted, this time not by the girl, but by a deep growl of an unknown beast prowling in the trees. The girl pulled out a dagger and went into a fighting stance. A four-legged beast jumped out from the trees and the girl jumps to meet it midair. The girl stabbed the beast with the dagger and in the blink of an eye it turned to dust and the attack was over.

The girl turned to me and said, "That is why we need to get back, because every human has a chaser and yours is loose; if we get you back, it will be restrained again."

"Why not just kill it like you did this one?"

"They do not die. They turn to dust and in three minutes reform into a stronger embodiment."

"Why stop them, though?"

"There are billions of them, like I said, one for each human; if they all get released they will take over the world; that's why we need to get you back to your normal life so your chaser is one less we have to deal with."

"I don't want to go back to that boring life, this is fun; I want to join whatever group you are a part of so I can defend the world."

"It does not work that way. Hey, I do not know your name; what is it?" she asked with a questioning look on her face.

"My name? My name is Corbin. What is yours?"

"Kylie. Now listen, we need to head back to your door before it's too late. Got it?"

"Got it," I said reluctantly.

We began to scurry through the forest trying to find the door that got us here. We finally found it in the middle of a huge oak tree. Kylie stood there waiting for something. As I was about to ask what, the beast charged the door and I screamed. She slammed the door shut on it and it turned to dust.

"They cannot reform if part of them is inside the hallway and the other is not."

"So that's one more chaser down," I said, trying to be optimistic.

"Yeah it is, so what is your room number? I will take you back home."

"Well seeing as I have no idea where I am, I do not know my room number."

"Oh great," Kylie said, sarcastically. "It looks like we need to go to the lobby to find out."

"Lobby?" I asked, confused. "This place has a lobby?"

"Well this place is a hotel," she said as she began walking the other direction of the dead end where we were, and I followed. After wandering for a long while and seeing the same thing the whole time, she stopped.

"Corbin, listen, if we ever get separated I want you to have this so I can find you," she said and reached into her pocket and pulled out a blue whistle and put it into my hand. "I can hear the sound of this whistle from anywhere and I will be able to find you."

"Okay, thanks," I said, staring at the whistle in awe.

"We need to keep moving."

We continued to roam for a long while until we both are stopped in our tracks by a sound no one wanted to hear... hissing. We both turned our eyes and looked at each other, scared, then turned around to see a black king cobra taking up the whole hallway.

"Run!" Kylie yelled. This time I didn't need her to tell me, and I was off and running right beside her. Realizing once again the only way of escape was through another door, Kylie busted one open to the right and we both ran inside. We slammed the door and leaned our bodies against it. The snake began to pound the door. Kylie and I looked at each other and then at the room. We were in a large warehouse with a conveyor belt leading to an incinerator. The snake stopped pounding the door and Kylie and I lifted off the door. We walked towards the incinerator and saw that we were on a balcony with a rusted railing and below us was a cement floor with controls to the incinerator. The door burst open and the snake began to slither in. Kylie, in her protective way, shoved me over the railing and I smacked the hard cement floor. I was in excruciating pain and could barely move. I heard Kylie and the snake in a struggle. It sounded like the snake was winning. I could move more now, but it hurt. I sucked up the pain and stood up. I ran over to the incinerator and climbed up a ladder and got on to the conveyor belt.

"Hey, snake!" I yelled, trying to distract it from Kylie, and the snake looked at me.

"Corbin, no!" Kylie yelled in a weak voice.

"I am saving you so you can save the world," I said, as the

snake began to slither towards me.

"But my job is to save you."

Standing there bravely and triumphantly as the snake approached to kill me, I said in my most confident voice ever, "My life is not important, it is just a cycle of the same thing every week; I am doing this so you can live your fun life and keep the world safe. The snake was just going to defeat you and then me; if I must die to save the world, I will feel like my life is not a waste."

As I finished, the snake tried to strike me and I dodged. It tried again. I grabbed inside its nostrils and fell into the hot fire, taking the snake with me. The last thing I heard was Kylie wailing.

I woke up startled and sat up so fast I smacked my mom in the face.

"Are you okay, sweetie?" she asked in a calm voice, "You were sweating and screaming the word hot over and over and I am just making sure you are feeling alright."

"I'm fine," I said, annoyed because I realized I am in the same life, and all that was just a dream.

"Were you having a bad dream?" my mom asked.

"No, it was the best dream I have ever had because I finally escaped this boring life."

"Oh," she said in a sad way. "I think being a high schooler is amazing and you should really try enjoying yourself."

"I tried my best, mom. It is just the same thing every single day and it is so boring."

"It will all pass soon. I am ordering Chinese for dinner, how does that sound?"

"Good," I said shortly, as I walked to my room to play video games. I sat on my bed and felt a lump in my pocket. I reached inside and pulled out the blue whistle Kylie gave me and smiled. I put it up to my lips and blew, and heard nothing. I threw it across the room in anger and began to set up my game. Sitting there in silence, I began to hear tapping on the wall of the house. I threw the controller down and ran outside. I went to the side of the house where the tapping was coming from and there was Kylie.

"Kylie!" I yelled, and out of character, ran to give her a hug.

"Hey, Corbin, glad you are okay."

"How am I okay?" I asked, confused.

"That is a long story; more importantly, do you want to join the organization to stop chasers? We need more operatives." And without a doubt in my mind I answered, "Yes."

43

The Search for Mommy

by Megan Taylor

Daddy was quiet for a long time. He used to be all smiles and happy faces, telling jokes and stories, but now he just sulked around the house carrying a square, shiny bottle in his hand. He also slept a lot, and his eyes were sometimes very red and his face very wet. He used to be at work on Saturdays, but one day he just stopped going. He told me he loved his job at the newspaper printing factory very much, so why did he stop going? At the time, I assumed it might have had something to do with the fact that Mommy hadn't come home.

She suddenly didn't come home one day while I was at school, and it'd been a few days since I last saw her. I often repeatedly asked Daddy where she was, and he told me she was away. I then asked where she went, and he'd say a faraway place, looking out the window with his mouth sagging to his chin. Then he would scold at me to stop asking so much about her. I wondered if Mommy went to a secret place, or a place Daddy didn't want to say. He had a lot of secrets he never shared with me or Mommy. But it hurt my brain to try and guess what place it could be.

I missed Mommy so much. I felt lonely without her around. I knew Daddy did, too. I sometimes sat in front of the door, waiting for her to enter so I could hug her. I sometimes fell asleep in that very spot and hoped Mommy came while I was asleep, but when I checked my parents' room, I found only Daddy in bed. I once practiced how I would greet Mommy when she would return home, but Daddy heard me and thought she actually did. He got very angry with me and kept me in my room for most of the day. I sometimes wrote letters to her and gave them to the mail man. At the age of seven, I didn't know that letters without a mailing address were never sent, but the mail man always smiled and took my letters anyway. Why take them if he was only going to throw them away later? That made me sad.

Every night, when I fell asleep in my own bed, I took a picture of Mommy with me. She had hair like mine, a long, fuzzy bundle of muddy hay. Her eyes were dark green, not like mine; I had Daddy's brown eyes. Her lips were a soft pink and teeth as white as fluffy clouds on a sunny day. I felt sad every time I looked at her picture, and so did Daddy. He sometimes cried himself to sleep. I wondered if he missed her more than I did.

I didn't want to see Daddy cry anymore. I wanted to have her wake me up in the morning by petting my head again. I wanted her to make me a yummy breakfast and walk me to school. I wanted to go out into the flower field with her and collect daisies in baskets to make flower crowns with. I wanted Daddy to be happy. So I made it my mission the next day, after church, I would go around town asking if someone knew where Mommy went.

The next morning, surrounded by a ring of crumpled papers, I finally drew my best picture of Mommy, basing it off of the photo I have of her. At the top, in red crayon, I wrote: *HAVE YOU SEEN MY MOMMY?* I remembered seeing a lot of posters of missing pets and old people around town, and people looked at them a lot. Maybe if I showed them my poster, they would look and know what faraway secret place Mommy went to.

Daddy stayed home, sloppily saying he didn't feel well, while I went to church with my Grandma. I told her on the way there about my mission to search for Mommy, and she laughed about it. Then she started crying. She must've missed Mommy, too. After our sermon and my Sunday school class, I told Grandma I wanted to go to the candy shop. Since it was around the corner, she allowed me to go by myself. But I didn't go for candy; I went to ask around and show my poster. It was harder than I thought; I hardly knew anyone in town, and Mommy always taught me not to speak to strangers. So when I walked into the candy shop, my determination to ask about Mommy vanished entirely. Instead, I slunk through the aisles of candy until the candy man at the counter asked what

I was doing, saying that if I wasn't going to buy something, I should beat it. This gave me the chance I needed to ask about Mommy.

I walked up to him and showed him my poster. "Have you seen my Mommy?" I asked shyly, standing on my toes to peek over the counter.

The candy man raised his brows at me and looked at my poster. After a moment, he looked amused and handed the poster back.

"Why, yes, little lady, I believe I have," he said, smiling.

"You did?" I asked excitedly. "Where? Where did you see Mommy?"

"I think I saw her head down Crescent Hill Street a few minutes ago."

"Crescent Hill Street! Thank you!" Gleefully, I raced out of the candy shop and looked for Crescent Hill Street. Maybe Mommy was already back from being at the faraway place! The candy man didn't specify which store or restaurant she went into on Crescent Hill Street, so I had to search through and ask around every store and restaurant from one end of the street to the other. I only asked employees if they had seen my Mommy when they stopped me, wondering what a little girl like me was doing wandering around by myself. When I asked, most of them smiled sadly and shook their heads no, and others thought it was a game and told me she was at this made-up place. I didn't find it very funny. Then the manager of the last restaurant on Crescent Hill Street discovered me and angrily ordered me to quit bugging his customers. I told him that I was looking for my Mommy and showed him the poster.

"What's your name?" he asked me.

"Sarah Louise Rockwell," I said.

His eyes and face weren't so angry-looking after I gave him my name. He looked sad. He must have known my Mommy. Did he miss her, too? After a moment, he gave me a free cookie and guided me out of the restaurant, telling me to go down Raven Avenue. I asked if he had seen her, and he nodded yes. "Just the other day," he said.

I thanked him for the cookie and the directions, and fled the restaurant for Raven Avenue. As I raced, I wondered if the candy man had seen Mommy more recently than the manager, or if he just confused another woman for her. I didn't let the thought puzzle me any longer; I needed to focus on finding Mommy so Daddy could be happy again.

Raven Avenue was always busy, especially on Sundays; it was when families endlessly went in and out of shops and restaurants after church. The eateries and stores were too crowded for me to enter and ask the employees, so I was resigned to asking people on the street, stopping and showing them my poster.

"Have you seen my Mommy?"

"No, sorry, little one."

"Have you seen my Mommy?"

"Afraid not, kid."

"Have you seen my Mommy?"

"Don't bother me, girlie. Ain't you got a home to get to?"

Every person I asked had either no idea where Mommy was, no answer to give me, or told me to scram. I didn't receive as many answers as I had on Crescent Hill Street. Daddy had always told me that Raven Avenue was among the dirtier parts of town full of rude people who smelled like they swam in a toilet. In spite of my bad luck, I continued wandering the street, showing my poster to those who passed by.

After what felt like hours of walking and asking, it was already late in the afternoon, and a wind storm was starting to develop. My legs ached and my throat was sore. I had no idea what part of town I was in, and I was sure Grandma was worried sick about me. Looking at the continuously busy crowd of people, I decided it was time to head home before it got too dark. I told myself I could try and find Mommy tomorrow.

Suddenly the wind blew past me, and my poster was torn from my hands. I gasped as it began to fly away. I couldn't let it escape. If it got away, I would lose my only hope of seeing Mommy again and have her come home! I chased it around town, frantically leaping into the air to try and seize it from the wind. I wished for someone around me to help and rescue it, but they seemed to pay no mind to what I was doing and instead went about their own business.

"Wait! Come back!" I implored my poster as it danced in the gusts. It fluttered down to where I could almost reach it, only to be snatched and risen higher into the air. Although I tripped numerous times, skinning my knees and elbows, I ignored the stings and continued to try and save my poster.

As the sky was rapidly consumed by dark storm clouds and the wind picked up, the poster flew beyond a black, rusted gate. I followed it by slipping through a large gap in the gate where a bar once blocked the way. I ran past mossy, flat rocks that stuck up out of the ground, avoiding them so they wouldn't make me trip. There were so many of these strange rocks, some of them much taller than me, that I felt I was trapped in a maze. I started to worry that I had lost my way, and my poster. Then, I caught sight of it from the corner of my eye and headed in its direction. It flew towards a dead, wilted tree and nosedived, getting caught against one of the rocks placed next to the tree. The wind kept it still and it covered one of the rock's faces. I finally had a chance to catch it.

I knelt down in front of the rock onto a fresh pile of dirt and shielded the poster from the wind with my body, so it wouldn't tear when I tried to remove it from the rock face. Once I had my poster firmly in my hands, I hugged it tight, glad to have it once again, then folded and tucked it under my shirt to prevent it from escaping me a second time.

As I was about to leave, I managed to catch a glimpse of the rock face. It wasn't dirty like most of the others. Beside it, there was a little vase of wilted daisies buried halfway into the ground, and a name was neatly etched into it. "Clarissa Hope Rockwell," I mumbled as I read the name aloud and wrinkled my nose in confusion.

I found it very odd that this Clarissa lady had the same last name as me.

44

Creator's Hope

by Ellaine Milan Tee

At the beginning of time, I was vibrant, young, lively, and enthusiastic like a hatchling just came of its shell. A great new start! A new life! And it all started with the dinosaurs.

Dinosaurs were my favorite; they lived for a few decades and complied with the great cycle of life. They were fun to watch and easy to manage. However, my sister Venus became very jealous of the vibrant life that I had. She plotted to destroy my beloved children in their peak of existence by betting our older brother Jupiter to pitch a few balls to Papa Sun. As usual, he missed and ended up hitting me multiple times. That was the end of the dinosaur era.

A few millenniums after that, I started to feel a little sick. Then, it didn't take long for me to realize that I was coming down with something. For a few millennia, I had the chills, and I first thought it was a cold. And it was. I have been working hard for centuries to recover from the hits. It took me so long to get the scenery back to the way it was. My huge land was broken into 7 pieces after those hits, and it took me so long to just get enough energy before I got started back again in producing life.

During this time, the mammoths and saber tooth tigers were crawling all over the place. They endured the long harsh chill for a few centuries. I dreaded the cold and dreamed of the warmth of the tropical sun and the sweat trickling down my face as I work.

I did not see an end to this long chill, so I made a deal with the nearby planet Mercury for a little heat. Along with this deal, I accepted to go house the failing species called man. In my mind, it seemed like a fair deal. Men were a great way to replace the fluffy mammoths and saber tooth tigers. Man came into the scenery and greatly accepted the cold air. Many of them thought of it as a great bargain as well. They used their wit and made their own apparel they called clothes. These men were quite funny looking. Like no one can pull off huge furry jacket without looking silly. They had the wit, but lacked in the fur and hair to survive the harsh cold that they had to borrow from the mammoths. Men are very odd creature. They were rather thankful for my great cold, but was later unsatisfied with their move to the new planet. I begin to notice that they had one fatal flaw: greed. I began to receive some heat from Mercury finally and the world began to heat up a little.

I was back to where I was before minus the dinosaurs. People were grateful for the warming up. I was finally restored to my greatest potential of producing animals. I began with the reptiles in memory of the dinosaur lives that were lost. I then created elephants and tigers in memory of the dear mammoth and saber tooth tiger of from my shivers. I continued on to create the rest of the animals from those appreciated in the zoos and those hidden in the farthest reaches of the deepest oceans and jungles. All of these animals are my children. Each living with a purpose to keep life of another to continue. Each one of them lives their own lives with souls affecting the other. All of them are connected including Man. Suddenly, Man began to tamper with my children and their system. It was alright at first. They tamed the souls of my creation. Took their true unique soul and bred them to satisfy the craving for their precious meat. Along with taming came one of the greatest threat to my children: farming. Here, Man began to tame the plants around them. They cut down the trees to make room for their domestication of the wilderness. They began to pollute my waters and poison my air. Man was then renamed People due to their grand increase in numbers. People multiplied like bacteria. They began to take over everything they touched.

People multiplied too fast and it was terrifying for my children and I, so I sent the worst thing I have concocted in the billions of years I have created things: a plague. This plague was terrifying. It was the worst thing I could have made because I was angry. I was angry that I was overpowered by the species that I have helped saved. This is what I got for this act of kindness and concern. Their action led to the destruction of my children and their homes for their benefit. The plague scared all of the People. Many of them went into their next life of their choice. The plague wiped out about thirty to sixty percent of their population. There was panic everywhere, but People still survived. They continued on living even if many of them died. The People who were dearest to me were the ones isolated away from the large land mass. The People from the so-called Afro Eurasia discovered the People, from the New Side of the world, took all the gifts I gave to the People of the New Side. These Afro Eurasians were greedy and took everything that they saw. They took the land and the trees and my poor bison and raccoons for their fur. Progress for People was my dread. I was helpless and hopeless. There was no end to their progress. My creations were suffering and dying. They were calling out to me for help, but I had nothing to help them with. Whatever I used to make my children are gone. Stolen by People. I was powerless.

As time went by, I watched my creation suffer. I began to get a fever. The heat that I borrowed from Mercury began to multiply as the people did. I began to sweat profusely while I was in bed trying to contemplate of a way to help my remaining creations. I was tired and done with People. My health seemed to have no hope on getting better. The feeling of despair succumbed my entire entity.

As time went by, my symptoms seemed to signal my end. I began to have fever chills. I ended up shaking up a whole city in the People's time 1900s. It was destructive. I also accidentally sneezed up a storm that demolished another town. That sneeze was named the Great Galveston Hurricane. The new generation of People began to notice new things about me. Well I guess that all storms have an end. They began to be more aware about my sickness unlike the previous generation. It all started during People Time 1970s. People called hippies were all about saving me. It was great. From there, the idea of recycling, where they remake things from old products, was helping me get a little better. People began to protect my endangered children. I felt something that I've never felt while the humans roamed earth. It was HOPE. It was a People emotion, (a sensation where they feel things inside of them). This Hope was like a light in the darkness of my tremors and fever. The future of mankind seems hazy right now. But through the darkest times I have seen the best People. They are builders, hunters, conquerors and most definitely survivors. Who knows when the next time I'll come down with something? *ACHOOO!*

45

Vacants

by Jan Tee

There were 3 houses on Sui Baker Street, and they all held mysteries. Mrs. Shuelmaker was the first house on the street and the oldest. She owned a small house but had a big backyard that was fenced off, which was strange. No one on Sui Baker fenced their backyard, but the rumor was that she had a mean dog in the backyard, and it only ate humans.

The next house was Allyssa Underton's house. She had blue eyes and hair the color of the night, which made her the prettiest girl I knew. She never came out on the weekends because her parents wouldn't let her. Nobody saw her parents leave the house or stick their head through their front door, which meant nobody knew what her parents looked like.

Then there was the house of my best friend, Sun. It was about two acres, making it the biggest house on the street. With his parent busy, he was lonely until we met. He always wore a pair of Wayfarers too. No one knew why.

Next to that house was an empty lot. On that empty lot was my trailer. That's where my family lived. Honestly, I don't know much about my family or my name. I never met my father and my mom was too tired to talk to me after a 12-hour shift, and the only reason I remembered my name, *Laulin*, was because Sun reminds me everyday.

There was also a forest. Sun and I called them the Greens. There wasn't much in the Greens. However, there's a vacant parking lot and an old abandoned record store behind it. Since there was not much there, we called it the vacants. We did stuff like reenacting our own versions of Huck Finn, but instead of having a raft to get around the Mississippi, he would have a speedboat. *The book would have been half the its length if he had and same is true for other stories.*

The store was shabby with boarded windows, but inside

was spectacular! There were stacks of records and old cassettes. Somehow, the power still worked in the store, so when we got tired of playing on the lot, we would hang out and play a random record inside. It would be like this for a couple of years until Sun was in third grade.

When he was in third grade, Sun wouldn't stop talking about school. He made school sound fun, which got me jealous. Sun said that school had many nice people, and if you were lucky enough to get the nice teacher, you were good for the year. This was also the year he wouldn't stop talking about Allyssa. He would tell me how they ate lunch together and played at recess together.

"You like her, don't you?" I asked him as we sat in the store.

"No!" he denied, looking away.

"C'mon man! Who am I going to tell?" I exclaimed. He shook his head, ashamed. "Alright, let's make a deal," I said, "If you tell me who you like, then I'll tell you any secret I have."

"Fine," he sighed. "I do like her," he said and blushed redder than a tomato. "But the thing is I don't know if she likes me or not!"

"That doesn't matter! We're only eight! We don't know anything about anything," I said trying to cheer him up. He scowled under his Ray-Bans and put his lip to the right side of his face - the face he made when he was trying to think real hard. When his face loosened, we decided to go back to our houses.

I was about to enter the trailer when Sun yelled from behind me, "So, what's that secret you promised you were going to tell me?"

"I don't have any," I lied.

The season changed. Fall turned into winter, and Sun's Wayfarers stayed on his face throughout the snowy weather. School ended and summer started, and the days began to grow hotter. Since the weather was so hot and the record store in the Vacants had no working central air, we decided to hang out in the Greens. We found a small creek there and decided to go swimming when it was too hot to play in the Vacants (which meant almost every day). When it was nearing the end of July, we decided to come back to the Vacants. When we got there, we saw a group of boys hanging out in front of the store. The parking lot was dirty because of the boy's trash. Sun decided to approach them, and I followed him.

"What are you doing here? This is ours!" Sun said firmly. The boys, who looked six feet and were most probably in middle school turned around and look down on Sun.

"Beat it kid, we found this place first," the tallest one said. Sun didn't budge.

"I said, beat it!" he repeated.

"Or what?" Sun asked.

"Or this!" he said and pushed Sun so hard when he hit ground, His Wayfarers fell off his face. I looked at Sun. His face was flustered and he stared at the group of boys laughing at him. Sun then picked up his glasses and put them back on his face and swung a fist towards the guy who pushed him down. It landed right on his nose. The guy flew to the floor and clutched his nose. Sun gave him a nosebleed.

His face changed from shock to anger. He pointed at Sun and yelled, "GET HIM!"

We turned around and ran towards the Greens. The group of boys began to chase us. Our feet were moving as fast as one could imagine. We continued to run and headed for Sun's back door. We tried to open it, but it was locked.

"Do you have a key?" I asked franticly.

"No!" Sun replied. We shook the door desperately, but no one answered. The group was getting near.

"Let's keep running," I suggested. Sun agreed and bolted. We didn't get very far until we reached Mrs. Shuelmaker's fence.

"Let's climb it!" Sun suggested.

"But there's a man eating dog in there!" I protested.

"Well, would you rather be eaten by a dog or get beaten up by some dummies?"

Without thinking, I agreed with Sun and climbed the fence. When we were on the other side, we peeked through the fence and saw the boys' horrified looks. They turned around and ran away. They knew about Mrs. Shuelmaker's pet. The backyard of Mrs. Shuelmaker was much more different than we would imagine it to be. We thought that her backyard would be filled with bones and remains of humans that mistakenly entered the place and were eaten up, but it was the opposite of that. The place was beautiful. It was filled with colorful flowers and plants and ferns all lined up in separate rows. Shades of purple, red, blue and even unidentifiable colors filled our eyes. We stood up and examined the plants. When we looked up, we saw Mrs. Shuelmaker watering her Azaleas. Her face looked surprised at first but then her face loosened and smiled afterwards.

"How did you get in here?" she asked calmly with a soft southern accent.

"We climbed the fence ma'am," Sun nervously replied.

"You trying to find trouble?" she asked sternly.

"No ma'am, we were running away from it," Sun quickly replied.

She turned off her hose and she invited us to her patio. There were only two seats, so I decided I would stand behind Sun. She went in the house at first and then walked out with a tray of lemonade and cookies. Sun grabbed a cup and started to drink.

After a few sips, Sun asked, "Mrs. Shuelmaker, how were you able to get a garden this big?"

"Well, when you're an old lady, there isn't much to do but tend to your garden. Sui Baker used to be my father's farmland until we had to sell because of competition with other farms. When my father passed away, we sold the rest of the land to a rich businessman, and was nice enough to keep this portion of land for me," she explained.

"But why fence your garden? This place looks real nice! I've never seen a garden this pretty! Why not show the world?" I asked. She didn't hear my question, but Sun repeated it for me.

"Well," she said. "Some places were just meant to be looked over by the human eye. This place is one of them. I wanted to protect it from harm. Just look at the forests. They were beautiful, untouched, and immaculate when humans did not see them. However, when they did, they chopped them down, their beauty stolen. People often overlook beauty when they don't understand it."

School began again, which wasn't a bad thing. The big kids who trashed the Vacants never returned so Sun, and I decided to claim back the Vacants and clean the place up. We picked up the trash and tidied up the record store. Broken records lay on the floor, graffiti of strange words appeared on the boarded windows. A place that was once beautiful became ruined. We understood why Mrs. Shuelmaker wanted to fence off her garden. However, considering the pitiful condition, we still played in it.

Since school began, so did Sun's love for Allyssa. One day, something strange happened. While I was waiting for Sun, Allyssa entered the Vacants. She was carrying her bright pink Jansport backpack. Leading her was Sun. I asked him how he got her here.

"I just did some persuading," he replied.

"With her parents?" I asked, surprised.

"No, just her," Sun said.

"Don't you think her parents will find out?" I asked.

"Not if she doesn't stay too long," he answered and turned to Allyssa. He gave her a tour of the record store.

The tour didn't last long. A tall man entered the store and said, "Allyssa! I want you home right now." His voice echoed throughout the store.

"Yes, Dad," she replied as she wilted towards her father. The two exited the store together. Sun and I decided to sit around and drink coke until it got dark, but a few minutes later, we were surprised to see Mr.Underton again.

"Did you trash this place?" he asked. We shook our heads.

"Who did?" he asked again.

"Big kids," Sun replied. Mr. Underton nodded and looked around the store, grabbed a coke and sat with us.

"I remember this place back in the 80s," he said "This is where I had my first job. Man, I thought I had the coolest job in the world. I had the coolest friends in school because of this job. I had a great time, but with all that fun, I ran into trouble."

"Is that why you keep Allyssa at home all the time?" Sun questioned.

He sat there for a long time, thinking. Then he finally said,

"I guess so, kid. Maybe I keep her inside because..."

"Because you didn't want her harmed?" Sun asked.

"Yeah, I didn't want her to end up like me when I was a teenager, a bum," he stated while taking a sip from his cola. "But being in here again is making me think maybe a bit of freedom wouldn't hurt her." He then stood up walked around the store with nostalgia in his eyes; thanked us for the drink and walked out. We never saw him again.

As the school year progressed, I saw Sun less. Some days I would for him to come to the Vacants, but he never showed up. There would also be times where he promised to come, but he never did. That's when I noticed I was being forgotten. When his fourth grade year was winding to a close, I decided to tell him my secret.

~

Sun and I were sitting in the parking lot watching the sun setting. He was telling his extravagant stories about his new friends and the crazy stuff he did with them. When it got dark, we walked towards the Greens but before we reached it I suddenly stopped.

Sun turned around and asked, "What's wrong, Saul?"

I sighed and stared at Sun. "Remember about a year ago you asked me what my secret was and I said I didn't have any?"

Sun nodded.

"Well I do have one," I said.

Sun stood there for a few minutes, scowled under his Ray-Bans and shifted his lips to the right side of his face. He nodded signaling me to continue.

"I know we've been friends for a long time, but I have to leave," I said.

"Where are you going?" he asked.

"I don't know, but I have to. You don't need me anymore, so that means I have to leave," I said.

"What do you mean? You're a friend, not a nanny," Sun replied.

"Don't you get it? I don't exist! I'm only in your head! You created me and you believed in me so hard you thought I was real!" I confessed.

He stood there with his head low and nodded. "I know

you can't stay, but I don't want to forget you," he whispered.

"You will. Once I disappear, I will be gone from your memory forever. I have to go now, or else you'll never be able to grow up. I helped you do that with your childhood. That was my job! That was why you created me! And I've done that..," my voice weakened.

I turned around and walked away, slowly. With each step I took, I began to fade. As I faded, I looked at the sun setting all the wondrous colors, like flowers on a sunny day. I also got a glimpse of the black night sky, and thought of Allyssa's dark hair. As I was thinking of these things, I solved all the mysteries Sui Baker Street held, but one. *Why did Sun wear Wayfarers all the time?*

POETRY

Star Poet

What It's Like

by Selene Ashewood

Being deaf in a world full of sound.
Being blind in this colorful universe all around.
Hearing 1000 voices whispering all at once in my mind.
Ignoring the chaos — leave them behind.
Head spinning,
Lights dimming,
As the distractions come near.
Focus killed,
Brain can't be filled,
Now the lesson is over, I fear.

Using my limitless imagination and sharp intuition.
Using the amazing traits I inherited from this condition.
Becoming sidetracked by daydreams I so love.
Blasting off with superpowers — fly from up above.
Creative writing,
Ninjas fighting,
As the energy gives me a lift.
Hyperactivity soared,
It can't be floored,
What a small price to pay for this gift.

A Performance To Remember

By: Sanchita Bhusari

As we approach the stage that glimmered and shined,
Our stomachs flutter with tiny little butterflies.

Stepping onto the stage with excitement and determination,
We get into our poses, our smiles giving off radiation.

We hear the music start from the loudspeakers,
As the spotlight turns to us, the main feature.

We start gliding to the music that we know by heart,
Our shimmering costumes glisten like a work of art.

Our graceful bodies twirl with practiced technique,
Our pirouettes have flawless style, there is nothing to tweak.

Then the time comes to elegantly leap and land to the ground,
The hardest part we have learned, my heart starts to pound.

I do the choreography that leads into the leap,
And extend my legs with perfect posture ready to land on my feet!

A splendid smile flashes across my face,
As I effortlessly land right in my place.

We finish with a magnificent pose,
While I think to myself, "I love performing in shows!"

As we end the dance we've worked on all year,
It felt amazing when the audience erupted in cheers.

As we come together to take our bows,
We start to exit the stage, away from the crowd.

As we all gather around, our dance teacher says aloud,
"Good job girls, I couldn't be more proud!"

Peace in the Womb

By Shruti Chakraborty

"Abort her!" I heard Papa say
Mama cried that's not the right way
She has a right to live
And to this world lots to give
But she is the second female
And the family needs a male
A son will carry our family name
He is the heir and will bring the family fame.
The uncertainty of life inside a womb
Will I live or shall this be my tomb?
My Mother was strong enough
Fought for me even though it was tough
Nine months passed, I came to this earth
The society I called home
Thought I will be of no worth.
Here girls were left uneducated
and always poorly treated
I never feared death
Maybe it was because I faced it from my first breath
I heard my father talking about World Peace
He wanted to kill me has he forgotten,
But I have; and unknowingly forgiven.
Today as my fame reaches far and wide,
I have become my family's pride
Love your daughter; she is your pride.
Stop killing the girl child!

The Peaceful Beach

by Audrey Chan

The egg yolk sun gleams around
The blue waters.

Her waves crashes along
The crumbled eroding sand.

The clusters of sand hold hands and dance,
Joyfully, under palm trees.

The palm trees sway in
The humid air.

Here on the peaceful beach,
The sun shines, the water twirls,
The sand dances, and the palm trees sway.

We Don't Live

Micah Glyn Clayton

My parents and I,
We don't go hungry
My family and I,
We hold each other's hands
Even when there's nothing in the pantry
And we're forced to forget our thought-out plans
We look at this frame
And we know it's not our home
And that's why we don't live
On bread alone.

My parents and I,
We do things wrong
My family and I,
We're far from perfect
But we've been forgiven all along
Even though we are not worth it
We look through this darkness
And know light is near
And that's why we don't live
In shame or in fear.

My parents and I
Don't look down, or even straight
My family and I
Set our eyes past the clouds
We can fit through the narrow gate
And shake off the everlasting shroud
We listen to hear
The triumphant bells
And that's why we don't live
Like everyone else.

My parents and I,
We understand ice
My family and I
Take care of each other
Even when windows are sacrificed
And we are forced to take cover
Death only gave
An empty threat
And that's why we don't live
In Heaven yet.

Battles (With Life)

By Amelia Fortunato

We all fight these battles with the world at some point
We all have the choice
To give up or keep fighting

We can't give up
We have to fight
We're warriors

We all have battle scars
No matter if they're on the outside or inside
We've all fought our own fights

Some people lose and give up
They think it's easier
But life goes on
And we have to push through

Constants
Keep us breathing
Constants as in people who are there for us
We all have reasons to live
So breathe and fight
Until the war is over

Our battles make us stronger
They fought, we fought, the world fought
And for that, we deserve to be recognized

Our battles make us human
So let's toast to the warriors

To My Sister Grace

by Katie Giveon

She is the ocean
The rushing waves are her hair
The smooth sand is her skin
The colorful seashells are her eyes
The unique tide pools are her lips
She is the sky
The shining sun is her smile
The peaceful moon is her soul
The bright stars are her laughter
The large planets are her dreams
She is the earth
The excited children are her energy
The exotic flowers are her scent
The unshakable mountains are her confidence
The stubborn trees are her determination
She is everywhere
She has filled my life from the day she came into it
And I don't ever want to know that emptiness again
So stay in the ocean and the sky and the earth
Stay in my heart and my mind and my world
And don't leave me to be by myself
Because I am so much better when you are around
I love you

Weaker by the Minute

By Jayden Gormley

Clenching Mother's trembling hand wishing to never let go
My eyes are flooding with tears
I'm trying so hard to hold them back,
like a wall blocking tidal waves
I'm taking little gulps of air,
hoping it's not the last breath each time
I'm weaker by the minute

Mother presses her forehead to mine,
feeling her warm tears flowing down both of our faces
I see her looking up at the ceiling praying to God
for me to live just one more day
I don't know how much longer I will live,
but I do know that it will not be long
I'm weaker by the minute

I've lived a happy life, but it now has to come to a painful end
Mother lowers her head and gives me a weak smile
as if she was telling me that everything is okay
I know it's not, but it is the best it will ever be
until the time comes and I have to go
I'm weaker by the minute

I take the longest sigh I can, breathing hard
with all my might and slowly close my eyes
I feel as if I no longer have any weight
and I am being pulled up to the sky
I still see Mother and I together holding close,
but I'm being pulled up above
I'm no longer weaker by the minute

I turn around to see angels grasping gently on
both of my arms taking me somewhere
though I am curious as to where I don't pull. I don't budge.
let them take me away from what matters most, but I don't know why
The bright light above the clouds fill me with joy and excitement
I'm stronger by the minute

The Magic of Words

By Jacob Guidry

I wish that I could do magic,
But it'd have to be with a card.
And however much I try,
It is very hard.

I wish that I could do magic,
But it'd have to be with a hat.
But I see the bunny that comes out
Is so squished and flat.

I wish I could do magic,
But it'd have to be with a wand.
Even if I make it dance,
My audience always yawned.

I wish I could do magic,
But it'd have to be with my hand.
And even if I "snap" and "clap,"
My tricks are ever so bland.

I can do magic,
But it has to be with words.
I try with other things
But they are left unheard.

The Last Supper Painting

by Annie Jones

460 by 880
Started 1495
finished 1498.
Leonardo's Christ
the Apostles, too.
Sitting round
amid startling shock.
Feel the silence
feel the outrage.
Thin halo crowns
atop the heads.
He's sure and still
they are not.
Broken into despair
Into outrage.
Death was coming,
and it would be –
by one of their hands.
Who could save them now?
Da Vinci sits.
Da Vinci stares.
A stroke of the brush,
a twitch of the hand,
Paint.
Paint.
Paint.

The Knight

By Alec Jordan

The knight gallant stands tall
Blade at his hip
Plate on his back
Polish, sharpen, hone
Noble and proud, he readies for battle

The horse pale stands proud
Bridle in his mouth
Knight on his back
Trot, canter, gallop
Regal and proud, he saunters into battle

The blade keen is brandished high
Hands on its hilt
Blood on its edge
Swing, parry, thrust
Hardened and cold, he sings his song in battle

The maiden fair waits long
Hair down her back
Hands at her breast
Wait, hope, pray
Anguished and loving, she waits for him after battle

The knight gallant returns home
Cries at his arrival
Victory by his hands
Carry, bless, lay to rest
Dead and cold, he is buried in the ground.

Perseverance
By Sachi Khemka

She watches time as it flies past her eyes.
She waits for a sign to relieve the pain.
But time cannot rewind the countless lies,
For the damage that caused all this disdain.

She only desires to make matters right;
But her conscience pushes her to move on.
She hopes that she can reignite the light,
But she knows that her chances might be gone.

She longs for forgiveness for all her sins,
And hopes that her strength will never give in.
She aims for a life of triumphs and wins,
And wishes to start a new life to begin.

Through the hardest of times strength is key,
Because hope will soon let her griefs be set free.

An Ode to My Books

by Mykaela Lawson-Ho

Ode
How I love my wonderful books
Your old and battered pages

Doorways that open to magical places
Forests or caves and even more

I don't know how many times I have stayed up with you
You have inspired me, brought me joy, and you have made me cry

You have kept me awake at night
You have slept on my chest

We have been together through thick and thin
Through seas and kingdoms

Now you occupy the space by my desk
You trace my life with happiness and joy

Leaf

By Maddy Nigrini

Ready to begin a journey of its own,
Not yet realizing what is out in the world
A beaming, olive green leaf sprouts.

The natural spring air as light as a feather,
The sun's rays hugging the earth like a blanket,
The animals interacting in the blooming grass.

Starting a journey of its own,
A vivid, vibrant leaf descends.
The wooden tunnel of bare trees howl with the wind.
Its yellows and crimsons dwindling down and down to the airing,
murky soil.

The autumn air brisk and chilling,
The sun cloaking itself behind the shady sky, animals starting to
vanish for their lengthy slumber.

In the midst of a journey of its own,
Crush.
Pearly and chalky snow packs onto the diminutive leaf,
now the unadorned colors of the miniature, curved breath of the
tree beige and brown,
the splatters of blunt pigment casing the leaf.

The winter air draft and freezing, sun tucked away from the sky,
plants and animals nowhere in sight.

Life starts to come back from sleep,
The sun starting to welcome the world again, spring air once
again light and sweet.

The small, withered leaf, covered in the melted snow and
morning dew,
now holding the wisdom of a successful journey, looked up to
the tree that it knew as home.

And as it did, admiring the new greens, it saw a new, green leaf,
just sprouted,

On a journey of its own.

Education

By: Avery Phillips

We need our education
We don't need more vacations
Perfect Education

Our education is so pleasant
Like a ribbon on a present
Priceless Education

Listen to your teachers teach
So you can relax on the beach
Education Vacation

When you come to school
You will have to follow the rules
Strict Education

Teachers give you knowledge
Which is great for your future college
Future Education

Even in another nation
We still need our education
World Wide Education

Voices Inside My Head

By Amaya Shah

I scream, I shout
But nothing comes out
All I hear are voices inside my head.

I'm odd
Since birth I was flawed
And nobody understands me.

Frustration builds up inside
I have washed away my pride
All I hear are voices inside my head.

I dream of fitting in
The words that come out are thin
But inside I have an intense hurricane of thoughts.

I am often alone
What comes out are moans
All I hear are voices inside my head.

The doctor says I'm autistic
Sometimes I cry and go ballistic
I just can't control myself.

Will people ever hear my voice?
I don't think I have a choice
Because right now all I hear are voices inside my head.

Seasons

By: Kaelynn Sims

No one stands in Season's way,
When it grows hot so you can play,
In the sunny summer day,
Don't step in Season's way.

The trees, their leaves all swirling down,
Catch them before they touch the ground
Look at the Red, the Orange, the Brown
Don't step in Season's way.

Sprinkling the trees with a cold breeze,
Brushing ice off their snow-covered knees,
People who think they're going to freeze,
Don't step in Season's way.

Flowers blooming from the ground,
But they might also drown,
The pretty colors all around
Don't step in Season's way.

Look outside, you might say "Alas!
How did all those seasons pass?
Those seasons came and went so fast!"
Don't step in Season's way.

Humanity

By: Lucía Vicéns

I believe in Music
In emotions being spoken
To the beat of the drum
And in the meaning

I believe in Science
In an explanation
For even
the strangest of things

I believe in Love
In a companionship
Like no other
A never ending friendship

I believe in Curiosity
In wandering through
Uncharted forest
In search of unknown items

I believe in a Future
Where people won't
Discriminate, bully,
Hurt, or kill each other

I believe in Humanity

Hope

by Dakota Widenor

I remember life as a child
Everything was so simple and easy to understand
All the adults told us, that the earth and the sky belonged to us.
That we could reach the stars as soon as we were a bit taller.
Dream they told us. For one day, all your dreams can come true.
So we held all those dreams with all our hearts.
Every wish upon a star,
Every coin tossed into a well,
Every fantasy imagined
We kept locked in our hearts through out all our childhood.
But then when we got older things, changed
No longer were we greeted with a smile and told to dream,
Instead we received harsh sneers and told to grow up! Get your head out
of the clouds. Stop acting like a child, God Sake, and get into the real world.
It was strange. Seeing how suddenly the world changed.
Maybe it was just our perception that changed.
Whether we liked it or not, any of us were shaken out of the dreams,
we were told to dream.
We couldn't afford to be children anymore, instead, we had to deal with the
problems the one before has created.
The world stopped being warm and kind, instead it became cold.
It was now like riding a steel slide in mid winter,
where at the base waiting for us was just a puddle of mud.
The world was no longer "what we made it"
But now, it simply was, what it was and nothing more.
And if we didn't like it, we would be left behind.
Labeled as "crazy or ridiculous"
I watched my friends grow just as cold and
uncaring as the rest of the world.
And for a moment, I almost did too.
Until, I remembered all the men and women
before me who accomplished great things.
They didn't know, they couldn't settle for how the world saw it.
People of fame are not the realist, they are the visionaries.
I understood that growing up did not mean I had to accept
the world for what most saw it as, but rather as taking the wisdom
I learned as a child, along with the knowledge I know now, and bring
it into the real world. And that was just what I was going to do.
And so, with a smile in my heart, and dream filled eyes, I shall continue to
see the world, not as how people tell me to see it, but as how I know it can be.
For I have hope.
And that is the stuff of what dreams are made of.
And no one will ever take that away from me.

Meet the Authors and Illustrators

 **Nelson Aiken** is the author of the short story, *Loss* (pg 109). Nelson is a 7th grader in the Greater Victoria School District. He wants to be a NHL Hockey Player when he grows up and his favorite school subjects are hockey and English. His favorite book is *The Monster Calls*.

 **Selene Ashewood** is the author of the poem, *What It's Like* (pg 265). Selene is a 6th grader in the Montgomery County Public Schools District. Her favorite subjects are digital literacy and English. Her favorite book series is *Ghost of the Graylock*. Selene wants to be a writer when she grows up.

 **Sofia Bajwa** is the author of the short story, *Shattered* (pg 113). Sofia is a 8th grader in the greater Houston, Texas area. Her favorite book series is *Harry Potter*. She would like to be an author when she grows up. Her favorite subject in school is swimming.

 **Finnley Benson** is the author of the short story, *An Important Lesson* (pg 11). Finnley is a 4th grader in the Garland Independent School District. His favorite subject is math. His favorite book series is *Diary of a Wimpy Kid*. Finnley wants to become an engineer when he grows up.

 **Sanchita Bhusari** is the author of the poem, *A Performance to Remember* (pg 267). Sanchita is a 7th grader in the Wilson West School District. Her favorite subjects are dance and English. Sanchita dreams of becoming a chemical engineer when she grows up. She loves reading the *Harry Potter* series.

Meet the Authors and Illustrators

Anna Boland is the author of the short story, *Rooftops* (pg 203). Anna is a 12th grader in the Cypress-Fairbanks Independent School District. Her favorite subjects are water polo and English. Her favorite book is *Of Mice and Men*. Anna aspires to become a writer or chemist in the future.

Zoë Brown is a cover artist for the *I Write Anthology* (pg 109). Zoë is an 8th grader in the Houston, Texas area. She wants to become a psychologist in the future. Her favorite subjects are English and art. Her favorite book is *The Fault in Our Stars* by John Green.

Tori Buege is the author of the short story, *Regretful* (pg 119). Tori is a 7th grader in the Mahtomedi Public School District. Her favorite book is *The Young Elites*. She loves reading and his favorite subject is English. Tori is striving to become a private investigator when she grows up.

Randii Carrell is the author of the short story, *The Story of the Saved Land* (pg 15). Randii is a 4th grader in the Garland Independent School District. Her favorite subject in school is writing. Randii would like to become either an author or chef when she grows up.

Shruti Chakraborty is the author of the poem, *Peace in the Womb* (pg 269). Shruti is an 11th grader in West Bengal, India. Her favorite school subjects are reading and computer science. She aspires to become an engineer when she grows up. Her favorite book to read is *Gone with the Wind*.

Meet the Authors and Illustrators

La'Jasha Champion is the front cover artist of the *I Write Anthology* (pg 60). La'Jasha is a 10th grader in the Aldine Independent School District. She loves studying electronic media. Her dream is to become an illustrator or graphic designer in the future. La'Jasha's favorite book to read is *Bubba, The Cowboy Prince*.

Audrey Chan is the author of the poem, *The Peaceful Beach* (pg 271). Audrey is a 4th grader in the Spring Branch Independent School District. Her favorite book is *The Tale of Despereaux*. She loves math and would like to be a heart surgeon when she grows up.

Bella Chramosta is the author of the short story, *A Fairy Different Person in a Fairy Different World* (pg 19). Bella is a 3rd grader in the greater Houston, Texas area. Her favorite activities are playing piano and writing. Her favorite book series is *Land of Stories* and she would like to become either an author or fashion designer in the future.

Bella Clark is the author of the short story, *Zinnia* (pg 125). Bella is an 8th grader in the Wilson West Independent School District. Her favorite subjects are art and writing. Her favorite book is *The Giver*. She wants to be a novelist, artist or forensic scientist in the future.

Micah Clayton is the author of the poem, *We Don't Live* (pg 273). Micah is a 10th grader in the Wylie Independent School District. Her favorite subjects in school are theater and Spanish. Her favorite book to read is *The Book Thief*. Micah hopes to become a writer in the future.

Meet the Authors and Illustrators

Wm. Patrick Cook is the author of the short story, *The Seven Leaders* (pg 25). Wm. Patrick is a 4th grader in the Garland Independent School District. His favorite school subject is science. Wm. Patrick's favorite book to read is *Warriors – Moonrise*. He would like to be a baseball player or author when he grows up.

Karen Corral is the author of the short story, *The Value of Life* (pg 29). Karen is a 4th grader in the Garland Independent School District. Karen's favorite subjects are swimming and math. She would like to work at a restaurant when she grows up. Her favorite book to read is *Esperanza Rising*.

Amelia Fortunato is the author of the short story, *Battles (With Life)* (pg 275). Amelia is a 6th grader in the Wilson West Independent School District. She is aspiring to become an author in the future. Her favorite book is *Eleanor and Park*. Her favorite subjects in school are reading and English.

Nia Gallagher is the author of the short story, *Inner Perfection* (pg 131). Nia is a 8th grader in the Wilson Independent School District. Her favorite book series is *Divergent*. Her favorite subjects are tumbling, art, English and Spanish. She would like to become either a doctor, author or artist in the future.

Katie Giveon is the author of the poem, *To My Sister Grace* (pg 277). Katie is a 7th grader in greater Houston, Texas area. She loves English and math. Her favorite book is *Ender's Game*. Katie wishes to become a lawyer and author when she grows up.

Meet the Authors and Illustrators

Adith Gopal is the author of the short story, *Run the Show* (pg 139). Adith is an 8th grader in the Wilson West Independent School District. His dream is to become an orthopedic knee/ankle surgeon. His favorite book to read is *Playing for Pizza*. He loves playing baseball and learning about history.

Jayden Gormley is the author of the poem, *Weaker by the Minute* (pg 279). Jayden is a 7th grader in the Wilson West Independent School District. Her favorite book series is *Divergent* and her favorite subjects are reading and writing. Emily wants to be a novelist when she grows up.

Jacob Guidry is the author of the poem, *The Magic of Words* (pg 281). Jacob is a 5th grader in the Garland Independent School District. He wants to be a mechanical engineer in the future. He loves robotics and his favorite book is *Eldest*.

Divya Gupta is the author of the short story, *Butterflies in the Light, Beasts in the Night* (pg 143). Divya is an 8th grader in the Blue Valley Unified School District. Her favorite subject in school is English and her favorite book is *Pride and Prejudice*. Divya hopes to become an ophthalmologist in the future.

Juliette Hess is the author of the short story, *My Big Blue and Green Eyed Boy* (pg 33). Juliette is a 4th grader in the greater Houston, Texas area. Her favorite book is *Because of Winn Dixie* and her favorite subject is reading. She loves playing volleyball. Juliette is aspiring to become a veterinarian when she grows up.

Meet the Authors and Illustrators

Zoey Hess is a cover artist for the *I Write Anthology* (pg 84). Zoey is a 6th grader in the greater Houston, Texas area. She wants to become a psychologist in the future. Her favorite subjects in school are art and English. Zoey's favorite book to read is *Wonder*.

Anna Hockett is the author of the short story, *Rest in Peace* (pg 57). Anna is a 5th grader in the Garland Independent School District. She wishes to become a book reviewer for the NY Times when she grows up. Her favorite book is *The Lunar Chronicles*.

PHOTO
NOT
AVAILABLE

Michal Ilouz is a cover artist for the *I Write Anthology* (pg 224). Michal is a 7th grader in the greater Houston, Texas area. Her favorite book is *Wonder* and her favorite subjects are reading and writing. Michal wants to become a lawyer when she grows up.

Annie Jones is the author of the poem, *The Last Supper Painting* (pg 283). Annie is a 4th grader in the Spring Branch Independent School District. Her favorite book is *The Heroes of Olympus* and her favorite subjects are reading and writing. Annie wants to become a paleontologist in the future.

Claire Jones is the author of the short story, *The Bookwyrm* (pg 209). Claire is a 9th grader in the greater Houston, Texas area. Her favorite book is *The Way of the Kings* and her favorite subjects are reading and math. Shana wants to be a theoretical physicist when she grows up.

Meet the Authors and Illustrators

Alec Jordan is the author of the short story, *As the Earth Slept* (pg 217) and poem, *The Knight* (pg 285). Alec is an 11th grader in the greater Houston, Texas area. He loves creative writing. His favorite book is *High Rhulain* and he would like to become an author in the future.

Kurt Kauffman is the author of the short story, *There's a Fly in My Stew!* (pg 149). Kurt is an 8th grader in the Fort Bend Independent District. His favorite activities are playing video games and reading. His favorite book to read is *Jurassic Park*. Kurt would like to become a professional basketball player when he grows up.

Sachi Khemka is the author of the short story, *Letting Go* (pg 225) and poem, Perseverance (pg 287). Sachi is a 10th grader in the Katy Independent School District. Her favorite subject is English and she would like to become a family practitioner in the future. Her favorite book to read is *Number the Stars*.

Alexandra Killgore is the author of the story, *The Winter Cabin* (pg 153). Alexandra is a 7th grader in the greater Houston, Texas area. Her favorite subject is English. She would like to become a vet tech when she grows up.

Harrison Kummer is the author of the short story, *The Smiths* (pg 229). Harrison is a 10th grader in the Los Angeles, California area. He would like to become a computer programmer in the future. His favorite subjects in school are robotics and physics. His favorite book is *Shannara Chronicles*.

Meet the Authors and Illustrators

Fiza Kuzhiyil is the author of the short story, *The Art of Friendship* (pg 159). Fiza is an 8th grader in the Harbor Creek School District. Her favorite book is *The Raven Boys*. Her favorite subject in school is writing. Fiza would like to become a journalist for the U.N. when she grows up.

Mykaela Lawson-Ho is the author of the poem, *An Ode to My Books* (pg 289). Mykaela is a 7th grader in the greater Houston, Texas area. Her favorite book series is *Harry Potter*. Mykaela dreams of becoming either a doctor in the future. Her favorite subjects are history, science and health fitness.

Haleigh Lechner is the author of the short story, *Forever Pompeii* (pg 61). Jade is a 5th grader in the Garland Independent School District. Her favorite subjects are dance and cooking. She loves the book, *Finding Danny* and would like to become a veterinarian when she grows up.

Maddy Nigrini is the author of the poem, *Leaf* (pg 291). Maddy is a 6th grader in the Wilson West Independent School District. Her favorite book is *The Giver*. Maddy dreams of becoming either an interior designer or architect in the future. Her favorite subjects are English and global studies.

Ethan Oropeza is the author of short story, *The Last Monster Hunters* (pg 37). Ethan is a 4th grader in the Garland Independent School District. His favorite book to read is *Warriors*. He wants to become an army soldier when he grows up. His favorite subject is science.

Meet the Authors and Illustrators

Arianna Papadakis is the author of the short story, *Meltdown* (pg 167). Arianna is a 7th grader in the Wilson West Independent School District. Her favorite book is *The Body in the Woods*. Her favorite subject in school is reading. Arianna wants to become a teacher and author in the future.

Isabela Parra is the author of the short story, *Going Down* (pg 65). Isabela is a 5th grader in the Garland Independent School District. Her favorite thing to do is eat food and her favorite book series is *Harry Potter*. Isabela wants to become an engineer when she grows up.

Nicole Pasterczyk is the author the short story, *Prove 'Em Wrong* (pg 175) and a cover artist for the *I Write Anthology* (pg 112). Nicole is a 7th grader in the Wilson West Independent School District. She wants to become a Penn. State Volleyball Player when she grows up. Her favorite book is *Out of My Mind* and her favorite subjects are reading, writing and volleyball.

Amanda Paz is the author of the short story, *The Fact of Life* (pg 233). Amanda is an 11th grader in the Alief Independent School District. Her favorite subjects are dancing and writing. Her favorite book is *The Lonely Hearts Club*. Amanda is aspiring to become an actress when she grows up.

Colin Pearce is the author of the short story, *The Day My Life Changed* (pg 239). Colin is an 11th grader in the Colorado Springs area. He would like to become a chemical/biological engineer or lawyer in the future. His favorite book series is the *The Hunchback of Notre Dame*. Colin also loves gymnastics and English.

Meet the Authors and Illustrators

Avery Phillips is the author of the poem, *Education* (pg 293). Avery is a 3rd grader in the Garland Independent School District. She loves cheering. Avery wants to become a marine biologist in the future. Her favorite book to read is *Tales of Despereaux*.

Victoria Pluviose is the author of the short story, *Never Alone* (pg 69). Victoria is 6th grader in the Wilson Independent School District. Her favorite subjects are gymnastics and English. Victoria enjoys reading *Tuck Everlasting*. She dreams of becoming a pediatrician when she grows up.

Jacqueline Poisot is a cover artist for the *I Write Anthology* (pg 152). Jacqueline is an 8th grader in the Houston Independent School District. Her favorite subject in school is science. Her favorite book is *Neuromancer*. Jacqueline hopes to become an artist, philosopher and psychologist in the future.

Mia Reyes is the author of the short story, *Life Takes Its Turn* (pg 73). Mia is a 5th grader in the Garland Independent School District. She enjoys reading the *Percy Jackson* series. She wants to become a marine biologist and her favorite subject is art.

Olivia Sacks is the author of the short story, *Neighbors* (pg 183). Olivia is a 7th grader in Houston Independent School District. Her favorite activities are lacrosse and running. She wants to become a graphic designer by day and comedian by night when she grows up. Her favorite book series is *The Hunger Games*.

Meet the Authors and Illustrators

Emily Santos is the author of the short story, *Unforgotten* (pg 77). Emily is a 5th grader in the Garland Independent School District. Her favorite subject is social studies and her favorite book to read is *Out of My Mind*. Emily wants to become a musician in the future.

Amaya Shah is the author of the poem, *Voices in My Head* (pg 295). Amaya is a 7th grader in the Wilson West Independent School District. Her favorite subjects are reading, writing and math. She is aspiring to become someone who makes a difference.

Genevieve Sheara is the author of the short story, *Way out West* (pg 81). Genevieve is a 6th grader in the greater Houston, Texas area. She enjoys reading *Hamlet*. Her favorite subject is English and her favorite activity is writing. Genevieve wants become either a writer or lawyer.

Joshua Sher is a cover artist for the *I Write Anthology* (pg 138). Joshua is a 7th grader in the greater Houston, Texas area. He loves reading *Casino Royale*. His favorite subjects in school are history, soccer and basketball. Joshua strives to become a Disney animator when he grows up.

Alani Simmons is the author of the short story, *You Are Still a Winner* (pg 41). Alani is a 3rd grader in the Houston Independent School District. She loves dancing and learning Chinese. Her dream is to become a dancer or singer when she grows up.

Meet the Authors and Illustrators

Kaelynn Sims is the author of the poem, *Seasons* (pg 297). Kaelynn is an 3rd grader in the Garland Independent School District. Her favorite subject is reading. She hopes to become a professional singer when she grows up.

Jackson Swindle is the author of the short story, *Reality* (pg 85). Jackson is a 5th grader in the Garland Independent School District. His favorite book to read is *Gregor the Overlander*. His favorite subjects are writing and science. Jackson wants become an inventor in the future.

Megan Taylor is the author of the short story, *The Search for Mommy* (pg 245). Megan is an 11th grader in the Cypress Fairbanks Independent School District. Her favorite subjects are digital media and creative writing. She is aspiring to become a writer and illustrator in the future. Megan's favorite book to read is *Their Eyes Were Watching God*.

Elian Tee is the author of the short story, *Child of Darkness* (pg 189). Elian is an 8th grader in the Lamar Consolidated Independent School District. His favorite school subjects are English and band. He would like to become a lawyer and musician when he is older. Elian's favorite book series to read is *The Mortal Instruments*.

Ellaine Tee is the author of the short story, *Creator's Hope* (pg 251). Ellaine is an 11th grader in the Lamar Consolidated Independent School District. Her favorite school subjects are science and math. Ellaine's favorite book is *The Great Gatsby*. She wants to become a chemical engineer in the future.

Meet the Authors and Illustrators

Jan Tee is the author of the short story, *Vacants* (pg 255). Jan is a 10th grader in the Lamar Consolidated School District. His favorite school subject is science and he would like to become a doctor. Jan's favorite book to read is *Of Mice and Men*.

Bethany Tran is the author of the short story, *Little Star* (pg 89). Bethany is a 3rd grader in the Garland Independent School District. Her favorite school subjects are writing and orchestra. She wants to be an orthodontist when she grows up. Bethany's favorite book to read is *Out of My Mind*.

Drew Turner is the author of the short story, *The Orb of Destiny* (pg 95). Drew is a 5th grader in the Garland Independent School District. He loves all school subjects and he also enjoys playing tennis. Drew's favorite book to read is *The Lightning Thief*.

PHOTO NOT AVAILABLE

Lucia Vicens is the author of the poem, *Humanity* (pg 299). Lucia is a 7th grader in the greater Houston, Texas area. Her favorite school subjects are language arts, science and world history. Lucia's favorite book to read is *Far, Far Away*. She wants to grow up to be a doctor or writer.

Alysa Walker is the author of the short story, *Hearts and Stitches* (pg 195). Alysa is an 8th grader in the Wilson West School District. Her favorite school subject is science and she also enjoys playing softball. Alysa's favorite book to read is *Ripper*.

Meet the Authors and Illustrators

William Wendling is the author of the short story, *The Prismatic Prank* (pg 103). William is a 5th grader in the Garland Independent School District. His favorite school subject is math and he wants to become a software engineer when he grows up. William's favorite book to read is *Out of My Mind*.

Dakota Widenor is the author of the poem, *Hope* (pg 301). Dakota is a 9th grader in the Colorado Springs School District 11. His favorite subjects in school are English and theater arts. Dakota strives to become a writer, actor or film producer in the future.

Elsie Williams is the author of the short story, *Bitten* (pg 45). Elsie is a 4th grader in the Anaheim Elementary School District. Her favorite school subjects are science and swimming. Elsie's favorite book to read is *Edenbrook*. She wants to become professional artist when she grows up.

Note from the iWRITE Founder

The iWRITE Literacy Organization started with a mission to encourage kids to read thirty minutes a day under the original name READ3Zero. After visiting with many budding young writers during my own school book tours, the organization quickly grew to embody both sides of literacy through reading and writing. I Write Short Stories by Kids for Kids has published some of the most creative pieces of work from young minds. The kids who have embraced literacy on this level continue to inspire me and our editors. Our authors and illustrators are smart. Intelligence shines through their creativity. They are witty and aware of the world around them. They are leaders through literacy. They get it.

In a short amount of time, our authors and illustrators have continued to build on their initial success. Many have gone on to start reading and writing clubs at their own schools. Others have started book drives, spreading as far as Mexico and the Philippines as our ambassadors. Many have entered their work into multiple contests and scholarships. Some of our kids have interned at iWRITE or have decided to pursue writing in their higher-level academics. We believe that early success is an important motivator to life long achievement.

I would like to thank everyone who has participated in the iWRITE program and the creation of our 7th anthology. I truly respect the parents, teachers and mentors who have become such a huge foundation to our growth. God has blessed this vision and created the opportunity for us to share our passion for literacy within our community. Thank you to the publishing team at iWRITE for your endless hours of work; Sharon Wilkerson, editor and interior designer, Tamara Dever and TLC Graphics, cover designer, Phuong Ha and Nicole Gautier. Ryan Shaw, thank you for working with our young thriving artists since day one. Thank you to our board, our sponsors and our amazing team of volunteers and judges. Of course we must thank our talented student authors and illustrators for working so hard to follow their dreams. We are so proud of all of you for being a part of this anthology. Thank you to the parents for sharing your children and their talents with us at iWRITE; your encouragement is the key to their success. If you would like more information for your school to be a part of the iWRITE program, please visit the website at www.iWRITE.org.

Sincerely,
Melissa M. Williams
Children's Author & Publisher

CPSIA information can be obtained
at www.ICGtesting.com
Printed in the USA
FFOW02n1127191016
28517FF

9 781941 515792